MASTERS OF SCIENCE FICTION PRAISE ONE OF THEIR OWN:

"R.A. Lafferty is one of the most original writers in science fiction. He bends or breaks normal story restrictions apparently at will, pokes fun at serious matters and breaks into a kind of folk-lyricism over grotesqueries. All this, plus the most unfettered imagination we've enjoyed in years."

—Terry Carr

"The Lafferty madness . . . is peppered with nightmare."

—Samuel R. Delany

". . . wild, subtle, demonic, angelic, hilarious, tragic, poetic, a thundering melodrama and a quest into the depths of the human spirit . . . R.A. Lafferty has always been uniquely his own man."

—Poul Anderson

"Lafferty's stories, like Philip K. Dick's, are not susceptible to being confused with the work of any other writer."

—Fred Saberhagen

"It is a minor miracle that a serious philosophical and speculative work should be written so colorfully and so lyrically."

—Judith Merril

"As with everything the man writes, the wind of imagination blows strongly . . . and we can settle back to appreciating the special magic proffered by the madman Lafferty."

—Harlan Ellison

Ace Science Fiction Books by R.A. Lafferty

ANNALS OF KLEPSIS

NINE HUNDRED GRANDMOTHERS

PAST MASTER

R.A. LAFFERTY

Annals of KLEPSIS

ACE SCIENCE FICTION BOOKS
NEW YORK

ANNALS OF KLEPSIS

An Ace Science Fiction Book/published by arrangement with
the author

PRINTING HISTORY
Ace Original/August 1983

ISBN: 0-441-02320-7

Ace Science Fiction Books are published by The Berkley Publishing Group,
200 Madison Avenue, New York, N.Y. 10016.
PRINTED IN THE UNITED STATES OF AMERICA

Contents

"The humanly inhabited universe, according to the best—or at least the newest—mathematical theory, *does* have a tertiary focus, and it is there that it is vulnerable. The humanly inhabited universe, with its four suns and its seventeen planets, is an unstable closed system of human orientation and precarious balance, a kinetic three-dimensional ellipse in form, with its third focus always approaching extinction. As with any similar unstable premise-system, the entire construct must follow its third focus into extinction. This is known as the 'Doomsday Equation.'

"The Equation has been bad-mouthed because it originated on an asteroid and not a planet; but must we forever believe that planetary mathematics is *always* superior to asteroid mathematics?

"The third focus of the humanly inhabited universe has been determined to be both a point and a person on the Planet Klepsis, on the *surface* of the planet, which is extraordinary in itself. Of the person, the human element of the anthropo-mathematical function, little is known except the code name the 'Horseshoe Nail,' and the fact that the person is more than two hundred years old. This is an added precarious element. Actuary figures show that only one in a hundred billion humans will reach the age of two hundred standard years, and that none will go far beyond it.

"What are the possibilities of combating the Doomsday Equation? The moving of some of the planets or suns to other positions and orbits to nullify the kinetic three-dimensional ellipse construct is very chancy, and it is also at the very limit of our technology. The transfer of the focus to another person is a million-to-one shot; and it has already been done once, from a notorious and discredited person to this same 'Horseshoe Nail.'

"There is a further complication in the essential balance of this critical person code-named 'Horseshoe Nail.' He cannot be allowed to awake, and he cannot be allowed to die.

"Unless mathematical advance in the field is made very soon, there is no hope at all for the survival of the kinetic three-dimensional ellipse which is the humanly inhabited universe. And the humanly inhabited universe—*that's us!* There are, however, very many possible universes that are more mathematically stable than the humanly inhabited universe."

"Come Bend Your Mind With Me"
—Karl Sayon

ANNALS OF KLEPSIS

FIRST CANTO

All the Peg-legged Irishmen

or

Salt for the Ocean

Remember these things, burn them into your mind, think of them always:

The Particular Universe, a kinetic three-dimensional ellipse with three foci and consisting of four suns and seventeen habitable worlds, from Gaea-Earth around Sol-Sun to the elegant planets around the Proxima and Alpha Suns, to the inelegant planets around the Beta Sun, the most inelegant of all being the three Trader Planets, Emporion, Apateon, and Klepsis. Of these three, Emporion has no law, Apateon has no ethics, and Klepsis has no history.

The Doomsday Equation, which threatens this Universe with extinction.

Klepsis itself, the Thief Planet, the Pirate Planet. Its government has always been a "Covenanted Piracy." The *Ocean of Klepsis,* which shouts "My Name is Adventure." The ship *The Dina O'Grogan,* which still sails that ocean. *Ravel-Brannagan Castle* on Klepsis, and the *Six Watchtowers* of the Castle,

1

named the Christopher, Januarius, Juda, David, Cloud, and Henry Watchtowers. These are named for the six successive rulers of Klepsis: Christopher Brannagan, Januarius O'Grogan, Juda O'Grogan-Brannagan, David Ravel, Cloud Ravel-Brannagan, and Henry Ravel-Brannagan. Five of the watchtowers are now inhabited by the ghosts of their namemen, and the sixth is inhabited by a living man.

Christopher Brannagan, the Founder, Discoverer, and Inventor of Klepsis.

The Ghost of Brannagan, a peg-legged specter who worries because Klepsis is two hundred years old and has no history.

Prince Henry the Pirate, he of the sixth bell tower and the present ruler of Klepsis. And his twin,

Prince Franco the Outcast, a much more pleasant person.

Princess Angela Gilmartin Ravel, the most beautiful woman on Klepsis (it says so on the coins) and the wife of the surly Prince Henry.

Tharrala Thorn, of the Royal Family but in disrepute because of having committed the unspeakable sin.

Long John Tong Tyrone, one of the Peg-Legged Irishmen who came to Klepsis, an historian who becomes the consort of Tharrala. This person is myself, the narrator of this account.

These persons and things are the hinges of the account.

Remember us, burn us into your minds, think of us always.

There were three peg-legs on the flight from Apateon to Klepsis. They went "swush thump, swush thump, swush thump" when they walked about the crowded ship—the sounds of their flesh legs and their wooden legs. Two young men and one young lady, all peg-legs, and they had come to Klepsis the Pirate Planet.

The tall tale of the peggies was that Christopher Begorra Brannagan, one of the earliest explorers of the Trader Planets, had been acted against because he had a wooden leg (and explorers are supposed to be physically perfect, how would it look else?), and because he was Irish (and explorers are supposed to be of the superior races, how would a person of an inferior race impress an alien?), and Brannagan resented his ill treatment.

Having been treated unfairly, Brannagan swore that, as soon as he had acquired a billion thalers, he would set up a fund whereby any one-legged Irishman anywhere in the universe could receive free transportation to Klepsis and could also receive any help he needed after arriving at that blessed place.

"How will we define 'Irish'?" the first administrator of the fund had asked Brannagan.

"If they have Irish names, they are Irish altogether," Brannagan laid it down. "Few of the other breeds would be caught dead with an Irish name."

Of the three peg-legs on the flight from Apateon Planet to Klepsis, one was clearly black, one was probably Gaea-Earth Eurasian, and one was plainly Latino; their names were Andrew "Gold Coast" O'Mally, Long John Tong Tyrone, and Conchita O'Brian. Gold Coast and Long John had their left legs missing, Conchita her right.

"When are you going to have *your* leg cut off, Terps?" Conchita asked Terpsichore Callagy. "There's several people getting amputated now down by the ship's handball court. You get a rebate on your passage after you get your leg cut off. You'd better go get it done now."

"I wasn't going to have my leg cut off at all," Terpsichore said. "I'm very much against the whole idea. It'd hurt."

"But you already got your name changed to an Irish one," Conchita reminded her. "That hurts more than having a leg cut off."

"Callagy is my real name," Terpsichore explained.

"Nobody's real name is Callagy," Conchita insisted. "What's your line, Terps?"

"Art. I'm into art."

"Then you came to the wrong place. Klepsis has the worst art anywhere. Yes, and on purpose! The rich people on Klepsis collect the worst art they can find in all the worlds, and they pay out big money for it. 'If it's bad, they'll buy it on Klepsis' is a saying."

"Yes, and I am going to look for the facts behind that saying," Terpsichore said with sudden determination. "Any art whose colors bark and howl out loud at you is worth studying."

Then a very gory incident took place, right there in the third-class luxury lounge of the ship. A man rose to his feet and began to scream in the most horrifying voice I have ever heard:

"The ten second warning! No, no, no! Give me time! I have the money with me. We will land on Klepsis in ten minutes and I can have the debt paid in fifteen. Give me time!" Then the man's head exploded. Well, it exploded all the way down to his waist, and only the lower members were left of him. There was a fine shower of flesh and blood all over us, a thing that was distasteful to all of us third-class passengers.

"My own line is coded technology," Conchita said with a merry lilt as though wishing to change the subject. But then she went back to it. "The time of most loans given by Klepsis moneylenders is one million seconds," she said. "When a loan is given, a mysterious sliver is inserted in the skull of the borrower. When he pays, the sliver is removed; but only the lender knows how to remove it. If the borrower does not repay the loan within one million seconds, his head explodes fatally. One million seconds is about twelve Klepsis days and nights."

"There isn't much coded technology on Klepsis," Andrew Gold Coast O'Mally said, "not what we mean by coded. I believe you have come on a wild merganser chase, girl Conchita. My own line is gold. And there *is* gold on Klepsis, billions of kilograms of it. I myself have more than one hundred treasure maps showing the locations of gold on Klepsis."

"What is your line, Long John Tong Tyrone?" Terpsichore asked.

"History," I said, for I am Long John Tong Tyrone, the probably Eurasian peg-leg. "Do we all have our salt? It's important that we should."

Slowing for our landing at Klepsis Third Port, we came over a little arm of the ocean. The oceans of Klepsis lack salt, and all visitors to the planet must make a token contribution.

"I don't have any salt," Terpsichore moaned. "I'd forgotten about that requirement."

"There's a man in the whiskey bar who'll sell you a hectogram of salt for one thousand Klepsis thalers," Gold Coast said with perhaps a touch of cruelty. "You can't leave the ship without making a ritual offering of salt, you know."

"Oh, oh, I can't afford one thousand thalers," Terpsichore complained. "And I can't afford *not* to disembark here either. Oh, oh!"

"I got some, pet," Conchita told her. "I thought I'd better bring an extra pack. Here. You have to pour it into the ocean yourself. Good. I bet that makes it a lot saltier. But there *isn't* any history on Klepsis, Long John Tong Tyrone."

"Then I'll find some," I said, "or I'll make some."

Klepsis is sometimes called the Pirate Planet. Many of the persons on Klepsis do indeed wear roughly formalized pirate costumes which are almost burlesques of those worn by stage pirates on Gaea or Astrobe. They wear loose, baggy shirts and loose, baggy trousers of Dahae mineral-silk in very bright colors, shouting yellows and oranges and scarlets, gold and bloodstone, sky-blue and sea-green, saturation-purple. They wear knotted head-kerchiefs that are brighter still. Oh, and they have eye patches and peg legs, short swords dangling in sword sashes, and earrings dangling in lop-ears. Most of the peggies have their wooden legs painted red and white, striped like barber poles, although other colors are used for them. And nobody on Klepsis wears sensible shoes. They wear slaughterhouse boots or cowboy boots, or they go barefoot. Wait, though—most of the barefoot ones have their feet painted in one of the bright primary colors, orange or scarlet or yellow. For a Klepsis farthing they can step into a trough that will color their feet with a color that will last all day.

Some of the people wear green-and-orange birds perched on their shoulders, as Gaea pirates used to wear Gaea parrots. These however are actually parley birds that may be sent to repeat oral messages to persons a reasonable distance away. But the birds can remember messages no more than two hundred words long, and they remember them for no more than two or three hours. And, if they are questioned for clarification of the messages, the birds go all to pieces.

Some of the pirate-dressed persons wear snakes also. Probably half of the sword-sashes are really living snakes. And these creatures are even brighter in their coloration than are the birds.

The bushes (there are no real trees on Klepsis) are brilliantly colored also, as is the land carpet of that world (it is not botanically related to Gaea or Astrobe or Camiroi grass) and all of the ocean meadows (floating-growing vegetation of eye-blinding brightness). Because of the sharp and stunning light, many persons wear colored wraparound goggles, and some wear colored monocles. These monocles do not seem to cut down on the bright colors, though; they amplify them. The people often flip the monocles high into the air and then catch them fitted perfectly into their eyes. Indeed, the young children practice this monocle-flipping as strenuously as they practice goat-roping or whip-popping or slingshotting birds.

The fact is that it is always bright on Klepsis, even at night. Klepsis has two moons and two suns other than its own Beta Sun. The Proxima Sun and the Alpha Sun are more distant, but they always turn the night into at least a cloudy day. Forever are there lights in the sky. These dazzle the people, even those born on Klepsis, and they made me dizzy for the first part of my journey there.

At customs there was a sign of greeting to all arrivals:

OH COME TO US AND CLAIM YOUR SHARE,
AND BREATHE OUR RANK AND LAWLESS AIR.

It sounded like a welcome, if you could take it by the handle. And at customs there were bowls heaping over with the most luscious grapes that I had ever seen or smelled or slavered over.

"My God, what are they?" I asked some customs people. "My God, what grapes! May I eat some? What are they really?"

"You may eat all you wish," the customs people told me. "You are encouraged to eat all that you can hold. And you have named them correctly, as does everyone who comes to Klepsis. The official and botanical name of them is the 'My God What Grapes!' grapes, though in the earliest times of Klepsis they were called simply 'Summertime Grapes.' "

I ate some of them, and then ate some more. All of the arrivals ate some of them. They brightened up everything for me. They gave a spring to my step and a sparkle to my eye. My God, what grapes!

'But I must locate myself and see where my prey, history, can best be hunted,' I told myself as I stood in line at customs. I scanned the booths that were nearby.

"Have you maps?" I asked a girl who had a booth, though I could not deduce what she sold from it. She did not seem interested in selling anything.

"Oh yes," she told me. "I have maps of almost all the sectors of all the worlds. We even have some city maps. Some of the worlds have cities, you know."

"I want maps of all the nearby sectors of Klepsis, and of any large neighboring cities on Klepsis," I said.

"We have no maps of Klepsis," the girl spoke as if I were out of my mind. "We are *on* Klepsis. Are you somehow confused about where you are? Why would anyone want maps of Klepsis when they are on Klepsis itself? One original is worth ten thousand imitations, as the proverb says. A map is only a formalized picture. Why should you look at a picture of a thing rather than at the thing itself? If you were out with a girl, would you be looking at the girl or would you rather be looking at a picture of the girl? Why do you want maps of Klepsis?"

"Pure perversity on my part, I suppose," I said. "But where could I catch a train or plane to the nearest large town?"

"Nowhere. There are no towns on Klepsis, and there are no trains and hardly any planes. People travel on water by boat. On land they ride animals if they are rich, or walk if they are poor. Are you rich, or are you poor?"

"I'm not sure, girl, I'm just not sure," I said. There did not even seem to be a town here at Klepsis Third Port. Most of us got through customs easily enough. All that the customs workers seemed to be looking for were "flagrant felons" whose records had got there ahead of them. The customs workers flagged seven of these conspicuous felons out of line, and an ambulatory judge convicted them and sentenced them to death on the spot. Then a customs worker came to the judge and reminded him that the gallows had places to hang only six persons at one time.

It was proposed that the seven felons play Tarshish roulette with a seven-shot revolver with only one of the cylinders loaded. That way, if they all shot at their heads in turn, one of them would be killed by the pistol shot and the other six would be hanged.

"That would be fair to everyone," the judge said.

"Fair, yes, but would it be sporting?" one of the felons asked. "How about us playing sudden-death poker: the winner takes all and goes free, and the other six hang?"

"Oh, I suppose that would be all right," the judge said, so the seven blatant felons were set down to play sudden-death poker with each other and with fate. We all begged to remain and watch, even those of us who had already passed through customs. And we were allowed to watch.

A couple of the felons were cravens who had no business playing sudden-death poker at all. But five of the fellows knew what they were doing. It was a superior game, and they dropped out one by one to their fate. But those who had lost still watched the narrowing-down of the game with great interest. Finally the two most impressive of the criminals were head-to-head with the heaped-up wealth of all of them between. And then the *most* impressive of them won. He was a man with a compelling look and a peculiar authority in his voice. He won it all. He went free with a stunning loot, for all seven of them had been well-heeled. And the other six of them were hanged on the gallows to flute music.

"I don't know where I want to go to investigate art," Terpsichore Callagy said. "There being no towns on Klepsis complicates things. Will I find art in the meadows or in the little houses of people I don't even know?"

"I don't know where I want to investigate coded technology," Conchita O'Brian said. "If they don't have towns, do they even *have* technology? Do they even *have* codes?"

"And I don't know where I want to go to hunt for history," I said. "History really begins with towns and writing. Can one have history without both of those things?"

"I *do* know where I want to go to hunt for gold," Gold Coast O'Mally said. "I have more than one hundred buried-treasure maps, and I want to go where they indicate. The map that most fascinates me is, I believe, the one for the site nearest this Klepsis Third Port. If I had someone who was familiar with these waterways just to the south and west of us—"

"I am totally familiar with all of them," said a man with a compelling look and a voice with peculiar authority. "Just let me see that sketch for the veriest moment. Ah yes, I know exactly where it is. We'll take a boat immediately, and we'll be there before the setting of the Beta Sun. Well, come, come, let us not tarry!"

I seemed to recognize this man, and yet I did not. It was as if I had known him when he was poor and did not quite recognize him when he was rich.

"Will there be a boat going in that direction at this hour?" Gold Coast O'Mally asked. "There are boats at the dock at the end of that inlet. I'll just go see about passage."

"Oh, I'll buy the biggest of those five boats," said that man with the compelling look and the peculiar authority in his voice. "I seem to be pleasantly in funds this afternoon. In fact, I feel like celebrating, so we will make a gala voyage of it. And if all four of you are not adroit seamen, I'll make you so within an hour."

Things went very fast then, suspiciously fast as it seemed to me. The compelling and joyful man had bills of million-thaler denomination—many of them. And the money of Klepsis is more valued than that of Gaea or Astrobe or any of the worlds. The man had pockets full of million-dollar bills, that's what he had. He bought the finest and largest of the boats with hardly any ceremony at all.

"Yes, Prince," a man said to him, "I have always preferred to deal in cash myself." And the cash was paid, and the boat was bought as easy at that. The man who had been called "Prince" then hired a crew of twelve seamen who seemed to be alert and knowledgeable. "Yes, Prince," one of them said. "It will be wonderful. It's been three years since I've sailed under you."

But the prince appointed the four of us, Terpsichore Callagy, Andrew Gold Coast O'Mally, Conchita O'Brian, and myself, Long John Tong Tyrone, to be ship's officers. We boarded ship only with what little baggage I had. We were quickly under power. We were out of that inlet and on the winding and devious oceans of Klepsis.

But it was not till we were well on our gala voyage that I realized who the compelling and authoritative man, the

Prince, the new boat owner, was. He was the seventh felon, he who had won the sudden-death poker game from the other six well-heeled felons and had then been given his freedom because there was no room for him to be hanged on the gallows.

Why had I not known him before? Because he had filled up with a new power when he had come out from under the gallows of death, and that had changed him a little.

"I am going home, and that is a great pleasure to me," he said, "though not everything will be pleasant at home when I get there."

SECOND CANTO

To Ravel-Brannagan Castle

The ocean seemed to shout, "My name is adventure." I heard it, and I believe that others did. There was a briskness and cleanness about the oceans of Klepsis that was not to be found in the oceans of other planets. One reason for this was that it was a freshwater ocean, the only one known on all the seventeen habitable worlds. There was also a narrowness about it that was not to be found in the oceans of other planets. This was because of the peculiar geography of Klepsis, because of the Ninety-Nine Continents of this world. These continents were really tentacled islands, of long extent down their peninsulas, but not of great area. Klepsis was, as any normal planet must be, three-quarters ocean in its area. And yet, from shipboard, three-quarters of that ocean area would be in sight of land. There were no real continents on Klepsis, and almost all of the transportation and travel on Klepsis was by water. The water itself looked like land for great extents, because of the floating "cork islands," their color-drenched meadows grazed by flame-pelted "cattle." Most of these "cattle" were really sheep, or goats, or deer, or chamois, or camels. And yet there was such a thing as the "cork island ox," very wild.

This pirate-planet Klepsis had never gone through the era of wooden ships. There were no trees on Klepsis for ship's timber, but there was a wealth of metallic ore, whole iron mountains and iron islands, and magnesium meadows. There was the memory, or at least the legends, of an interval of stone ships, but they could not be verified. Metal ships seem to go back to the beginning, even if there were stone ships at that same early time.

The iron and magnesium and lead and tin and other metals were easily smelted with the hot-burning peat and coal and lignite in the Brannagan Smelters. Christopher Brannagan had been a smelting man and a designer of smelters before he found his true calling in space piracy and settlement. The secret of the wonderful magnesium-steel with which Brannagan had built his ocean ships was an additive known as "sulphur-and-secret," the exact composition of which really was secret. The secret of the wonderful magnesium lattices with which Brannagan had built his space ships was this same sulphur-and-secret additive with an inert substance blended in for the sole purpose of doubling the price to non-Klepsis purchasers. The sulphur-and-secret additive had also been introduced by Brannagan into the sperm of Klepsis men of the heroic class, probably as part of an initiation rite. And it did result in ocean-and-space ships and ocean-and-space men who were without equal.

"I don't know how it is accomplished today," one of the seamen said to me, "but it *is* accomplished. I have only to look at myself to see that I am superior to the men of other planets, and yet I am a poor peg-leg who was born not on Holy Klepsis but on Gaea-Earth, as were you.

"I am Jerome Whitewater. I have heard from one of your company that you, Long John Tong Tyrone, have come to Klepsis hunting for history. You have been told by now, I am sure, that there is no history on Klepsis. Yet, if we are going where I think we are going, to a Prodigious House that calls itself a castle, to a Prodigious Monument, to a Prodigious Cave; if we are going to that region, we will find something nearer to history than can be found anywhere else on this planet. History, of course, is a state of mind. You are supposed to say 'What isn't?' there, Long John. But really, you will come to the *smell* of history at least."

"I hope so," I said. "I can feel the very rocks of this world stirring and groaning as if they were ready to break open and let history seep out."

"If we are going where I think we are going," the seaman Jerome Whitewater continued, "we will find another strong and throbbing thing that is often associated with history."

"And what is that?" I asked him.

"Bloodshed, mortal bloodshed," he answered me. "Our shipowner, Prince Franco the Outcast, isn't a bloody man, but he is a catalyst for bloody happenings. Before the second moon shall rise tonight we are likely to see bloodshed and bloody death."

Jerome Whitewater went aloft into the ship's rigging then. He climbed well, in spite of being a peg-leg. He began to unfurl a sail. The sails on the Klepsis ocean ships are furled in a manner that I have never seen on any other world. The Klepsis ships are a combination of sail and propeller and underwater jet. The oceans of Klepsis are everywhere populated with winds and crosswinds, and these winds are a basic fuel.

I was really picking up quite a bit of the things that history is made of from the seamen, and I was not convinced that there was no history on Klepsis.

This was the winelike ocean that the poet Omer (or Homer) of earlier Gaea had sung about. But how did he know about it? Was the Aegean still a freshwater sea when he composed his epics? Had it only recently left off being a lake, and were there as yet only narrow passages from it to the Mediterranean? On Gaea, the Baltic Sea (on the shores of which I spent a part of my boyhood) is a small freshwater ocean. But such bodies of water are rare. Saltwater oceans have dozens of colors, but only freshwater bodies are ever genuinely wine-colored.

The flying fish of the Klepsis Ocean are clearly not related to the flying fish of Gaea-Earth. They are brighter-colored; they are like pulsating fire; they are toothed and will fight you; and they are meatier. The seamen shot them with bow-and-arrow, and they pulled them in by the cords that were attached to each arrow. I did not see any seaman miss a shot. They pulled in seventeen of the fat fish, for there should be seventeen of us to supper on the ship. And name of the ship was *The Dina O'Grogan*.

The sense of visual proportion was violated on this narrow ocean. For one thing, it was not nearly as narrow as it seemed. We saw dolphins leaping in schools, but one of the sailors said that they were not dolphins at all, but right whales. I studied them through the glass and decided that they were indeed those huge Gaea cetaceans.

"Christopher Brannagan brought seven right whales from Gaea-Earth," the seaman Bartolomo Portuguese told me. "For this he built seven spaceships (the bottle-nosed Brannagan's Folly Ships) at very great expense. He did it because he wanted whales on his world. And of course, he could use the Folly Ships for other things after the whales were hauled. These Folly Ships paid for themselves many times and are still in use. And the whales have filled the oceans and are the most valuable crop on Klepsis. Besides that, they unclogged the oceans of Klepsis, for these were originally choked by their overgrowing vegetation. Know you that whales do much better in freshwater oceans than in saltwater oceans. This is the only chance they've had to prove it, but they've proved it resoundingly."

A young man on a cork island blew a whistle at us, and we pulled alongside. He had a cork island heifer, tethered and hobbled, for sale. Our authoritative ex-felon shipowner bought it; and we brought it on board with a sling to slaughter it and barbecue it. The young man had a crumpled newspaper. I asked him if I might have it, for I had seen no newspaper since I had been on Klepsis. He gave it to me readily enough.

"Take it and read it, as much as you can, before it disintegrates," he said. "I did all of it myself except a few quips that my wife told me to put in it before I left this morning. She said that she felt it in her liver that the Ink-Stained Wretch would come by my cork island today, and my wife has the most dependable liver of any person I ever knew. She's better than bird entrails."

"What is the date of this?" I asked him, for I could find no dateline on it at all.

"The date is today," the man said. "Can anything be done on any date except today? As to the actual date, I haven't enough education to calculate it. Few around here have."

"It is just about to crumble into dust," I said. "It's eaten up with acid."

"So is the day itself," the young man said. "You are an off-planet person, so let it be known to you that things that are not of outstanding importance may be printed only on paper that will self-destruct by the following night. This prevents our world from being choked by its own paper. The only things of possible importance in my paper are some of my wife's jokes, but I do not understand them, nor do other people. Even the Nine Imperial Gazettes of Klepsis are printed on paper that will last for only four days. The Ink-Stained Wretch prints the Imperial Gazettes too, but he takes about an hour longer for one of them than for a little paper like mine."

"The morgues of the newspapers of Klepsis must be slim pickings then," I said, "especially for an historical man such as myself. But your paper does not show the place of printing, either."

"Yes it does. See! 'The Ink-Stained Wretch Printery,' that is the place of printing. It is on a little boat that travels constantly, so naturally the bearings of the place of printing cannot be given. He comes around every day or week or month to the cork islands of this neighborhood and prints for us such little newspapers as we wish to have. This keeps us from slipping all the way back into the slough of illiteracy.

"This is my own newspaper that I sometimes have the little old Ink-Stained Wretch man to print for me; it consists mostly of local news and jokes and report of the fish and the whale runs. And always there is at least one paid advertisement. If I do not have at least one paid advertisement, I will not have my newspaper printed. 'There will be a paid advertisement today,' my wife said, 'about the slaves.' My wife is smart. The little old Ink-Stained Wretch always picks up the advertisements and the money for them and brings them to the people who sometimes have newspapers printed. The money from the advertisement is always the same as the cost of having the paper printed. So the little old man simply moves the money from the right pocket of his pants to the left, and I barely get a glimpse of it while it is being moved. There is only one paid advertisement in the paper that you hold in your hands, but it is a good market advertisement. It's about a sale."

The advertisement—it struck my eye immediately—started off with a garish headline:

BIG OLD-TIME SLAVE SALE TONIGHT AT RAVEL-BRANNAGAN CASTLE

And below this was the text of the advertisement:

> This is the first big sale here since early spring. This is a prime crop. There are one hundred fifty-two genuine human persons from Gaea, Astrobe, Camiroi, Tarshish, and some of them from Klepsis itself, most of them young and talented and attractive. There are forty-three short-tailed human persons from Tarshish and the other hidden worlds. And there are more than two hundred intelligent and hardworking humanoids from the furthest reaches. There will also be storytellers plying their trade, and barbecue and fireworks. And possibly there will be fireworks of another sort. If you like a good scuffle, you'll love this. This is an authentic slave sale *like they used to be*.

Yes, that was a startling advertisement for this day and age, even for Klepsis. Or so it seemed to me. Slave trading was strictly forbidden even on the Trader Planets.

"Where *is* Ravel-Brannagan Castle?" I asked the seaman Jerome Whitewater, who had now finished unfurling the sails and had landed lightly on the deck like a cat—like a cat with one wooden leg.

"I believe that it will be our destination tonight," he said. "They say that you're interested in history. Isn't that rather in the class with the ignorant things like astrology and cockfighting? What do you find so interesting about history, Long John?"

"History is the peopled worlds," I lectured him in my schoolteacher manner. (I was once a substitute schoolteacher for one year.) "History is ourselves in our clearest aspect. Only in history do we find the substance that is our justification. History is the account that we will give to God when, on the last morning, He will ask us to give an account of ourselves in species and persons. Only in history do we find the clarity that is our purpose of being."

"Unadorned clarity is pretty bland," Whitewater said. "I always loved a little obscuring fog with it, a little mist, a little blown foam and froth, a few torrents of shouting rain. I suppose that's why I like Klepsis. Clarity is kept under control here. I always like whole skies unbottomed to let out the distorting lightning and thunder to overwhelm us. You will find a much stronger meteorology here than on Gaea-Earth. You'll find weather to scare you. It is weather to form barbarians by. Clarity is the penny whistle of single and shrill voices. I want the mystery and un-clarity of orchestras, monumental and mountainous and rhapsodied, and not very good. And I want a great number of them. As to God and His last morning, He already has everything stacked in His favor. Do not help Him by handing Him the history of ourselves. Let Him guess!"

"You are not an ordinary seaman," I said.

"I was once, Long John. Then, three years ago, I said to a friend, 'I'd give my right hand to find a new life and get

out of this rut.' 'I know how you can give your left leg and
find a new life and get out of this rut,' he said. 'Really, I
have an item about it here.' So I gave my left leg and became a peg-leg to get my passage paid to Klepsis, because I
was tired of being ordinary. And Klepsis isn't an ordinary
world. It is often grotesque, but change is easy here. Situa-
tions develop faster here than on any world except
Camiroi. In a prehistoric world like this, things may happen without any preparation at all. For instance, we now
sail into a little area where it is raining without clouds. The
cloud buildup is skipped. Clouds are only warehouses for
holding water anyhow, and why should the water not fall at
once when the proper spirit moves it?"

And it did rain on us without clouds, for a distance of
about two sea miles as we sailed obliquely through the
meta-storm. Yes, the weather appeared to be quite offhand about things on Klepsis, irresponsible even. But the
people were even more so.

Friendships and enmities could be formed quickly and
with no preparation at all. The natural scenery could
change instantly, and the artificial scenery (that of human
construction or arrangement) was subject to sudden
change and invention. For instance, we now came abruptly
to the Regions of Manors or Mansions or Castles. We had
just rounded the headland of one continent, and the buildings made an incredibly ornate shore on the next continent.
Oh, what wealth! What decay! What new decay still under
construction!

"Oh yes, you have never come onto this vista before?"
Prince Franco the Outcast, our shipowner, said to me. "It
is elegant decay, is it not?"

"A thing we have often said about you, Prince," the seaman Jerome Whitewater said with easy impertinence.

"They are like the Old-South Plantation Houses of the
former Confederate States of America of Gaea-Earth," I
said. "And at the same time they are Palm Beach, they are
Newport, they are Money Manors. They are the epitome
of the nouveau riche. More than that: it's as if they had

been nouveau riche for two hundred years, growing
brasher all the time."

"Not bad, not bad," the unordinary seaman Jerome
Whitewater commented. "And you have the two-hundred-
year time era almost exactly right."

"They are like the houses of British dukes and Italian
princes," I said, "and they are set in gardens that are a mixture of the high English and the high Italian. They are Castles in Spain, especially in Estremadura. On Camiroi they
would be symbols of inferiority and bad taste. But here
they represent a taste that is taken in giant bites. They are
like the ancient Haik Castles in high Armenia, also on
Gaea-Earth, castles so huge that each of them, sticking its
head out of the snow, is mistaken for the remnants of
Noah's Ark, each of those castles at the head of a mountain
valley, each of them formerly drawing tribute from that entire valley."

"Not bad, not good," commented our princely shipowner, that man with the compelling look and the peculiar authority in his voice. "We come now to the finest and largest
of these Haik Castles, Mr. Tyrone, that in which I was born
and raised, the one that shall be my own when I come into
my kingdom. Seaman Whitewater, take charge of the landing, and then represent *yourself* as the owner and captain
of this ship. I myself will become 'vague' for a little while.

"And you four ship's officers, Terpsichore Callagy, Andrew Gold Coast O'Mally, Long John Tong Tyrone,
Conchita O'Brian, let me explain what I mean by becoming 'vague.' I will tell it in my leisurely fashion, for there is
no hurry about it. I am a lord of time, and I will not allow
there to be a hurry.

"When human male twins are born on Klepsis, one of
them will usually have what is either the gift or the weak-
ness of becoming 'vague.' This is so, no matter what the
original descent of the twins, whether their ancestors were
from Gaea or Astrobe or Analos or wherever. So this trait,
though there are traces of it on the original worlds, must be
partly borrowed from the ambient here; and I suspect that
my ancestor Christopher Brannagan had something to do

with putting it into the ambient, so that others might have the gifts that he had somehow acquired. To be able to go vague is really to be a sort of biological freemartin, but how does such biology get into a twinned person here? How, if it wouldn't get into him if he were born on one of the other planets? I believe that the trait turns up in one out of thirty thousand male twins on Gaea-Earth, and in three out of four sets of male twins here.

"Some of the animals on World Abounding are able to go vague, and we know that father-and-founder Brannagan brought many sorts of plants from World Abounding to Klepsis. There is a sort of ghostliness about a twin who can go vague. And the vague twin will always outlive the normal twin, a fact that gives me pleasure in my own case. But will a vague twin outlive a normal twin by two hundred years? Do you believe that possible?"

"No," I said, and the other three ship's officers also said no. We were in a little captain's room off the wheelhouse.

"Christopher Begorra Brannagan, the founder of Klepsis, was twins," said the authoritative ex-felon and prince. "That is the most loosely kept secret on Klepsis. There were two of him, so it's said. But even after these two hundred years, it remains neither verified nor unverified. In the Brannagan case, the special archemodal case (for Brannagan was born on Gaea-Earth and not on Klepsis), the two twins were essentially the same person. It may be so with all these special male twins born on Klepsis. In a monumental grave by our landing that we come to very soon, the bones of Christopher Brannagan may be seen in their coffin through its clear onyx glass. And all the bones of the left leg are there, along with all the other bones of the body. But the perhaps-ghost of Brannagan lives in the same monumental grave, and it is the ghost that has a wooden left leg, substantial and unghostly."

"May he be blessed by all peg-legged and deep-colored Irishmen forever," black-faced Gold Coast O'Mally said piously and seriously.

"Sometimes I sit on the stones with him in the tomb and talk to him, to the ghost of him," the Prince said. "I give

him Bandicott cheroots of hallucinatory weed to smoke,
and he smokes them: and they are smoked. I question
whether a ghost needs hallucinatory weed to hallucinate
more than he is already doing, but he likes to smoke them.
I give him Tarshish Gin Slings to drink, and he drinks
them: and they are drunk. Can a ghost consume things of
substance? He knows who I am, who everybody is. He
knows that I am his great-great-great-grandson. He insists
that I am so in the true bloodline, though in the conven-
tional accounts of the family I am so only through the interlopers John Summers and David Ravel in the first and
fourth generations of Klepsis."

As we came into the channel to the docks, there was one
of the buoys with a scarlet-on-yellow message printed,
"Something good will happen to you today." But the next
buoy had the painted message, "Something not necessarily
good will happen to you tonight." Providential buoys, but
were they to be believed?

"What is the name of the biggest house that we come to
now," I asked, "the one in which you say you were born
and raised, Prince?" I was impressed by the height of the
building, by the six very tall watchtowers, and by the other
tower still taller and stranger than the six. I was impressed
by the Italian gardens with their water pastures and their
herds of hippopotami, and by the English gardens with
their herds of elephants. I was impressed by the violet and
lavender and purple and red fields, which I knew were colored by their growing "Summertime" or "My God What
Grapes!" grapes. No castle ever offered a more beautiful
prospect from the sea.

"It is Ravel-Brannagan Castle," the Prince and ex-felon
said. "Gaze on it. Let yourself enter into it. Let it enter into
you. You are the historian, Long John. Ravel-Brannagan
Castle contains all the history that there is on Klepsis, and
it isn't in an easy form. This Castle *is* Klepsis. Everything
else on this planet is extension of it."

We were nuzzling into a little quay. A large right whale
was berthed in the slip next to us. It was sedated and

grinning and happy. It would be the main dish at the gala that night.

"What is your own official name, strange Prince?" I asked the shipowner.

"Oh, I'm Prince Franco Ravel-O'Grogan-Brannagan the Outcast, First Earl of Klepsis, Grand Duke of Tarshish, Honorary Citizen of Gaea, Astrobe, Camiroi, and Analos, sometime student of Georgetown University on Gaea and of the Collegium Omnium on Analos. I am the twin brother of Prince Henry Ravel the Pirate, who is now the illicit ruler of Klepsis. I am under sentence of death by my brother. And now I will lay me down on this cot in this little room off the wheelhouse, and I will go vague. Leave my clothes just as they are on the cot here. I will go out from them, and later I will come back into them. There are persons who do not mind returning from vague naked in the midst of crowds; but they are vulgar, and I am not."

The Prince did lie down on the cot. Then he disappeared from out of his clothes, and they went slack and saggy on his departure from them. Prince Franco had disappeared. That is what he had meant by "going vague."

"Look, look," Terpsichore cried out in delight. "It is Queen Zenobia, the Barbarian Queen. Who says there is no art on Klepsis? She is sheer primitive and barbaric art!"

A party came on board our ship as soon as we were tied up at the little quay. This party was led by the most beautiful woman on Klepsis. And how could one be sure that she was the most beautiful of them all? I had a new and local gold coin in my pocket, and I looked at it. Yes, she was the one. Her face was on all the ten-thaler gold coins of Klepsis, and her nomenclature, "Princess Angela Gilmartin Ravel, the Most Beautiful Woman on Klepsis," was on all of them too. She was the most beautiful woman because the coins said that she was. That's how we knew it. But it seemed to me that she had a little more class than a "Queen Zenobia the Barbarian."

"She looks about eighteen years old," I said to Jerome Whitewater, who was seeing to the landing as well as playing the roles of captain and shipowner.

"It is all those baths in hippopotamus milk that keep her young and glowing," Jerome said. "But she is about eighteen, in Klepsis years. That would make her about twenty-six in the years of Gaea-Earth."

"Hello, Whitewater," Princess Angela said as she came on ship. "I am glad that you are working for Prince Franco once more. Where is he? I knew that he had bought the ship and was on it. A wing-weary parley bird told me so. He has owned this ship before. I have been on it before. Franco, Franco, are you in the little captain's room here behind the wheelhouse? We must plot together. It is all yours if only you will reach out for it. It really falls of itself. Franco, my secret love, your clothes are here but you yourself have gone vague. How could you, when you know that it breaks my heart to miss you? Franco, Franco, you know that Prince Henry is only my husband and you are all the world to me. And you have never touched me. This must be settled. I swear that it will be. After the coming encounter, there will be no more of Prince Henry and his horrible cruelties. There will be only one of the twinship left alive, weird yourself!"

THIRD CANTO

Oh, Hospitality Most Strong!

"I am not sure that you are welcome here," Prince Henry Ravel the Pirate was saying to the bunch of us who had come off the ship *The Dina O'Grogan*. "All of you are creatures or partisans of my despicable brother False-Prince Franco the Outcast. His smell is all over the bunch of you. I have been wondering what I would supply for additional entertainment at the slave sale and gala that I am hosting tonight. My problem is solved. The public execution of the sixteen of you will be that additional entertainment. Sixteen is a good square and solid number, and sixteen executions will allow me room for creativity and innovation."

"You will not do this, Prince Henry! Curse your whole damned planet if you do!" Conchita O'Brian cried out in sudden fury. "There is the flag of the Ambassador from All the Planets flying over your Castle, and that indicates that he is present under your roof. And you have signed every sort of treaty in favor of civilized behavior. And besides, the Hospitality of Klepsis is an institution that you may not violate. The blood of all your hospitable ancestors would boil in your veins if you would do so. Now, you will assign sixteen good rooms to the sixteen of us, out of the six hundred guest rooms that are in that Ravel-Brannagan Castle

yonder. And you will give us everything that we ask for.
We have come to be guests in this princely house of
Klepsis. Treat us as guests. Have us shown to our rooms at
once."

Prince Henry looked exactly like his brother, Prince
Franco. Only the disposition was different. I'd have be-
lieved they were the same person if it had not been for
Prince Franco's recent talk about his being a twin.

"Peg-leg girl with a false moniker," Prince Henry said
furiously to Conchita, "I know the homely anecdotes of my
ancestors, and you know them not. Each of us of my line
has broken the hospitality a few times, out of anger or out
of irony, or just for the plain truculence of it. The blood of
my ancestors has boiled in my veins many times, and I still
live. Not to your *rooms* will I have you shown, but to your
room, to one room only for the sixteen of you."

And then this Prince Henry turned and spoke to a ser-
vant: "Show them into the strong room, into the strongest
room of them all, called the Whispering Room, though I
never knew why. Sometimes I hear screams of people long
since dead coming out of that room, but my ears do not
bend low enough to hear whispers. Use whatever force you
need to put them into that strong room."

We were immediately surrounded by a crowd of husky
servants. Three of them took each of us, one for each of
our arms and one to follow after with an electric cattle
prod. We put up only sporadic resistance and generally
went along with them easily, all of us except a very tall and
strong seaman named Sparaticus. Ah, but they put six men
on each of his arms, and behind him went three men with a
cattle prod so heavy that the three of them could barely carry it. "It is not a cattle prod, it is an elephant prod," one of
those tough men said in answer to a question from the seaman Fairbridge Exendine. "And this elephant of a man
will learn to step lively when it is behind him."

We were taken through a giant cellar of Ravel-
Brannagan Castle to a still lower cellar. We were herded
into a large enough iron room there (crowding was the one
thing we could not complain of), and the iron door and

darkness swung shut behind us. Then we heard bolt after bolt slammed into its cylinder, and lock after heavy lock being turned against us. It was as dark in there as midnight, midnight on Gaea-Earth, which is the only one of the worlds that has only one sun and one moon.

Among the sixteen of us locked into that room were the four new visitors to Klepsis:

Terpsichore Callagy, who was into art.

Andrew Gold Coast O'Mally, who was into gold and treasure maps that showed the way to buried gold.

Long John Tong Tyrone (myself), who am into history.

Conchita O'Brian, who said that she was into coded technology (but I had already begun to suspect that "coded technology" was only a code for what she was really into).

And then, with us in our lockup, were the twelve seamen from the ship *The Dina O'Grogan:*

Jerome Whitewater, a peg-leg who was clearly a partisan of Prince Franco.

Otis Landshark, who was an adventurer from the Trader Planet Apateon.

Kwong Ti, a Sino who was born right here on Klepsis.

Karl-the-Great Orka, who was a treacherous man from Astrobe.

Bartolomo Portuguese, a pseudonymous man from Far Tarshish and other places.

Hektor Lafcadio, the "Greek God" from World Abounding (Aphthonia). Hektor looked as if he had been carved heroically out of ruddy-tan marble, and he also talked as if he were, which is to say that he didn't talk very much.

Kate Blithespirit, the "Amazon" from Camiroi, though she was not at all typical of that very intellectual planet. She was really too blithe for it.

Fairbridge Exendine, the penny philosopher from the Trader Planet Emporion.

Frank Shea, a peg-legged black man from the planet Gaea-Earth.

Sebastian Jamaica, another Klepsis native.

Sparaticus, a giant escaped slave from Far Tarshish.

Hogson Roadapple, an undistinguished person from Hokey Planet.

If that is not twelve of them, then I have forgotten some. There was a lot of varied experience among the bunch of us, and probably there were reserves of real talent.

"We are really a crosscut of all types," Terpsichore ventured to say.

"Aye," Bartolomo Portuguese gave her the answer. "We are a crosscut, from the small end of the log. If our execution is to be the added entertainment feature of the slave sale, I'll bet it will be good entertainment at least. I've been in death cells before, and I've been dragged out of them to my execution before. And in both of those cases I put on a memorable show. I'm well-voiced, and the proper words and rants are given to me in my hour. It was sort of an anticlimax in each case when my execution was changed to marooning-without-hope-of-escape on a desert world. I never stay marooned for very long."

"Water is rising about us here in the darkness," said Hektor Lafcadio the Greek God in a small and fearful voice. He was called the Greek God because of his beautiful and heroic appearance. But that appearance was now hidden by the darkness, and his voice was not at all heroic. "We'll be drowned here without ado."

"No, we will not be," the seaman Otis Landshark gave the opinion. "There would be no entertainment for the multitudes for us to drown here in the darkness. We will be worried and tortured here with much ado among ourselves. And then we will be led out to give our entertainment."

"Talk less and listen more, all of you," Conchita O'Brian told us. "This stone strong room with its iron reinforcing is the perfect sounding fork for everything that goes on in the Castle and on its whole estate. Listen!"

Indeed there was a strong and constant murmuring that could be split into the sounds of dozens of different activities and conversations, if only we had the discriminating ears for it. And most of us did have that equipment.

"Doesn't Prince Henry know that we can hear everything down in this room?" Conchita asked. "He said that this was called the Whispering Room, and he said that he didn't know why. Is this audibility something that can be turned on and off?"

The Castle was filling up with guests so that it seemed that even its famous hospitality would be strained. And many of the arriving guests were commenting on their host as soon as they were in their rooms. They were impressed by the luxury of their rooms and suites, yes, though several of them affected to find elements of bad taste in the excessiveness of that luxury.

"It is plain bush. Nay, it is cheesiness to overdo it this way," one voice said. "Oh, it's cheap, cheap, to go so expensive."

And then there was a voice that we knew, or thought that we knew, speaking apparently to several different groups. It was either the voice of Prince Henry or that of Prince Franco, who had gone vague before our very eyes on the ship *The Dina O'Grogan*. The voices of the two brothers were identical when their moods were similar. It was either Prince Henry being agreeable for reasons of policy, or it was the regular voice of Prince Franco.

There were voices and noises from the castle grounds and from its verdant gardens and fields and waterfronts. There was the coded whistling of ships' whistles, which most of the seamen amongst us could understand. There was a clanking and ringing of iron mixed with a rebellious babble of voices. The giant crewman, the big escaped slave Sparaticus, said that it was the noise of the arrival of groups of slaves in chains. Then, seemingly within the castle again, there was an interesting dialogue.

"Prince Henry," said one very much displeased voice, "the last time this happened, just one third of a year ago, you gave me your absolute oath that it would never happen again."

"*Cave iusiurandos praedorum*, 'Beware the oaths of pirates,' " said the voice that had to be that of Prince Henry. "You do know, do you not, incompetent Ambassador, that Dog Latin is the diplomatic language on Klepsis? It gives us a touch of elegance, you know. No, no, we are not to be trusted at all. But this slave-sale-and-gala this evening is, for reasons of falling profit, the last slave sale that I will ever hold at Ravel-Brannagan Castle or anywhere else on Klepsis. I'll hardly break even tonight. I give you my highly qualified oath that it'll be the last one, Ambassador.''

"Declare the previous one to be the last one and the one tonight to be canceled, Prince. You know that slavery by any name is strictly forbidden in every democracy, oligarchy, regency, tyranny, kingdom, benevolent dictatorship, plutocracy, and people's republic in all seventeen of the habitable worlds. Strictly forbidden, Prince. And any government that permits it can be occupied and placed under trusteeship.''

"The government of Klepsis is not any of those types you have named, Ambassador. Our government is a covenanted piracy. And it would not be easy to occupy us and place us under a trusteeship.''

"But you, personally, have signed the no-slavery agreement!''

"I personally sign almost every paper that comes to my hand, Ambassador. I sign the things out of my desire to live in peace with all mankind and quasi-mankind. I spend a pleasant half hour every day signing official-looking papers.''

"But you have subscribed to all the basic freedoms.''

"Yes, Ambassador, to all of them. I am the only ruler in all the worlds who has subscribed to the ultimate freedom. And the ultimate freedom is the freedom to own slaves. There is no freedom more ultimate than this, to own and traffic in the buggers. You know, Ambassador, that I have a good double for you, to take your place if anything happens to you. He is an actor from Camiroi, where acting is one of the fine arts. Now, go! Go out and mingle with the people, Ambassador. Go out and be seen everywhere at the slave-sale-and-gala. And smile, damn you, smile. Your very life depends on how sweetly you smile among the people tonight.''

Then the conversation between Prince Henry and the

Ambassador became more bitter, but also less audible. And finally it was heard no more.

"I wonder whether people throughout the castle can hear us here in the strong room, since we are able to hear them so well?" Gold Coast O'Mally asked.

"No," said a voice that I did not immediately recognize. After all, there were several crewmen from *The Dina O'Grogan* whom I had not yet heard speak. "No, it is all done with one-way amplifiers. No sound from your strong room can reach the outside, except to one place. Nobody outside of your strong room, except myself, can hear you at all. I built it that way when I built this castle."

"Who are you? What voice is yours?" I asked. "Are you not one of our party? Are you not in our strong room? Where are you then?"

"I am a voice crying in my monument, and I will not be stilled. But now I will turn off the amplifiers, for you will be going to more comfortable quarters at once." And the murmuring sounds from everywhere ceased. "Come talk to me in my tomb after the storytelling is finished tonight," the voice said.

"We don't know who you are or where your tomb is," I complained.

"You will know; you will know in good time," said the voice.

People came to the door of our strong room then and opened it. It was the Princess Angela Gilmartin-Ravel with an armed party. The water rushed out of our room when they opened the door, and it drenched them.

"Ah well, there's no way to deal with a moisty and pauky situation without getting wet," the Princess said. "There has been a mistake, a deliberate mistake made by my husband, Prince Henry. You must have better quarters than this. These are completely unacceptable for you good people. Come along, and you really shall have sixteen rooms, one for each of you, rooms of true luxury and convenience. Aye, and a great entertainment hall, and a game room also. I would beg the pardon of all of you, except that persons of my high position never beg.

"But the truth of it is that you are a nuisance to me. You may bring on a confrontation before I am ready for it. No matter. I can't let honest people languish in a dungeon, or be taken out of it and killed."

We were taken to very fine quarters, and we could find no fault with them at all. In every hospitality guest room of Ravel-Brannagan Castle there was a little font hanging on the wall, and in it was money for the guest who happened to be low in funds. A guest must not be embarrassed. In the princely room that was assigned to me, there was a princely sum of twenty thousand Klepsis thalers. To me, a poor scholar in history, this was an extraordinary sum. I put the twenty one-thousand-thaler bills into my pocket before my luck should somehow evaporate. The picture of Princess Angela Gilmartin-Ravel was on the one-thousand-thaler bills just as it was on the gold coins. And so also was the script that this princess was the most beautiful woman on Klepsis. Well, she had made a beautiful gesture anyhow, if 'twas she who did it.

The sixteen of us gathered in the great entertainment hall and game room that pertained to our sixteen rooms. Comparing our experiences, we found that we had all done about equally well with the money left in the rooms so discreetly for guests who might be in need.

We found tables heaped high and lavishly with "My God What Grapes!" grapes, and we stuffed ourselves on them. We mixed drinks for ourselves at the well-stocked wet bar. We played darts there, and we shot pool. We picked up the news broadcasts from Aphthonia, or World Abounding. There was only a thirty-eight-minute lag in the radio-wave transmission from World Abounding to Klepsis at this season. All the planets of the Sun Beta hold rather tight orbits.

I went into the library. It hadn't many books in it, and the dust of two hundred years was on those few that were there. There was a Septuagint Bible. However had it come there? There was the *Rule of Saint Klingensmith*, a little devotional booklet. There was the *Big Book of Pirates for Boys*, from Gaea-Earth. There was a book *Spaceship*

Building by the Natural Intuitive Method, by none other than Christopher Brannagan, the founding father of Klepsis. And that, believe it or not, was the total of the books in the Castle Library. I went back to the big entertainment hall where the others were still gaming and talking.

"When there's a circus in town, it sure is hard not to have at least a glimpse of the circus parade," Kate Blithespirit the Amazon commented with a certain wishfulness.

"Since slavery is totally wrong, it would be very wrong for us even to steal a look at the slave sale," Conchita O'Brian chided her.

"Since we are all in a position of peril here at Brannagan Castle, I believe that it behooves us to be as informed as possible about our surroundings," Sparaticus declared. "You are saying, gracious lady, that we should not notice a burglar who is fiddling at our front door, since burglary is quite wrong?"

But it wasn't these and several other little arguments that were tossed into the pot that brought us out of there and to the spacious Castle grounds and gardens. It was, more than anything, the calliope band that brought us out there. Sure, it was gross. Sure, it was in bad taste. Sure, it was so bush that it could only have happened on Klepsis World. But one hundred steam calliopes, from more than a dozen different continents, all playing at top steam together (no, no, not playing together, but all playing at the same time, not *in* the same time), playing the rowdy-dow circus music from half a dozen worlds—well it stirred something primeval in our blood. And, besides the calliope band, it was the nose-bursting aroma of the whale being barbecued whole that brought us out there. This was the right whale, and it weighed 136,000 kilograms or 150 tons. Whalers are very conservative and still refer to a whale in tons. Well, 150 tons of whale barbecued whole sets up an aroma like nothing else in any of the worlds. Oh, the smell of it, the smell of it! The Polynesians on Gaea-Earth have the legend about various people offering sacrifices of fatlings of cattle and sheep and such. The odors ascended to God, and He accepted them in good humor, and He granted small favors to show that He appreciated the sacrifices. Then He was enraptured by the towering and powerful smell of a great fat whale roasted whole by some Polynesian persons of extreme piety.

"Because of this," God said, "you People of the Whale will never have to work or toil again. For you the coconuts will fall off the trees; for you the taro roots will jump right out of the ground; for you the wild pigs will run directly into your snares; for you the fat fish will leap into your outrigger canoes till they fill them nearly to sinking; for you the bananas will grow without toil; for you a dozen island fruits of which I do not immediately recall the names will burgeon and thrive."

"Well, that's what God said in the legend," I defended it, for I was the one who told this simile. "I am an historian and historians cherish legends. Some of them are only two short steps from history."

Oh God, the smell of it, the smell of it! Ten thousand fat pigs roasting would hardly equal it. And as a matter of fact there were, not ten thousand, but about one hundred eighty fat pigs roasting for the gala.

This was all much larger than we had supposed. The advertisement that I had read in the disintegrating newspaper had mentioned one hundred fifty-two genuine human persons from Gaea, Astrobe, Camiroi, and other places; forty-three short-tailed human persons from Tarshish and the other hidden worlds; more than two hundred intelligent and hard-working humanoids from the farthest reaches. But that was only the list offered by Ravel-Brannagan Castle itself. Prince Henry of Ravel-Brannagan Castle was hosting a slave sale like they used to have, and his own list was only one of about a hundred. Oh, there was something like ten thousand genuine human beings to go on the slave blocks, and further numbers of not quite genuine humans. It was a grand assembly of clanking and ringing iron, and of roaring and ululating human voices.

And there were the touts, like those at the racetracks on

Dahae Planet, telling us for a small fee where we might find
the very best of the slaves taken from the top ones of all the
lists. So naturally, we paid the touts their small fees and
went to top block, where the top stock was offered.

What, what, there was big Sparaticus enslaved again!
How had they caught him up into the slave network again,
and on what warrant? But no, Sparaticus was still in our
company. Then, who was the other one who looked so exactly like him, of the same huge size and of the same pas-
sionate look?

"Oh, it is only a scurvy brother of mine," Sparaticus
spoke with some scorn, and the enslaved Sparaticus hung
his head. "He is worthless. He will not work, and he has no
talents. It costs a fortune to feed him. But, because he is my
own blood brother, I will offer ten Klepsis thalers to have
him out of bondage."

"Ten thalers for him," said the auctioneer. "Do I hear a
higher bid?"

"Ten thousand thalers for him," said a rough man. And
both the Sparaticus in chains and the Sparaticus in our
company groaned.

The auctioneer offered ten slaves at one time. He got
several bids on one of the slaves, then let the bidders think
about it for a while as he opened the bidding for the next,
and then the next slave after him.

There were several beautiful women among the offer-
ings. Andrew Gold Coast O'Mally, Otis Landshark,
Jerome Whitewater, and Bartolomo Portuguese all got in
on the early bidding for one or other of the beauties. Terpsichore Callagy and Kate the Amazon Blithespirit bid on
attractive or exuberant male slaves. And I, I did not bid on
any of the beautiful women offered. I bid on one who was
not quite beautiful, who was not quite superb, who was sul-
try rather than flaming, who was hang-head rather than imperial. Well, she looked at me, so I bid for her. I bid a thousand thalers. I bid five thousand for her. Then I bid twenty
thousand. And another man bid twenty-one thousand. The
auctioneer let it dangle and went on to the next slave. But I

surely did not have twenty-two thousand thalers to top that last bid.

"Eleven thousand thalers," Sparaticus said when the auctioneer came back to his brother again. "Oh, why do I do it? I know him. He is worth no money at all."

"Eleven thousand thalers," the auctioneer said. "Do I have a better bid?"

"Twenty thousand thalers for that big one," the gruff man said. And both Sparaticus and his brother-in-chains groaned in their wretchedness. The crewman Hogson Roadapple went to Sparaticus and gave him something.

"Twenty-one thousand thalers," Sparaticus bid.

"Thirty thousand thalers for that big one," the gruff man said. And both Sparaticus and his brother-in-chains groaned again.

There were intervals in the bidding for slaves (about a hundred bidding blocks were going on at a time). In the intervals there were short calliope concerts. There were equestrian exhibitions. There were some really sensational bits of advertising and entertainment that broke the flow of the sales. Now there was the announcement that a man would leap without a parachute from an airplane twenty thousand meters high. Without a parachute? What would he use, then? Twenty thousand meters is very high. Klepsis people began to fit telescopic monocles into their eyes, and a kind lady loaned me such a monocle. I got a good focus on the kicking man just as he left the plane. And he hurtled down, down, down!

"Without a chute how will he handle it?" I cried in alarm.

"Oh, they have it all calculated exactly," the kind lady said. "Did you never see an advertisement like this before? They have the plane's speed and direction calculated, the wind drift at the various levels, the timing of his leaving the plane (he did not jump, of course, he was pushed), even the hysterical threshing of the man in the air (they have all his probability-reaction patterns). It is all calculated. And he will hit almost exactly in the middle of the glowing red X that is painted on the beach. Whoosh, you can hear the whistling of his coming through the air even now, although he is falling much faster than sound. That is known as the Whittlesby Phenomenon."

The man did hit almost exactly in the middle of the glowing red X that was painted on the beach. He hit so hard that he splashed. Then he actually exploded. And there was not left unbroken of him a bone upon a bone.

"But, but, but it *killed* him!" I blurted.

"Sure, it killed him," the kind lady said. "Do you expect a man to fall twenty thousand meters and hit like that and walk away from it? Give my monocle back to me. You sound like some kind of gooney bird."

"But, but, but *why?*" I cried out.

"It's an insurance company advertisement," the kind lady explained. "It will tie in with the slogan *The Happy Valley Insurance Company Hits the Spot Every Time.* I don't believe that insurance will ever catch on here on Klepsis, though. In insurance, as I understand it, you pay somebody else to take risks for you; and taking risks is about the most fun of anything I know of. But some of the big insurance companies from Astrobe are making pitches here. They think that because we are all so rich on Klepsis we will be easy pickings. I bet we're not. *There* is the widow of the dead man now. I know her; she never was much. And there is the insurance company promoter and sales-man. They are going to make a pitch-and-talk together on that little platform there. Hear that whistle blowing! That is from the time the man hit the ground; it started to blow then. The insurance man is supposed to hand the check to the widow within one minute of the time the man hit the ground. That's when the whistle will stop blowing. It's go-ing to be close, but I bet he'll get the check made out in time. He's making it seem closer than it really is."

It *was* very close, but the insurance man *did* get the check made out and presented to the widow within one minute of the man hitting the ground. The whistle gave a still stronger blast, and then it fell silent. A burst of many-colored fire-works was set off. It was a very effective insurance adver-tisement, and yet several persons told me that insurance would never catch on with the people of Klepsis World. This seemed strange to me, as insurance was big on all the other worlds I knew of. Would the people of Klepsis really prefer to take risks themselves? Did they indeed find the taking of risks to be more fun than anything they could think of? What a strange mind-set they did have! I went to my slave girl, the one I had been bidding on.

This slave girl was too broad in the beam, if I may use an ancient seaman's term for it. Her eyes were set too far apart, also. Her hair was much too orange-red in color. This was counted a vulgar color on most worlds. The girl had the "Thorn" sign on her magnesium-steel collar. Did this mean that she belonged to the Thorn clan? Or that she might be done to death by thorns? How historically curious that this sigh of the "th" sound in Old English should have reappeared on Klepsis World! I thought this might be the first sound of her name.

"Seventy-one thousand thalers," Sparaticus was bidding for his brother-in-chains. That was big money even in this slave market.

"Ah, he can have the big fellow," the gruff man said when the auctioneer turned to him to see whether he had another bid. "I'll go no higher on him."

So, to the great joy of all of us, Sparaticus and his brother were united. Sparaticus and his brother were absolutely identical when they stood together after the brother had been unchained. But for the difference in clothing, you'd never have been able to tell them apart.

"You'll find that your friend Sparaticus has blue eyes and his brother has green eyes. That's the way you tell them apart," the slave girl I had been bidding for said in a low and pleasant voice. It was almost as if she had been reading my mind.

"You gave to Sparaticus twenty thousand thalers to help him buy his brother, did you not? This was the money that you had already bid for me. Now how will you buy me? That was almost all the money you had, and my price will go somewhat higher. But the auctioneer knows when money has gone out of a man. They have a device to read what

money a man has in his pocket, and what credit. You have
no credit and not much money left. Do you not feel his eyes
upon you? Now they will hang you up by your thumbs and
whip you. And what will happen to me?"

"I don't know," I said glumly. I had gone to this slave
girl to look at the roots of her hair. I wanted to see whether
they were of the same flaming orange-yellow-red color as
the rest of her hair. They were.

"Even my soul is of that same flaming orange-yellow-red
color," the girl said as if reading my mind again. "This
flaming color is accounted a vulgar color and persons af-
flicted with it may not ascend to the nobility. I will tell you a
secret, though. Some persons fake it and hide it. They go
about with their hair an acceptable color. Here's Princess
Angela; ask to see the roots of her hair. Ah, poor man,
you'll be hanging by the thumbs now."

The auctioneer turned back to my slave girl. "I believe
that the penultimate twenty-thousand thaler bid for this
girl was a false bid," he said. "Young man, it is officially
doubted that you had that sum. If you did not have it, then
you'll be hung up by your thumbs and whipped to death.
That's to keep the cheap-shotters out. Did you have it?"

"I had it when I bid," I said truthfully. "I do not have it
now."

"Then, out of compassion, we'll give you a hundred
lashes only."

Four strong men came and hanged me up by my thumbs,
and the strongest began to lash me with a horrifying cat-of-
nine-tails whip. I'd be dead by fifty such blows, and my clay
would be desecrated by the last fifty. Doomsday Lightning
had begun, and three bolts of it killed three different persons within ten seconds.

"Oh, this is wonderful, Long John," the voice of Terpsichore Callagy was suddenly at my side. "This is raw art,
primitive art, art with all the hair on it! It was to find this
that I came to Klepsis. It was to find such as this that I was
born. Oh, you are wonderful with your pain-racked face
and the bright blood running down your withers. Dying
people often show these flashes of art. And Doomsday

Lightning coming now is a stroke of genius. Oh, what an inspiring piece of art you are, Long John!"

"Any more bids for this carrot-topped slave girl?" the auctioneer called.

"Yes, yes," a musical voice chimed. "The young man being whipped bids thirty thousand thalers for the girl." It was the voice of Princess Angela Gilmartin-Ravel, who was now standing beside my girl slave.

"If the young man didn't have twenty thousand thalers before, he can hardly have thirty thousand thalers now," the auctioneer said. "And my instruments indicate that he does not have it."

"Nevertheless, he wishes to bid thirty thousand thalers for her," Princess Angela insisted. "Your business is to take the bids. Take his."

"But his means and fortune will be checked immediately," the auctioneer said. "And if he doesn't have the money, he will immediately be whipped to death."

"I know," the Princess said. "That is the fate of so many young men on Klepsis. Enter his bid."

The auctioneer entered my bid. The Princess came and stood by me where I was being whipped, being whipped out of my mortal body, as I thought.

"Tharrala says that you wish to see the color of the roots of my hair," she said. Then she put her head so close to mine that the whip of the whipper opened her cheek and brought a rush of red blood from it. She parted her hair, and I saw that the roots of it were indeed that flaming orange-yellow-red color that is accounted vulgar and ignoble on so many of the worlds. She put something in the inner pocket of my tunic. Then she kissed me—the first time I had ever been kissed by a Princess. "That is for your simplicity and your suffering. Those whips really tear one apart, don't they?" she said.

"Who is Tharrala?" I asked her.

"The slave girl, of course, the object of your bidding. Tharrala or 'Courage' is her name. She has a lot of it, to come back here even as a slave after committing the unspeakable sin. I love her, but I do not approve of persons committing unspeakable sins."

"What is her unspeakable sin?" I asked, but the Princess had left me.

Men came to me. "Have you the money to support your bid of thirty thousand thalers?" one of them asked me.

"Yes, in the inner pocket of my tunic," I said, hoping it was so. It was. The men took the money back to the auctioneer.

"I put the money in escrow," the auctioneer said. "The bid is valid. Thirty thousand thalers. Are there any other bids?"

"Thirty-one thousand thalers," said the man who had bid the twenty-one thousand thalers.

"We will come back to this merchandise," the auctioneer said. "Give the thumb-hung young man a whip stroke now and then for his past misconduct, but let him not die. He seems to be a person who has swallowed the golden goose, as the old nursery rhyme has it. When we come back to this item, we will see whether he regurgitates any further gold certificates. But do not kill him. What, what? You say that a Resuscitating Man from Broxley Continent is here at the sale and gala? Well, go ahead and kill him then, if you wish. The Resuscitating Man can always bring him back to life."

FOURTH CANTO

The Slaves at the Sale

*The slaves at the sale are the best slaves ever.
(Listen, my soul, to the sound of the seas.)
I'll buy me a wife, a more beautiful never,
Sound in the noggin and sound in the knees.*

Klepsis Slave-Sale Song.

Somebody put a piece of hot-roasted whale fat in my mouth, and I was very thankful for it. It was good. It was elevating to my spirits. Then somebody invisible put a piece of barbecued cork-island heifer in my mouth. I knew by his aura that he was Prince Franco the Outcast, still vague and invisible. I recognized him though I could not see him.

"Be of good hope," he said quite clearly. Of course I was of good hope. The roiling of the crowds was stimulating to my spirits. The calliope music would have heartened anybody, especially when it went into the rousing "Second Moon Rising." One hundred calliopes goes over the line of the critical mass needed for stimulation and excitement. And if they did overdo it and kill me with their whips, there was still the practitioner from Broxley Continent who was able to bring persons back from the dead.

"I'll bring you whatever you need," the invisible Prince Franco said.

"I need to be freed from this thumb-stringing," I told him. "It chokes my breathing, and I'll likely die just from hanging like this."

"Be very easy with this person," Prince Franco told the strongmen who had control of me. "Ease him till the time of his release. It will be soon."

"Yes, Prince Franco," said the strongest of the strongmen, he who had been whipping me to death. "We have already been going rather easy on him. Now we will go still easier." This man then raised me up so that there was no weight on my tortured thumbs and so that my chest was not constricted. He could not see Prince Franco either, no more than I could—I was sure of that—but he seemed to belong to the Prince Franco Faction. And when, now and then for the sake of appearances only, one of the other men gave me a stroke with the horrible whip, it was almost like a caress in its gentleness. Somebody gave me some "My God What Grapes!" grapes to eat. I heard talk that there were twenty metric tons of these grapes for the gala, and they did make me feel very good.

My mind and my ears and my eyes had become quite sharp. I garnered a multitude of details from the rich scene. It was like the rotation of hundreds of interlocking kaleido-scopes: the crowds and the activities of them. There were these tumbling vistas of sight and sound and smell, ever changing, ever brilliant. Now all I needed to get the true picture of what was going on around Ravel-Brannagan Castle was to fit the several million evolving details togeth-er correctly; for the true picture of the castle and its envi-rons would be a jigsaw-puzzle picture all of whose pieces were in the state of high-speed change.

The bid came to me again and again for the girl slave named Tharrala or Courage. "Sixty thousand thalers," I bid excitedly once, and immediately I felt the invisible hand of Prince Franco put something into the inner pocket of my tunic.

"I will verify this bid before we go on," the auctioneer said crisply, and he came over and took something out of the inner pocket of my tunic. "Ah yes, this will bring it to sixty thousand thalers," he said. "I'll put this in escrow with the rest of it. This lad has indeed swallowed the golden goose. The bid is valid. Are there any other bids?"

"Sixty-one thousand thalers," called the voice that had been bidding against me. We went up and up, with intervals in it when the auctioneer was bidding other slaves in.

"Ninety thousand thalers," I bid sometime later, and I felt the unseen hand of Prince Franco add the sum to the inner pocket of my tunic that would cover my latest raise. The auctioneer came and took the increment out of my pocket. But why were two members of the royal family aiding me in bidding for this slave girl whom I had never seen till a half hour before?

"Ninety thousand thalers," the auctioneer said. "The bid is validated. The golden goose that the lad swallowed still yields gold notes. Any more bids?"

"Ninety—" began the voice that had been bidding against me; and then that voice was cut off with a gurgle and a moan.

"What ails that bidder?" the auctioneer asked. "Oh, dead is he? Yes, it is almost as if he were strangled to death by invisible hands. The neck is broken and the throat is bruised with livid marks of fingers and thumbs. Well, I cannot accept a bid that is incomplete, and I am not sure that I can accept a bid from a dead man anyhow. The bid of the young man hanging by his thumbs is therefore accepted. Let him down. And unchain the girl also. What, you want to keep the magnesium-steel collar that is around your neck, girl? All right. Unfasten her collar from the running chain, then, slave-master. She is yours, young man. You yourself look a little bit the worse for the wear. I trust there are no hard feelings for the treatment you have received. An auction must be run on firm lines."

"Yes, I hold very hard feelings against you because of this," I said honestly.

"However you want it, boy. I can get harder than you can."

I wondered: Could Prince Franco have killed the other man as thoroughly and convincingly as that? Had he such power in his invisible hands?

I went to Tharrala or Courage or Thorn to take possession of her, but I had the most curious feeling that she was taking possession of me. I looked at the magnesium-steel collar still around her neck, and at the Thorn sign on it. She could not be strangled while wearing that. It was too broad and snug fitting. Had the sight of the strangled man induced her to keep her collar on? I wished that I had such a collar myself.

"Come," this slave girl said to me. "You seem to be in terrible shape. I will have to fix you up. I do not like to have such damaged merchandise on my hands if there is any way to make it better." She led me away from the throng then, to a quiet corner in the monumental garden. She put unguent on my thumbs and back. She had kind and healing hands.

"Now that I have bought you," she said, "I will tell you my few simple rules that you must live under. We will get along very well if only you learn primary obedience. If not, well then it will be hard with you."

"But it was myself who bought *you*," I interrupted.

"Keep that little fiction if you wish. I guess it can do no harm. We will see, we will see about it," Tharrala or Thorn said with a strange smile. But now there were droll things that had taken place in Tharrala herself. She was no longer too broad in the beam; it had simply become the case that most other women were too narrow. Her eyes were no longer set too far apart. It was that the eyes of most other women were now set too close together. Her hair was still that flaming orange-yellow-red color, and so was her soul. But now that color did not seem as vulgar as it had seemed before. It was possible that it had all been a moronic prejudice.

"Heal quickly," she said. "I hate people who dawdle

about things like that. I want you to be pleasant and powerful and alert so that you can enjoy the executions that will
begin in about an hour. We will have to learn to enjoy
things together. I want to be proud of your appearance. I
believe that what you need now is the wine treatment."

"Yes, a glass of wine would be nice now," I agreed.

"If one glass is good, a hundred thousand will be better,"
Thorn said as if she were teaching a class in logic. "So, now
I will see to it that you will be saturated and healed in one
hundred thousand glasses of the common but holy wine of
Klepsis 'Twill be in bulk, though. Oh come, come! If you
are to belong to me, you must move faster and react
faster."

"Where are we going, droll girl?" I asked her.

"Oh, into the Ravel-Brannagan Castle. Into a cellar of
it."

"I have already been in a very dismal cellar of that
Castle."

"Yes. Where we will go now will not be very far from the
Whispering Room where you were held for a while. We
will take a cut through this trashy courtyard here."

"Do you know the Castle, Thorny Person?"

"Yes, I was born in this Castle, Long John Tong Tyrone.
We cut through this corner of the Sleeping Beauty Courtyard. Isn't it trashy though! And that is the Sleeping Beauty Door to the Castle. Really it is named the Sleeper's Door
and the courtyard is named the Sleeper's Courtyard. But
we will not use that way in, not now. We will pass through
only this corner of the courtyard. Is it not fun to walk on
matted weeds and on cobwebs that are a meter thick! And
we will go in by the Wine Door here. You didn't even see
the Wine Door, did you? And yet it's large and heavy and
ornate. It is said that persons very deep in their cups can
find it, but others will pass right by."

"Is there a sleeping beauty in the Castle, Thorn?"

"Yes, I think so, a sleeping person anyhow. Quasimodo
is its name."

"In a Gaea-Earth Roman-Grotesque, Quasimodo was a
male, a dwarf, a hunchback, and no beauty."

"So, he was almost the same here. But on Klepsis the deformities are not so noticeable. Many of us here are of a funny shape. He is a dwarf, he is a hunchback, and he is my friend. And all my friends are beautiful. He is a beauty in mind and in disposition. Long ago, he was the closest thing that the Brannagan ever had to an executive officer; that was in the years when the Brannagan was the monarch of this world."

"But, Thorn, that was two hundred years ago, when Brannagan was the ruler of Klepsis."

"Oh, you the historian, you know the history of Klepsis which has none? It was even said that Quasimodo was with Brannagan during at least part of the seven years of his exile or marooning. It was said that some transfer of occult power from Brannagan to Quasimodo was made during the marooning. And after that Quasimodo was not seen. It was said that he was on a special mission. It's almost two hundred years that he's been on 'special mission.' But some persons believe that he is The Sleeper in the Castle. I know that he is. Oddly, the code name of the sleeper in this Castle is Horseshoe Nail."

The courtyard where we had stopped to talk for a moment was the most overgrown place that I had ever seen. It was several meters deep in what I can only call disuse. The cobwebs, the cobwebs—there must have been a million kilograms of that light stuff scattered about that courtyard and portico and heavy door.

"It would take a million spiders spinning for a million years to produce such a mass of webs," I said, but Thorn only pointed to something dark. It was a spider twenty times as big as a house cat, bigger than a large dog, as big as a small pony.

"It would not take as many spiders as I believed," I said. "And I see that the strands of the webs, before they are separated, are very, very thick."

"They sometimes use them for ships' cables," Thorn said. "Oh, the place is trashy, but it's its business to be so."

"The Sleeping Beauty department of the Castle looks to be just about out of business," I jibed.

"Yes, just about out of business," she said seriously. "This may be the last week of it." We entered the Castle by the camouflaged Wine Door.

"Come along, my love; come, come," she spoke.

We went down iron ladders through a fetid darkness to reach a giant cellar of the Castle. We went past a hundred iron doors, and then we went past an iron door I remembered. It was the door to the Whispering Room where, for a while, I had been prisoner. On Klepsis there are no duplicates of anything, no two of anything; surely no two iron doors could be alike.

"I wonder what poor unfortunate prisoners are in that hateful room now," I mused out loud. "I hope the room is empty."

"The Whispering Room is seldom empty for very long," Thorn said. "I believe that there are sixteen persons in that big room now. I believe that they will be taken out of there quite soon and executed for the entertainment of the well-born visitors at the gala. Prince Henry has always been quite proud of his executions. Such creativity as he has he pours into them."

"But there were sixteen of us held in that room as prisoners this very evening," I jabbered. "We were to be held there till it was time for *us* to be executed. There is something very wrong about this. I hear voices that chill me. Thorn, I'm dizzy. I'm very, very sick. I believe that I am suffering from the 'unreality syndrome' that afflicts many persons who visit planets not their own. It is the hallucination sickness that cannot easily be resolved. It is the only sickness that cannot be cured until it is proved wrong. As a disease it is very serious: many people die from it. And, as a part of it, there's the terror of falling, down, down, down, out of the unreality and into the reality, to be dashed to death on the reality. I'm wrenched almost apart. If only I didn't recognize some of those voices!"

"Oh, we all get the unreality sickness on Klepsis, my love. It's a warning, and it's a signal to—well, I forget just what it is a warning and a signal for. Let us go into the room of the giant wine tun. You can be healed of almost anything there."

"Thorn, there are voices in the Whispering Room," I stated with more alarm, *"and I recognize those voices."*

"Do not let it worry you, my buried treasure. It is only another reality, and it must be avoided. Come and swim in the giant tun."

"Thorn, that is the voice of Gold Coast O'Mally sounding in the Whispering Room, sounding in fear. And he came out of that room when I did. There are the voices of Conchita O'Brian and Jerome Whitewater and Bartolomo Portuguese and Hektor Lafcadio and Kate Blithespirit the Amazon. Thorn, that is my own voice in that room, my very own voice. Thorn, I'm shaken by this. It crumbles everything."

"Come to the giant tun, my love. It will uncrumble you. It will heal you and make you right and sane."

We went to the big wine cellar which was quite near. The giant tun was the main thing in that room, for there wasn't space for much else. We went up a tall ladder to a catwalk that circled the lip of the big tun. Yes, it would surely hold a hundred thousand glasses of wine, and perhaps its capacity was twice or thrice that. But the level of the wine was about a meter below the edge of the tun.

"How do you drink from it?" I asked Thorn. "We have brought neither bucket nor pitcher."

"Plunge right in, my love. Then you can drink any way you will!" Thorn yiped with sudden merriment and she tumbled me into the big vat. I sank. Then I rose to the surface again.

"Help, I'll drown!" I called out. "No, I suppose I won't," I quickly amended. "But I did envision myself as drowning for a moment there, or as falling more and more rapidly through the wine to be dashed to death on a bottom many kilometers below. There is something very pinnacled about wine in extraordinary quantities. The quick fear of plummeting down barely missed being ghastly."

"Oh, cut it out, kid," Thorn hectored me. "Only goofs

have that fear of falling. Only tedious Lucifer had it really bad. And so he fell *down* when he was thrown from the skies. Why in the world would anybody fall down if he had a choice? He forgot that he was a winged creature and needn't fall at all.

"But, Long John my love, *we also* are winged creatures. Let us never forget that. And let us have no more odd notions for the moment. The wine heals you."

Yes, the wine was healing me, was healing my skewered thumbs and my shredded back, healing my confused mind and my pawky spirit. It was *not* soothing me, no. It healed in an opposite manner. It excited me and lifted me up. Through my brain there paraded vast and happy rhapsodies of wine and of wine spirits. I still heard the voices of familiar persons from the Whispering Room that was very near to us. I heard my own frightened and fluttering voice among them. But the me who swam and sported in this spirited ocean of wine was neither frightened nor fluttery. The duplicity of voices was only an interesting puzzle, no more.

"Thorn, you weaponed loveliness," I called up to her. "If I knew what sort of person could distinguish reality from unreality, I would follow that person to the ends of the galaxy."

"So would I do, so will I do," she said. "There is only one sort of person who can tell the real from the unreal, and that is the historian."

"But *I* am an historian."

"I know it. I wouldn't have you be anything else. And you have the green stone in your brain that can distinguish reality from unreality. It was for this gift of yours that I came looking for you until I found you."

"Thorn, you are kidding, are you not?"

"Oh, a little bit, yes. I kid quite a bit."

"Who are you really?" I called up from the healing ocean of wine. "And how did you happen to be born in Ravel-Brannagan Castle?"

"I am named Tharrala Thorn-Ravel-O'Grogan-Brannagan really, and one must be born somewhere."

I was afraid to look and I was afraid to feel, but I believed that all the bloody wounds and broken bones of my
back and ribcage and thumbs had healed.

"Of course they are healed," Thorn said, matching her
words to my thoughts as she had done several times. "You
now have beautiful scars on your skewered thumbs and
your shredded back, but you are healed."

"How is it done?" I asked. "Is it only the wine? It is common red wine. I should bottle such wine as this, and sell it
as a cure-all, and get rich."

"A big enough bottle of it would impoverish you, my
love. It is the wine that heals, yes. But below a certain critical mass it will not heal. If the mass is below five thousand
barrels, forget it. There are only critical masses of wine at
about a dozen places on all the planets, and at half of those
places they do not even know about the curing properties.

"Come now, my love, there are entertainments going
on. There are plots and intrigues taking place. There are
people being chopped down like weeds. There are ro-
mances springing up like April flowers. There are new
things being done in music and eloquence. There are huge
treasure chests to be discovered under the ground in the
company of your friend Gold Coast O'Mally and some of
your other friends. And we *will* find those treasure chests,
for I know exactly where they are. We will hear a genuine
Tarshish storyteller in a theatre of the sort that you could-
n't guess in a million months. Historian my love, his stories
are such things as history is made of.

"There is a metamorphic encounter that we are to hold
with a Green Robe of the order of Saint Klingensmith. We
will have a meeting with my own great-great-great-
grandfather. Well, you *do* want to meet my family, don't
you? We will talk with Christopher Begorra Brannagan
himself. Is he alive or is he dead? Well, he seldom leaves
his tomb nowadays, but I believe that he is alive. And he is
interested in you. We will find history for you, Long John,
as it coils and uncoils in its nest. Let us go now, my love, or
we may miss part of the fun."

I could not reach the edge of the vat. I had visions of

staying in the big vat of wine till I drowned or at least died. The depth of the critical mass seemed to have diminished by at least a meter, and it was now two meters from the lip of the vat down to the surface of the wine.

I dove deep (in the depths a voice spoke to me, "What is the date?" "The twenty-eighth of the month of Arpad," I said. "Then, tonight is the night that I come out of this place," the voice spoke). I came up with a rush, leaped out of the wine, reached my hands up, and Thorn reached her hands down. She caught mine and she lifted me up easily.

Thorn and I climbed O'Grogan's Mountain when we had gone out from the Castle. Januarius O'Grogan, he who had married a Margaret Brannagan who was the daughter of Christopher Brannagan, the founding father of Klepsis, this Januarius had many things named after him here. O'Grogan's Mountain wasn't a high mountain. It was a long and gentle hill that rose about a hundred meters above the surrounding country, at the highest. But the easy rise of its kilometer-long slope gave comfortable seating or lounging room to more than a hundred thousand persons at one time. And there were probably a hundred thousand persons on it now, watching the colorful doings around Ravel-Brannagan Castle below them. But the highest points of the Castle rose almost exactly even with the highest point of O'Grogan's Mountain.

The highest points of the Castle were the six watchtowers named the Christopher, Januarius, Juda, David, Cloud, and Henry Watchtowers. These were named after Christopher Brannagan, Januarius O'Grogan, Juda O'Grogan-Brannagan, David Ravel, Cloud Ravel-Brannagan, and Henry Ravel-Brannagan, the alpha men, the true-liners, and the interlopers of the six generations of the first family of the Planet of Klepsis. There were really nine families on Klepsis which claimed to be the first family, but none of them was more first than the Brannagan clan.

Even higher than the six watchtowers, even higher than the highest point of O'Grogan's Mountain, was the *En-*

Arche Bell Tower. Nobody now living knew just what it was for. Nobody knew how the giant bell, which had never been rung, could indeed be rung. There was a complex mechanism to ring it, but who now understood that complexity? There was a sort of taboo on this highest bell tower. People did not raise up their eyes or their voices to it. They ignored it, or they tried to. But what was it for? And who was *En-Arche?*

Five of the six regular watchtowers were inhabited by ghosts. Those were the Five Royal Ghosts of Ravel-Brannagan Castle. (There were about a hundred other ghosts associated with the castle, not an unusual number for such a large and storied place.) The sixth of the towers was sometimes inhabited by a man who was very like a ghost in his carrying on, Prince Henry Ravel-Brannagan the Pirate. The first five named of these towers had no stairways. The stairs had been taken down from each of them on the day that the namesake had died, on the same day that construction began on the watchtower of the new ruler. If the name-ruler came back as a ghost, it was reasoned, he would not need a stairway. Brannagan's Ghost, however, was said to climb painfully up the stone shaft from which the stairway was taken, much hampered by stiffness and by having a wooden leg. And yet the Brannagan Ghost could go through walls in the true ghost fashion.

In each of the first five watchtowers there was nothing except the eight broad-field telescopes, one at each of the eight corners of the wind; the big swinging warning bell—without the bell-pull rope which was also taken away on the day of death of its patron; and the lantern—without oil.

But the staired sixth watchtower, that of the living Prince Henry, had all the amenities, for he spent much of his time up there.

"There is a light in the Juda Tower," I said to Thorn.

"Hush, my love, hush," she said. "It is bad manners to mention it. Juda believes that his light is unseen. Juda's Ghost is the most gentle of all of them. He never angry-

faces the people below. He never sets his warning bell to
roaring. He never sets it to banging or pealing at all, but
sometimes he plays little tunes on it with a hammer. He
produces the different notes by striking the bell at its different curvatures. He plays pretty little tunes such as 'Oh
Death Irregular that Comes Betimes' (his own death was
irregular and came betimes), 'Rosa, Rosa, Rosa' (his wife
was Rose Lunaria), 'Wait Here Until the World Begins,'
'Oh Sheba Played the Harp a While a Hundred Years This
Morning' (Juda's daughter-in-law was Sheba McSherry),
'Oh Darkened Skies that Once Shone Bright,' 'Nineteenth
Continent Rag,' 'I'll Wait for You a Hundred Years/I'll
Wait for You Till Morning.' I believe that Juda O'Grogan-
Brannigan, who has been dead just over a hundred years, is
lonesome. And Juda is not at all a portentous ghost. No
direful meaning is ever given by the people to his
appearances."

"Bad manners it may be to mention it, Thorn," I said,
"but now there is a light in the David Tower also."

"The ghost of David Ravel, the Elegant Interloper (that
is really the official title that he gave to himself), is often
not a gentle ghost at all. At times he goes into rages, and I
suspect that he will do so in just a minute, when he checks
his tower and finds what is missing from it."

"And what *is* missing from the David Watchtower,
Thorn?"

"These two telescopes. David had them made on Gaea-
Earth in Germany, where the best telescopes were then
made. This one, from the southeast-corner-of-the-wind
station is for me to use tonight. And this one from the
southwest-corner-of-the-wind station is for thee to use. It
has always been known that the finest of the telescopes are
from the David Tower."

"How and when did you get them, Thorn? If there is no
stairway in that tower, you would have to have climbed the
sheer tower itself. And there was no time that you could
have done it."

"But there was time when I could have done it, Long
John, my love (if there is no time, then I make time), and I

did climb the tower itself, up the outside of it."

"You climbed that sheer one-hundred-meter height that is all stone-built? And the mortar of it is loosened, as I can plainly see through the telescope."

"I climbed it so, yes, my love. Look at the Januarius Tower now. The ghost of that greatest O'Grogan is sitting in the dark there with his lantern unlit, and he is looking through his telescope of the west-corner-of-the-wind directly at the two of us. Turn your glass on him, my love, and you can even see the specks in his magnified viewing eye."

"And he in ours, Thorn."

"Oh, I hadn't thought of that. Of course he can."

"Thorn, do you know that there were several human bodies floating in the lower levels of the great wine tun where my wounds were healed a short time ago?"

"Yes, there are six of them, and each one has its own story. I was hoping you wouldn't see them and be frightened. The popular account is that one of them is not dead. This is the one who was flogged till he seemed quite dead and was then thrown in there by Cloud Ravel-Brannagan, the father of Prince Henry the Pirate and Prince Franco the Outcast and of my mother. Cloud did not believe in the healing properties of that vat of wine. 'Heal yourself, revivify yourself if you can,' he mocked at that person when he threw him in. Now Cloud Ravel is long dead, and his victim perhaps is not. That body, that person, heals slowly, but he heals. When he has been there for fifty years (so the popular story of him goes, and he has now been in there for forty-nine years and an uncertain number of months), his healing will be completed and he will come out."

"Thorn, your tongue is crooked. You made it up."

"I did not make up the living body in that vat. He spoke to you, and you to him. I heard it. And the story I told about him *is* the popular story."

There were five bears on O'Grogan's Mountain that evening, and they did not look like Klepsis bears, so the bear-watchers said. These were two big bears and three little bears of a deep golden color and very good behavior.

They sat up straight there on O'Grogan's Mountain, just as people do, and watched all that was going on. Then Prince Franco let them use his telescope for a while, and they passed it from one to another, all enjoying it. But the father bear had to show one of the little ones how to focus it.

"You look like the Five Royal Intelligent Bears who disappeared so mysteriously from the Golden Garden on Astrobe recently," Prince Franco said to them conversationally. "A completely new species and immensely valuable. Two big bears there were, and three little ones. Astrobe authorities say that there was no way you could have got off that planet, for all transportation there is monitored. Are you the same bears?"

The father bear seemed to nod assent.

"We can't talk very well," one of the little ones said. "Our mouths are made different from people mouths."

"Well, how did you get off Astrobe?" Prince Franco asked them.

"Jumped," the father bear said. He said it very thickly. They really couldn't talk very well.

Was that really Prince Franco sitting between us and the bears, when there had been nobody sitting there a moment before? It sure did look like him.

"Are there archives in the Castle, Thorn?" I asked her.

"No, historian John, not written archives such as you could transcribe out as history. They are in other forms. Oh, hear the angry bell that David Ravel the Interloper has set jangling in the David Tower, my love. 'Thieves in the Night, Thieves in the Night' is the tune it peals. Did you know that a silver-bronze bell was capable of such anger? Hear that refrain 'Robbery, Robbery!' It peals, but nobody will look for the robbers. People are afraid to get mixed up in the affairs of ghosts. Are these not wonderful telescopes, my love?"

Yes, they were. We could read the facial expressions of people as far as two or three kilometers from us. But we felt ourselves watched, at the same time, by a person (not yet a ghost) only half that distance from us. It was Prince

Henry the Pirate watching us from the Henry Watchtower, and he had his southwest-corner-of-the-wind telescope trained directly on us. His own look was one of anger and unease.

"Yes, Prince Henry is looking directly at the two of us," Thorn said, following my thought and observing what I observed.

"No, he isn't," interposed Prince Franco the Outcast. "He's looking at me. I'm not sure that he's noticed the two of you at all."

So Prince Franco had come back to visibility. It had been an odd, even a taboo, interval for me. I hadn't known whether I was *supposed* to have noticed that Prince Franco had come back. What if he believed that he was still invisible?

"Yes, there is sometimes a touch of embarrassment in it," the Prince said. "I do slip at times and not realize that I have become visible again. Or I come back gradually. And other species have a wider range of seeing than do humans. For instance, these intelligent bears here could see me before you could."

Prince Franco was no longer vague. With his glass he studied his brother with irony, and his brother Henry studied him in lowering anger.

"Henry will have to leave his tower at once," Prince Franco told us. "Baron O'Tolliver has just completed the last of his executions, and now our Prince Henry must try to top him in the originality and creativity of his own. He will do so in numbers, but will he do so in originality? And I have heard that some of Henry's victims have escaped and must be substituted for. Things like that throw Henry into a turmoil."

"Whence?" Thorn asked Prince Franco, indicating his telescope.

"Oh, from the Henry Tower, of course, though they are slightly inferior. Everything of my brother's is slightly inferior. It infuriates my brother when I steal trinkets of his, and it's quite easy to do. Since we look exactly alike, I come and go pretty much as I wish. I must only be careful that I am not pent up in an inescapable place when I go vague."

What seemed to be the last of Baron O'Tolliver's executions was a striking vignette of a man being torn to pieces by sixteen horses, eight of them pulling with great force on each leg. Oh, but he was a muscular and well-made man! Those horses heaved and strained, or they seemed to. Then I noticed an oddity about the act. Those sixteen horses were ham actors, and nothing is hammier than a trained horse. These horses were trained especially for this act. They were putting on a show of pulling, but they were pulling hardly at all. Oh, and then the man's left leg came off and eight of the horses went galloping away with it. It took the crowd a moment to realize that the leg that had come off was an artificial leg. The man was a peg-leg clear to the hip. He laughed and hopped after the horses that were dragging his leg away, and the crowds laughed too. It is good to have a comic touch after all the bloodiness. I doubted that Prince Henry would have the light touch with any of his executions.

And now the Prince Henry executions were on.

The first of Prince Henry's victims was wearing a mask, and it was a perfect mask of the seaman Sebastian Jamaica. Then one of the executioners removed the mask for a moment, and the real face of the man was not like that of Sebastian at all.

"I wonder what his real voice is," I asked.

"Oh, it will be his own voice, Long John Tyrone," Prince Franco said. "There is not as much hokus in these things as people are inclined to believe. You yourself were apparently taken in by the voices you heard coming out of the Whispering Room when you were going to the Wine Room. If you'd been able to hear them better, you'd have recognized the conversations. Prince Henry records all the conversations of prisoners in the Whispering Room. When he discovered that his wife, the Princess Angela, had released the bunch of you on her own authority, he went to the Whispering Room and played back your conversations to hear whether there was anything subversive or informative in them. He was in the Whispering Room when you and Thorn went to the Wine Room, a close encounter. Now he has had to scrounge up sixteen (or less) substitutes to execute. He got the best mask-man on the continent to fix up masks, but the mask-man was able to get a good look at only about half of you."

There was some business with dogs about the execution of the person who was wearing the Sebastian Jamaica mask, and I chose not to look at it.

"What is your relationship to your brother Prince Henry?" I asked Prince Franco boldly. An historian must often ask bold questions.

"We are full-blood brothers, historian John. That is our relationship. I avoid all other relationships, especially now when he has all the power in his hands and has put me under sentence of death."

"And what is your relationship to your brother's wife?" I asked still more boldly.

"I covet my brother's wife," Prince Franco said.

The executions were crude, to my mind at least. I had heard that the high people of Klepsis, and Prince Henry in particular, took great pride in their executions. There was much pomp to them, but I could not see anything to take pride in. There were the One Thousand Trumpets that raised their brazen and blaring voices before and after each announcement. But, from my place, and scanning things with my excellent glass, I estimated this one thousand really to be no more than about a hundred and twenty trumpets and trumpeters.

"Hearken all to the beheading of a traitor to the realm and a partisan of the interdicted Prince Franco the Outcast," came the announcement. (No amplifiers were used on Klepsis; the proclaimers were huge-chested men who had been trained in loud proclaiming since their childhoods.) "This is the seaman and schemer named Hogson Roadapple whose death we call you all to witness. May the

death he suffers here be only the first of the ten thousand
deaths he will suffer in Hell in just his first hour there.''

Hogson was the second of the victims of Prince Henry. I
believe that it was Hogson Roadapple himself that they
had there now. He had let himself be retaken somehow.
The blade of the black-masked executioner was burnished
to a high silver, and it caught the light of all the torches and
spotlights, of the two moons that were bright in the sky,
and of the distant Sun Proxima. The burnished blade de-
scended to the merry chortling of calliope music, and the
head rolled. Men quickly raised it up on the point of a
heavy spear. Then the head grimaced and spoke, and a little wave of horror swept over the people who were close
enough to hear him. After the head had spoken, it closed
its eyes and died.

Prince Franco was chuckling: "He cursed them with my
own curse out of his severed head, and they reeled back in
horror. So we have psyched them a little bit with that set-
to. Those evil ones are more and more in fear of me now."

"How do you know what words he spoke?" I asked.
Prince Franco looked at me in amazement.

"You mean that you cannot read mouth?" he sputtered.
"You, an historian, cannot read mouth? I would guess that
ninety percent of all primary history is garnered by reading
mouth at a distance through a spy glass, often through a
Glotz-Kimmel glass that sees through walls. Long John,
there is really no other way to discover true history in its
delicto moments. Thorn, this poor historian belongs to
you, does he not? Teach him to read mouth at least."

"Yes, I will. I hadn't realized that he was so inept in his
own trade."

"What is *your* relationship to Tharrala Thorn here?" I
asked the Prince in what I believed was a sly manner.

"I am her uncle," Prince Franco said. "Also her Dutch
uncle. And, to some extent, her funny uncle. And I am her
godfather. The next victim—I thought for a moment that it
was a girl from your party, but I see that it is a substitute."

It was a girl in Terpsichore Callagy's red-and-gold wrapper, but it was not Terpsichore. She was thicker than Terpsichore. The girl, the pseudo-Terpsichore Callagy (she was a stronger and more determined person than Terpsichore), was to be crushed to death by elephants. Well, Prince Henry did have a prime herd of those beasts. The girl was staked out on her back, hand and foot. Then a large elephant was brought to stand on her with all four feet.

"Women are much more durable at this than men are," Thorn told me. "I am a one-elephant girl myself, but this will go far beyond that."

When the beast was led off her and the executioners came to check whether she was dead, the girl erupted from her staked-out position. She pulled those four stakes right out of the ground. She rose resurgent to her feet and, with arms akimbo, she cursed her executioners vehemently.

I began to get into this business of mouth-reading with enthusiasm. I understood half of the girl's fiery cursing, and I guessed at the other half.

They staked her down again with heavier and longer stakes. They hammered her head with the same mallet they drove the stakes with. They placed a long, wide, and very heavy plank across her body. They brought out four elephants and had two of them stand on each end of the plank for three minutes. I found that the odds on the girl surviving even this were two-to-one. She seemed to be known in the revolutionary or some other movement.

"They'll not kill her, not her," people gave the opinion. "It will take more than elephants to kill her." The executioners led the elephants a few paces off her then and came to see whether she was really dead. And once more the girl erupted from the ground. She tumbled the big plank off her body, pulled the four larger stakes out of the ground, rose to her feet, and cursed her executioners sevenfold.

"Oh, oh, oh!" Thorn cried out. "Poor stubborn Ischyrognomon! Will they run out of girl first, or will they run out of elephants first?"

"They will run out of girl first," Prince Franco said sadly. "Castle Ravel-Brannagan will never run out of elephants."

They staked the girl down again with *three* big stakes at each of her hands and feet. They banged her much more relentlessly on the head with the same stake-driving mallet; and this may have been decisive. They brought four more elephants, making eight in all. They had four of the elephants stand on each end of the plank for a full nine minutes. Then they led the elephants away and came to the girl to examine her. She was dead.

The usually stolid Prince Franco was crying. The girl must have been a partisan of his. "She is a true daughter of Klepsis," the Prince said then, "stubborn, tough, resurgent, fearless, but not of towering mentality. A little bit stupid, really, to be so decidedly in support of such an indecisive leader. Long John Tyrone and Tharrala Thorn, come along with me for a while. We have an important and happy item of business to transact."

"I want to see the execution of the one who is rigged in place of me," I said.

"I believe that he will be very near the last one of them," the Prince stated, "and possibly we will be able to return in time for it. But our happy item of business is more important than the executions. Come."

We went down a flank of O'Grogan's Mountain. We went through an almost impenetrable wasteland, a mixture of rock and swamp and jungle, that was nevertheless very near to the Castle. We went into a large monument or walk-in tomb, and we saw an old man with a powerful and interesting face. He was sitting on a transparent coffin from the old days of Klepsis glassblowing. It had been blown as a single bubble.

"Come you now, that all things may be done by law and order and ancient custom," the old man said. "Here is a Green Robe of the order of Saint Klingensmith. Begin it, Green Robe!"

The Green Robe was a large and friendly looking man, with both his hair and his beard of that flaming, vulgar, orange-yellow-red color.

> "To God the Father glory be,
> And to His Son in Kingdom Come,
> And to the Spirit One in Three,
> *Nunc, et in omne saeculum.*"

So did the Green Robe intone it in a musical way. This was a charade, and I love charades.

"Do not be nervous," Thorn said to me. "It will be easy. It will be quick. And it will be wonderful for all our days."

> "Oh, will you take or will you decline?
> Or will you stay or will you go?
> Now comes it to the mine-and-thine.
> Do you accept?"
>   *"Accipio."*

The Green Robe had intoned all of this except the last word of it, and Thorn and I had spoken that last word together, *"Accipio,"* though how it happened that such a word, which was strange to me, tumbled out of my mouth is something that I do not know. The charade became more interesting.

Prince Franco gave a gold ring to me and one to Thorn. Thorn put hers on my finger, and it was so loose it wobbled. I tried to put mine on her finger, and it would not go.

"Oh, how grotesque, my love," Thorn chirped. "My fingers are thicker than yours are. Let us reverse them."

We reversed the rings, and then each of us had our fit. What is the primary meaning of rings in charades? Something, something, but I could not remember it. Then the Green Robe intoned another verse:

> "Oh, be to each a unity,
> And flesh of flesh and bone of bone.
> All blessing to be on thee! And thee!
> *Conjúngo vos in Matrimón.*"

I knew that it was very clever, though I did not quite understand it. The charade seemed to be over with. Well, I would figure it out or I would give up on it and ask somebody for the answer.

"Come again later in the night and talk to me," said the old man with the powerful and interesting face, he who was sitting on the transparent glass coffin. "I am in better form later in the night. And here is your pedigree, pup. You belong to the family now."

The old man gave me a paper filled with names and generations. "This is possibly the first scrap of written history that I have found on Klepsis," I said to myself.

"Oh, history," said the old man, just as if I had spoken the word out loud. "And historians. I sent for you as historian, but can you do anything about the Klepsis jumble? Historians are the only ones who do not know what is happening when it is happening, and do not know what has happened when it is over with. And there is much happening here right now."

What did this old man mean when he said to me, "I sent for you as historian?"

"We will be back, father of my fathers," Thorn told the old man. We left the big walk-in tomb then and went back towards the foregrounds of the Castle, to the area of the action.

"I still haven't guessed the answer to the charade," I said as we walked. "What is it?"

"Oh, we just got married, my wobble-brained love. We just got married," Thorn told me.

"Oh? What? That'd fit the charade all right. It would be a valid answer, but I'd never have guessed it. Do you mean married in fact?"

"In fact and in fancy, my love, and in all ways. It isn't that I'm all that taken with you. It's just that—well, I'll be able to manipulate you better if I'm married to you, and you are one of the pieces that we'll have to manipulate. Oh, don't look so glum, my love. I will guarantee you that you'll enjoy it."

I had heard of "getting married" before, of course. I *am* an historian. But I could not quite recall all the details or meanings of it.

From the almost impenetrable wasteland and swamp and thicket and Tartarus of stones on our right hand as we came from the big walk-in tomb and monument to the area of action nearer the Castle, there was the sound of digging. There was the sound of spade and shovel, of mattock and rock-splitter, of muck-shovel and of bailing-bucket. It was the sound of digging through sand and quicksand, loam and muck and slate-mud and gumbo clay all in the same place. Somebody was digging in the near dark in that thicketed wasteland. But who, and why?

The gala had made considerable inroads into the provisions. The huge barbecued whale, lying on its side, was now a half-empty shell of its former self. It was a cavern. Lights flickered inside it. It looked like a theatre with a strange, slotted, fleshy door to enter by. There were torches and whale-oil lamps burning inside the hulk, and somebody inside the carcass was speaking compelling words.

At the execution site we were barely in time. I found that it was my self, the last of the victims, who was ready to be done in.

"I must leave you two, Princess Tharrala Thorn and Duke Tyrone," said Prince Franco the Outcast, and he dashed off somewhere.

"What, am I a duke now, Thorn?" I asked. "Is that a part of this 'getting married' business?"

"Yes, you are a duke now. And it *is* a part of your getting married to the Princess Tharrala Thorn."

"Why am I not a prince if I am married to a princess?"

"Because you are only my consort, until somehow and someday you seize the power of a prince. And you are not immediately a prince because all princes on Klepsis, except Prince Henry, have been put under sentence of death by this same Prince Henry."

That man about to be executed was my self. There was no facial detail in which he was not. And then I saw that he was no more my self than the sturdy and stubborn Ischyrognomon had been Terpsichore Callagy. This man was too thick to be me, too tall, too strong, too springy, too robust. But he was wearing my face, and he was bawling out in approximately my voice:

"Kill me, kill me, and the very stones will rise as rebels against you to take my place. Kill me, and there will be ten more sturdy men in place of me."

His strange form of execution was announced to trumpets and calliope skreeing. He was to be taken up to the top of the absolutely taboo *En-Arche* Bell Tower, and he was to be hurled down from it to his death.

But that other and more robust me, standing defiantly in the circle of strongmen executioners, seemed to be surrounded by a lightning of spirit, and he made them all quail back from him a little bit. And he bawled out in my almost-voice:

"You believe that I am weaponless? I have but to ask the True Spirit of Klepsis, and the weapon will come to my hands. I do ask it. It does come!"

And a Ricco-recoil handgun (it was a handgun for a man who was man enough to handle it) was moving through the air towards the defiant prisoner who was on the execution spot. The man, the more robust me, grabbed it. He held it in both hands, and he—

("Oh, it is only Prince Franco gone vague again," Thorn whispered to me. "He brought the weapon to your double." "But who *is* my robuster double, and how did he get that way?" I asked. "Oh, maybe it was the first disguise he thought of, to look like you. He must have seen you with Franco or myself. And it would give everything away for him to die with his *own* face.")

—and he fired the gun with a booming chatter. He mowed all those strongmen executioners down. Then suddenly there were a hundred weapons being fired, or a thousand. There were presumably two sides to this sudden battle, but who could tell friend from foe?

"We have got to find cover," I said. "We are unarmed, and we are in the line of fire. The line of fire is everywhere. Where can we go?"

"Into the whale," Thorn said.

FIFTH CANTO

Tales of Tarshish

The empty hulk or the shell of the whale (if it might be so called) made a perfect, though somewhat greasy, theatre. It was partly open at the top, and the stars might be seen. It was open where we entered in the belly, but that was not a large entrance. The walls of the carcass were tolerably sound, still two meters or so thick with meat, and the bone structure was intact. Bullets and exploding pellets from the Ricco-recoil handguns and other weapons thudded powerfully against the fleshy-fatty walls of the whale, but few of them penetrated into the inner cavern.

There were a hundred or so persons inside the whale, two thirds of them children. Half a dozen whale-oil lamps were burning and flickering, and a number of devilfish torches. People still munched and swallowed pieces of the whale in which they were assembled.

In this theatre-in-the-whale, a Tarshish storyteller was the whole program. He was a grizzled and lined, but powerful man. Was he blind? Of course. All good storytellers are blind. But he was one of the new blind-men-who-can-see. He was technically blind, yes. But he wore one of the expensive and sophisticated Eumolpe Pierce-Brain Light-Harvester arrangements as a heavy glass-and-metal mask over his eyes. This gave him a measure of surrogate or artificial sight. The prods of the thing *did* pierce into his brain, and they did offer him a simulacrum of sight. "The Pragmatic Equivalent of Sight" is the way the Eumolpe device was advertised.

The Tarshish storyteller was beginning another story just as Thorn and I got settled in the crowded theatre-in-the-whale:

"This is the way they tell it:

"The first things that jumped were tumbleweed thistles. As they rolled over the prairie land of one planet, they would pick up seeds and spores of all sorts of plants and trees, and nits of insects, and even nests full of eggs of the smaller birds. Then one of these tumbleweeds, rolling along on one planet, would immediately be rolling along on the surface of another planet around another sun maybe even in another system. This is the way that the distant planets were populated with plants and insects and small birds.

"Then it happened to the fish. Fishes would be swimming along in creeks or lakes or oceans or seas or rivers of one planet, and then they would be swimming along in the corresponding waters of another planet. So were the waters of all the planets populated with fishes, except the whales, which were too big to jump.

"Then the larger prey birds got into the act and petitioned that they might as well go to other planets as migrate, summer and winter, on just one world. They made a very great noise about it, and it was finally allowed. 'For the hardness of your hearts it is permitted to you, but in the beginning it was not so,' God said. Then all sorts of animals, coneys, chipmonks, beavers, bears, monkeys, got the same grudging permission. And finally the short-tailed humans of Tarshish got it by a mistake. God, for a moment, forgot that they were humans and thought that they were monkeys.

"These short-tailed humans of Tarshish learned to jump ships when they jumped. A ship with even one of these short-tailed humans on it could be sailing along on the waters of one planet, such as Tarshish, with a dozen humans of the regular sort on it, and then it would be sailing along in the waters of an entirely different planet. This was before spaceships had been invented. When God noticed that this was being done, He said 'No more of that, no more of that; I forbid it.' Everybody obeyed this prohibition except the pirates, for the pirates will obey nobody. Then it was only the pirate ships, with always one short-tailed human from Tarshish on each of them, that would raid and scuttle in the waters of one planet, and would then evade pursuit by armored ships by jumping to another planet and sailing along in its placid waters just as if nothing had happened.

"That is the story. That is the end of the story. This is the way it has always been told."

I liked the story. We historians say that there is history deeply hidden in every good story, but what history was hidden in this one? Thorn, strangely, said that it was all true.

"Yes, the pirates in my ancestry, the Eleven High Pirates of Klepsis, used to jump their ships by means of a gifted short-tailed human on each of them. They *did,* Long John my love, and it was by means of such tricks that they were able to bring so many shiploads of treasure to Klepsis."

The Tarshish storyteller began another one.

"This is the way they tell it:

"Tarshish has no mean civilization. It is the nexus of the whole cosmos, the world that is the bellwether of all the worlds. When the call 'Awake! Awake!' comes (as it will come some morning soon), somebody on Tarshish will awake immediately. The other worlds do not even know that they are asleep, so how could anybody on them harken to the cry 'Awake! Awake!'?

"The civilization on Tarshish is more intuitive than are other civilizations. As befits sleeping persons, we operate entirely by intuition and we do not use any reason at all.

This is not a handicap to us, although we of Tarshish are as unconscious and unborn as so many machines. We build things in our sleep, in our unborn state. Spaceships, for instance, can be built entirely by intuition, just as easily as a Wanken's Wasp builds its nest entirely by intuition. In neither case is conscious science or technology or engineering used. And we on Tarshish, we who are entirely unconscious and unborn, we build better spaceships than do persons of any other planet."

"Storyteller, if you're completely unconscious, you don't even know that you're here," a superior young boy who had "born on Klepsis" written all over him protested.

"That's right," the storyteller agreed. "I do *not* know that I'm here. I do not know that I'm talking to you. I'm pretty sure that *you're* not here, little boy. I do not hear or understand your question, but I answer it by intuition. We of Tarshish do not know anything else, but we do know that we're unconscious. Other persons on other worlds do not know even that much. There is no thing anywhere that is conscious, that knows where it is and what it does. There is no such thing as life, or matter, or planet, or space, or time, or mountain, or river. There will not be any of these things until time and space and matter begin. And none of these things has begun yet."

"You penny Socrates, you halfpenny Klunkhausen, *I* am conscious," said a second little boy. "Here I am, and I know I am here. Here on Klepsis, all of these things have begun. Life on Klepsis began five generations or two hundred years ago. And the universe itself began at least fifty years before that, for Christopher Brannagan was fifty years old when he first brought life, his own, to Klepsis."

"No, no," the storyteller argued, almost as if he had heard and understood what the little boy had said. "These ideas that the worlds already exist or have existed for a long time are all wrong. On the Planet Skokumchuck they insist that the universe is four hundred years old, on Aphthonia that it is eight hundred, and on Astrobe that it is twelve hundred years old. And on Gaea-Earth (get this, people!) they maintain that the universe is *two thousand, two hundred years old*. And they say that they are now living in the year *twenty-two hundred*. But all of these things are only imaginings in minds that don't even exist. The universe has not begun yet."

"Well, when *will* it begin, storyteller?" a third little boy asked.

"In just a moment, little boy, in just a moment," the storyteller said. "Since there are no intervals of time before time begins, everything that happens in the preexistence is just one moment from the beginning. So time, and all that goes with it, will begin in just a moment."

"You are laughing at us, you farthing Fripple," a little girl said. "Your face is straight, but your stomach shakes and bounces, so I know that you are laughing at us."

"That is impossible," the storyteller insisted. "Since I have neither face nor stomach, I cannot be laughing either internally or externally. There is no laughter yet. There is nothing yet. Not till the 'moment' comes."

"And what is it that will happen when the 'moment' arrives?" the girl demanded. "What happens when things all begin?"

"Oh, it will be a grand race then. The great command that will be given at the beginning of time can be translated as 'Wake Up' as well as 'Let There Be Light.' And, no matter how close the race is, one thing somewhere will wake up before anything else does. Then that one thing will be the only thing in existence, the beginning-thing of the world. All things else will be no more than items in the mind of that first thing that wakes up. So, all of us here (no, not here, there is nobody here), so all of us, in just a moment, will be no more than items in the mind of a dog, or a bird, or a grasshopper, or a swamp, or a parasite in the stomach of a fish. For this one first-to-awaken thing will be the only thing, and all else will be but imaginings of that thing."

"Can a fish be only an imagining in the mind of a parasite

that's in its own stomach?" a grown man asked. "That's against all geometry."

"Oh, absolutely it can," the Tarshish storyteller insisted. "There is not any geometry and there will not ever be. The first thing, whatever it is, will not entertain any geometry in its mind.

"That is the story, that is the end of the story, this is the way it has always been told."

"I have heard him before, on Thirty-Third Continent," a man said. "He always tells that story, but I believe that it is no story at all."

Six persons with flutes played little tunes then, as a sort of intermission to the stories. One of the little tunes they played was "The World Begins Too Soon."

The Tarshish storyteller then told these stories:

"The Bloodiest Piracy of the Ship *The Dina O'Grogan.*"

"The True Story of Maybe Jones City. 'Tis Not What Maybe Believed It To Be."

"The Three Daughters of King O'Hara."

"The Weaver's Son and the Giant of the White Hill."

"The Fisherman's Son and the Gruagach of Tricks."

"The Thirteenth Son of the King of Tarshish."

"The Story of the First of the Three Ladies of Sikestown."

"The Young Man Whose Hands Were Cut Off."

"The Story of the Lovers Neameh and Noam."

"The Story of the Magic Horse."

"The Thirteenth Voyage of Es-Sinibad the Pirate."

"Irem the Tarshish Paradise."

"The Death of Pentheus."

"The Treasure Caves of Klepsis."

"The Stubborn Girl Who Was Crushed to Death by Elephants."

The storyteller explained that this latter story was new,

and that he was telling it for the first time, and that it would get better with the retelling.

After this, the storyteller declared a recess. I felt that this had been the best part of his repertoire. Anything after this would be a falling off.

Through the holes in the top of the whale we could see bright fires burning and the reflections of them in the sky. The only thing around there big enough to maintain such fires was Ravel-Brannagan Castle itself.

"But Brannagan Castle is built of stones and of bricks, and it has no wood except a few pieces of brushwood," I protested. "How could stone and brick burn so brightly?"

"Nay, Duke Tyrone," a man said. "It's mostly made of peat-bricks; and nothing, not even pieces of coal, burns as intensely as peat-bricks."

"How do you know my name and title?" I asked. "And how could there be peat for peat-bricks on Klepsis if there have never been any trees here? Peat is formed out of old and decayed trees. How could it have formed here?"

"That is the sort of question that only an historian could answer," said the man.

"Ah, I think I'll just go outside, come what may," another man said. And half a dozen other men went out with him. "We have to be where things are doing," they said. The fire and crossfire outside of the whale were still murderous, and several of the men who went out were immediately shot down. But none of that bunch seemed to want to return to the safety of the whale.

For some time we had been aware of a strident screaming that entered even into the secluded interior of the whale. And, from the reflections in the sky as we saw them through the holes in the top of our whale-hulk, we knew that a taller and more crowning fire was burning now.

A wounded man tottered into the whale. "It's the David Tower that's burning," he said, "and it's something to see. Oh, the horrifying reek and heat of it! And the strident and incredible screaming is that of the cranky ghost David Ravel who is caught in the tower and its veritable inferno, and he seems to believe that he is burning to death. He burned to death the first time, you know, the first time that the David Tower burned."

We heard digging under us.

"They are mining the whale," a fearful person said. "They will blow us all up in what we believed was a place of safety."

But the shooting outside was dying down like water turned off at a water tap.

"What can the matter be?" I asked.

"They're running out of ammunition," my Princess Thorn said. "Klepsis is like a banana republic, without the bananas that will not grow here. They do not think things through here. They plan poorly. Every civil war they've ever had here has collapsed for lack of ammunition. When we come into our power, my love, we will travel to worlds that have proper and sustained wars. Well, it's back to the dagger and the short sword and the arrow and the piano-wire garrote, now. I've always liked the silent and deadly scuffle better, anyhow. Oh, poor Ghost of David Ravel the Elegant Interloper! He believes that he is in horrible agony. And so he is, subjectively. I don't know why I feel such sympathy for the arrogant person, except that he's my great-grandfather."

"David Ravel, the Elegant Interloper into the Brannagan Recension, is *your* great-grandfather?" I asked uneasily. After all, this was *my* family too now. I saw with disappointment mixed with pleasure that the Tarshish storyteller had fallen asleep.

"Yes, my great-grandfather," Princess Thorn said. "And I myself, in this latter day, have returned to my own house and home as an interloper. I lack only elegance to be an Elegant Interloper like my ancestor who is now screaming his long-dead throat out."

"*I* think you are elegant, Thorn," I said awkwardly. And then I flushed with shame. Oh corn, oh corn, come and cover me up!

"Really, that screaming is not elegant of him," Princess

Thorn complained with a certain embarrassment. "He is long dead. He is a ghost. And there is no way that a ghost could feel real pain."

I noticed that the sleeping storyteller cocked one ear at that.

"I'll waste no feelings on him," Thorn maintained. "A ghost can no more feel pain than a stone or a hill or a river or a metal ingot can feel pain. A ghost can no more feel pain than a piece of machinery can feel it."

I noticed that the Tarshish storyteller cocked his other ear and woke up at this. The digging under our whale had become nearer and louder.

"All these things *do* feel pain," the storyteller said firmly. "And, being on a time scale that may be a billion-to-one to ours, they may feel a billion times as much pain as we do. But let me not forget to use the designated formula:

"This is the way they tell it:

"Imagine a soul in Hell. It is in everlasting agony, so everlasting that a billion years of it is only as one drop of water compared to the time-ocean of pain in store for it. Then imagine the pain if a human soul were concentrated into something no bigger than a mu-meson. The concentration of pain would be many billionfold what it had been before, and there are other subatomic particles that have even more capacity for pain than the mu-meson. I believe that subatomic particles do commonly feel pain trillions of times more intense than any human will ever feel. I believe that this concentrated pain is the motivation of the universe. If a human would hop around so lively that he would be in as many as six hundred places at one time (see Bluffer's Thirty-Third Equation) we would suspect that he was in great pain. If he writhed and staggered to such an extent that he went backward in time (and subatomic particles do often stagger backward in time), we would know that he was in agony.

"And large things as well as small things may feel exquisite pain. Consider almost any mountain upthrust. What

writhing agony must have brought it about! What screaming deep in the ground must have accompanied upthrusts
as much as nine thousand meters high! Oh, the screaming
planets and the hysterical mountains of them! A ghost cannot feel pain, you say? A ghost can feel more terrible pain
than flesh can ever feel. It can feel the pristine pain
undiluted by the body."

But the ghost of David Ravel the Elegant Interloper had
stopped screaming. Somebody said that the Castle Boys
Volunteer Fire Department had put out the fire in the David Watchtower.

The digging below the whale was much nearer now.
Soon there would be a breakthrough.

"You say that a stone or a river or a metal ingot or a
piece of machinery cannot feel pain?" the storyteller was
continuing, but he was very sleepy. He was looking for an
end.

"Do not forget the designated formula," I said.

"That is the story. That is the end of the story. That is the
way it has always been told," Princess Thorn recited it for
him.

"Thank you," said the Tarshish storyteller, and he fell
into untroubled sleep.

A sharp-bladed spade came up through the bottom of
the whale. Then the black head and face of Andrew Gold
Coast O'Mally came up through the bottom of the whale.

"Oh, it's Long John the Historian!" Gold Coast cried
out. "Where have we come up?"

"In the middle of the whale," I told him. The children in
the whale all gazed at him in glee. They had never seen a
man come up out of the ground before, surely not a man
like Gold Coast O'Mally.

"He is a Tellurian giant, the creature who lives in the
middle of the world," they all said. "See his black face from
living in the middle of the world! I bet he knows more stories than the storyteller does, living in the middle of the
planet the way he does. And he has gold. All underground

dwellers have gold. Give us pieces of gold, Tellurian giant!"

And Gold Coast O'Mally gave each of the children a big gold coin. All of his pockets were full of them.

"Ah, Long John the Historian, come on down with us and bring your slave girl with you," Gold Coast said. "We'll plug this passage behind us. We've hit it rich, real rich. The treasure maps were true."

Princess Thorn and myself followed Gold Coast O'Mally down into the passage that was under the whale. We plugged the passage behind us.

We know, though, that one of the stories the Tarshish storyteller told is true, and we know which one it is.

It's not the one you think.

SIXTH CANTO

Treasure Caves of Klepsis

This is the ancestry and descent of the first and foremost house of Klepsis, the high house of the Brannagans. This is the "pedigree" that the old man gave me in the walk-in tomb just after I had gone through a charade that was not in fact a charade, with Tharrala Thorn.

Christopher Brannagan is known as the Father of Klepsis. He was a peg-legged man, and it has been stated that he had no children of his own. In my own person and ghost I deny this. I had several children; my daughter, the only one on Klepsis, is the only one that pertains to this account, my daughter Margaret.

I, Christopher Brannagan, married *Margaret Summertime*. She had been named Margaret Thyme, and she was the widow of John Summers, who was one of the party of Christopher Brannagan on the first arrival at Klepsis. Margaret compounded a surname, Summertime, for herself from Summers and Thyme. This is the first generation of Klepsis.

Margaret Brannagan was the daughter of Margaret Summertime-Brannagan, the wife of the great Christopher Brannagan. It is said that this Margaret was the daughter of John Summers and not of Christopher Brannagan, but are those who say it sure of their facts? I say that she was my daughter. This daughter Margaret married *Januarius O'Grogan* from Tarshish. This is the second generation of Klepsis.

The children of Margaret Brannagan and Januarius O'Grogan were:

Juda O'Grogan-Brannagan, a gentle man who married Rose Lunaria.

Ruben O'Grogan-Brannagan, a pirate who went and ravaged World Abounding nine times.

Levi O'Grogan-Brannagan. Levi was Bluebeard the Pirate. He had thirteen wives and more than one hundred children from the thirteen of them.

Simeon O'Grogan-Brannagan. Simeon accumulated and buried somewhere near Ravel-Brannagan Castle on Klepsis ten thousand large chests filled with gold and gemstones.

Dan O'Grogan-Brannagan, a cruel and crafty pirate.

Nefthal O'Grogan-Brannagan. He put ten thousand persons to the sword.

Gad O'Grogan-Brannagan. The "Gold of Gad" is proverbial.

Aser O'Grogan-Brannagan. He gave up piracy (when the game was about worn out) and became an Ocean Marshal.

Issachar O'Grogan-Brannagan. He was killed while still a youth.

Zabulon O'Grogan-Brannagan. He also was killed while only a youth, but he did a lot of killing of his own first.

Benjamin O'Grogan-Brannagan. Benjamin has gone into the Klepsis story as a "good-guy pirate." He did his own publicity, but he was not as good as he painted himself.

Joseph O'Grogan-only. ("No," Margaret testified for the record once. "Joseph was my son only by adoption. He is the son of Januarius by his previous marriage. He was the eldest of my tall sons, though from his boyish look you'd take him for the youngest. He and Juda are the only ones who never broke my heart.")

There was also a daughter of Margaret and Januarius, *Dina O'Grogan-Brannagan*. All of the sons except Juda and Joseph were pirates, as was their sister Dina. These were the high pirates of the great age of piracy on Klepsis. Their eleven tall ships, named the *Ruben, Levi, Simeon, Dan, Nefthal, Gad, Aser, Issachar, Zabulon, Benjamin*, and *The Dina O'Grogan*, were the terror of all the oceans and continents of Klepsis; and they also had themselves transported to sail and ravage the seas of almost every other planet. The crews of *The Dina O'Grogan* were more savage than the crews of any of the other tall pirate ships of this family. This is the third generation of Klepsis.

John Hethite Brannagan was the son of Juda O'Grogan-Brannagan and Rose Lunaria. For wife he took *Sheba McSherry*. He was murdered however by:

David Ravel the Elegant Interloper. David not only took the life of John Hethite, but he took his wife's, Sheba McSherry's, also. This was the tangled fourth generation of Klepsis.

Cloud Ravel-Brannagan was the son of David Ravel and of Sheba McSherry. Cloud's own wife was Brigid Hearn. Cloud represents the fifth generation of Klepsis.

Cloud Ravel-Brannagan and Brigid Hearn had three children:

Princess Placidia Ravel-Brannagan. She married an adventurer named Tarquin Thorn who had

some idea of being the second Elegant Interloper
in the Brannagan line. He failed in this, however,
and was murdered by one of his brothers-in-law.
Princess Placidia and Tarquin Thorn had only one
child, a daughter named Tharrala. She was driven
into the wilderness for a sin too unspeakable to
mention.

The other two children of Cloud Ravel-
Brannagan and Brigid Hearn were the twin
brothers:

Prince Henry Ravel-Brannagan the Pirate. He
is a great robber, but he is not personally an
ocean pirate. He doesn't know one end of a ship
from the other. His wife is the Princess Angela
Gilmartin-Ravel-Brannagan.

Prince Franco Ravel-Brannagan the Outcast.
Prince Franco has no wife.

These children of Cloud Ravel and Brigid Hearn
are the sixth generation of Klepsis.

Princess Tharrala Thorn says that she is the
seventh generation of Klepsis, but I, the old
ghost, and Prince Franco the Outcast, and possibly Princess Angela, are the only ones in the family who will have anything to do with her. She stays
mostly in the wilderness for her unspeakable sin (I
do not know what it is, but she says she will tell me
some day), and she is hardly well enough estab-
lished to be a generation. If she wants to be considered a generation, let her generate!

Nevertheless, she is a favorite of mine. I have
committed unspeakable sins myself. . . . This is
written by my own ghostly hand.

Christopher Begorra Brannagan
The Father of Klepsis

We were down in the galleries and arcades and passages
and caves and caverns, partly natural limestone, partly
hewn rocks. Going by the treasure maps, Gold Coast and

his band had dug out one old shaft at one end of the complex. Then they'd traveled two hundred meters of the galleries without going into any of the side passages, and had then dug their way up through a filled-in shaft that had once been topped by an inn called "The Queen-of-the-Ocean Haven and Hostel for Tired and Irregular Farers of the Heights and the Deeps." The map showed the "Sign of the Whale" as the sign of this old inn. But the whale in which Thorn and myself had found haven had been roasted only that afternoon. Was it a symbol after the fact? Was it a female, and could she be called the "Queen of the Ocean"?

"Sure she was a female," Thorn said. "Can't you tell things like that? Even gross Prince Henry wouldn't serve tough male whale at a gala."

With Gold Coast O'Mally were eight other friends who had sailed together on *The Dina O'Grogan* for however short a time. They were:

Terpsichore. She now wore seaman's tattered blue instead of her red and gold wrapper. "Oh, this is the soul of art itself!" she gushed with the same rich gushing sound that gold coins make when poured out. "There is no art anywhere like thrown-open chests of gold, except piles of loose gold. Oh, magic art! To see such as this I was born!"

Jerome Whitewater. He had old ties with the first family of Klepsis. But did he have old ties with these caverns also?

Bartolomo Portuguese. He had the pseudonym of an old Gaea pirate, and he had the look of one. But he was from Tarshish originally. He wore his hair in a tarred pigtail, and he had a tailpiece at the back of his seaman's trousers. He'd had all these attributes when I first saw him, but it was only now that he gave me an uneasy feeling.

Hektor Lafcadio, the Greek God. He was a statue of a sort, of the sort that had not yet shown much real life.

Kate Blithespirit, the Amazon from Camiroi. Aye, but she was a dropout from Camiroi. The heartiest friend ever, though.

Fairbridge Exendine, the Penny Philosopher from the Trader Planet Emporion.

Sebastian Jamaica. He was of Klepsis, a Klepsicle.

Sparaticus. The green-eyed one, not the blue-eyed one.

Eight of them; and Gold Coast and myself made ten of those who had arrived on *The Dina O'Grogan.* So seven others: Conchita O'Brian, Otis Landshark, Kwong Ti, Karl-the-Great Okra, Frank Shea, the blue-eyed Sparaticus, and Hogson Roadapple, had been killed by Prince Henry's killers.

Hektor Lafcadio was cutting the names of those seven on blank plaques in the wall. Several hundred names were already there and the title above them was, *Those Who Have Died In Irregular Seas And Skies.*

"We have words to put on the plaque of Conchita," said three parley birds who flew in. "She was a specialist in coded technology, but only we parley birds really understood her code. We have cold qualms about her dying so lively and so young. She is a cult figure to us, and these are cult words."

"No, no, no!" the Ghost of Brannagan roared as he made an appearance. "We'll have no more qualms nor cultishness on Klepsis." But Hektor Lafcadio quietly cut the cult words of the parley birds for Conchita.

Ah well, those of us who were left made up a happy band. And Tharrala Thorn, my princess with the flaming orange-yellow-red soul, became the ornament of the band. Gold Coast O'Mally included all of us share-and-share-alike in the project of the caverns, even though it was he who had the treasure maps and who had followed the quests all his life.

I didn't know whether these gallery-caves held the "ten thousand large chests filled with gold and gemstones" that had been accumulated by the pirate Simeon O'Grogan-Brannagan, or whether they held the proverbial Gold of Gad of Simeon's brother, the pirate Gad O'Grogan-Brannagan, or whether this was the treasure of the other nine pirate brothers and sister.

These large chests in the caverns were very large, shoulder-high to a tall man, and their height was their smallest dimension. Fifty or so of them had been opened at random by Gold Coast and his friends, and they were all full of gold and gemstones that cascaded out when their lids were thrown back. They had been stuffed full-up even under the bowed lids. It was mostly gold coin, though there were also brow-arching and blood-wakening artifacts.

'There is history in these gold coins at least,' I told my own person. 'The scripts on them are about the first written history I have found on Klepsis, though hardly any of the coins are from Klepsis. Maybe the dragon coins are from here.'

I was very pirate-gold-conscious just then, having read, while in the whale, the "Ancestry and Descent of the Foremost House of Klepsis" as previously given to me by (possibly) the Ghost of Christopher Brannagan himself, having gotten a hint in that document of the piracies of the eleven high pirates of the third generation of Klepsis, and having moreover just heard the story "The Bloodiest Piracy of the Ship *The Dina O'Grogan*" from the Tarshish storyteller (it was his best story). This all excited me because I had just become related to the eleven great pirates of Klepsis by marriage and interlopership. And I had sailed on that ship *The Dina O'Grogan* herself for several hours of the afternoon of the day past. I had even been named by Prince Franco the Outcast as one of the officers of that ship.

And I had also heard the story "The Treasure Caves of Klepsis" from that same Tarshish storyteller (it was his second-best story). These two stories (the finest in his repertoire) were enough to whet the appetite of anyone for high piracy and treasure.

"Are these the ten thousand large chests of gold and gemstones of the great pirate Simeon O'Grogan-Brannagan, do you suppose?" I asked Gold Coast O'Mally and the rest of them, "or is this the proverbial gold of Simeon's brother Gad?"

"What do you know about these things, notable historian?" Gold Coast asked me. "All of us have agreed to pool our knowledge of the *res piratica*—of the pirate 'thing' or 'institution.' How about yourself?"

So I related to them all that I knew about these things and also let them read the document that Brannagan's Ghost had given to me.

It has been stated in books of elementary science and of explanations for the young, that gold and gemstones do not shine from their own light but only from reflected light. But the gold and gemstones in the caverns did shine of their own light. They glittered, they gleamed, they sparkled. In sufficient mass they do kindle themselves and shine by their own light, and it may be that these caverns are the only place where that sufficient mass of them is to be found.

The people also had begun to kindle and shine by their own light from being inspired by the cavern treasure. There is this gold-and-gemstone light in every person, and it only needs to be evoked. All of them, all of us, shone through our bones and our skins. We gleamed. We glittered.

The Princess Thorn added considerable knowledge to the golden caldron. She said that the signature-and-seal "T.E.H. C.O.P.O.K." stood for "The Eleven High Covenanted O'Grogan Pirates of Klepsis." So, treasure of them all was here. This signature-and-seal was to be found on every one of the maps.

My brain itched to have a copy of the covenant that the eleven high pirates had agreed on among themselves. I'll not be content till I have read this pledge of the Eleven.

And the number eleven was prominent in these galleries. There were eleven side passages in these galleries, each of them guarded by a very large dog of non-Gaea species. They looked like Astrobe mastiffs. Gold Coast and his friends had just decided that these large dogs were mechanical dogs, but the things seemed no less threatening for that.

The dogs became activated whenever one of us came within three meters of one of them. The red lines behind their eyes would shine and pulsate, and they made very

loud sirenlike growls and howls in their throats. Their
mouths would loll open to reveal several hundred frightful
fangs in each of them.

"Good God! Those are homing rockets in their mouths,
rows of them!" Bartolomo Portuguese howled, and
Bartolomo was a knowledgeable weapons man. "Those
other fangs are Incinerating Ray Attack Nodules. Those
third ones are Beauclaire Blasters. And these nozzles are
of Instant Inactivating Nerve Gas. Notice their shape, and
how they will throw a figure-eight spray! All of the dogs are
swiveled three hundred sixty degrees. How do you say,
'We are friends. We don't mean to intrude,' to a mechanical dog?"

"I suppose that I could probably deactivate them," my
Princess Thorn spoke in a musing way, as if trying to recall
the details of something. "We had one such dog in the Castle when I was a small child. It was the best friend I had in
this world, an indication of what my early childhood was
like. You folks may not realize it, but these 'Deviced Dogs'
are probably almost as valuable as the treasures they
guard. They were made about a hundred twenty years ago
by an artisan and gadgeteer of genius who took 'Prester
John' as his *nom de gadgetier*. These have now become collector's items for the very rich and exclusive people of all
the planets and private asteroids. Of the six known Deviced Dogs, out of the nineteen that were made by Prester
John, you could hardly buy one for a billion thalers. And
here are eleven of the fabulous lost dogs all together in this
cavern.

"And I will tell you this about them. They will grow used
to you. After you are around them for a little while you will
become 'people who belong' to them. You will be able to
make friends with them in time. Work around them for
several days (after all, there are thousands of chests of gold
and gemstones in the main gallery that are not guarded by
dogs), but do not for a while come too close to them and
their treasures. Things will work themselves out in rapport
and friendship."

"Thank you for the advice, Princess Thorn, but it will not be easy to follow," Gold Coast O'Mally croaked in an avid and nervous voice. "Those glittering heaps and hills are like magnets to my eyes and hands. They draw me, they draw me! Forbidden gold has an attraction that free gold can never match. I want to revel in those heaps right now, and I do not care all that much whether a mechanical dog should gun me down from behind."

Indeed, some of those glittering gold mountains were like magnets. The thousands of chests and barrels full of fortune in the main gallery were one thing. The bare and uncontained gold in heaps and piles and small mountains behind the arsenaled dogs was another thing entirely. Who could resist them? There were quite a few human skeletons among that heaped gold behind the eleven contrived guard dogs. Those dogs, activated and swiveling, were killers. We were not the first people to find our way into these treasure galleries. "But, with luck, we may be the first intruding people to come out of them alive," Kate Blithespirit the Amazon added the hope of all of us.

Kate Blithespirit was attracted to something more than the riches, however.

"There is something full of rotten power in this side passage here," she said. "I could possibly trade all the treasures for it. It is rot and shame and death. But oh, the power of it, the attraction; it's hellish."

"This is the side passage of the Pirate Levi O'Grogan-Brannagan," Thorn said. "He was the Bluebeard the Pirate who had thirteen wives and more than a hundred children by them. His body is here. The bodies of seven of the eleven covenanted pirates are in their guarded side passages here. Levi (Bluebeard) O'Grogan-Brannagan has more stories about him than any of the others. The rest of them are reduced to mere skeletons, but Levi Bluebeard has hunks and globs of flesh still on his bones, putrid and rotting flesh. He became a leper in the last decade of his life.

"Let me repeat the story that the Tarshish storyteller

told when I heard him at a wilderness settlement three years ago. It goes thus:

"This is the way they tell it.
"Bluebeard the Pirate, in the treasure caves of Klepsis, has not foregone his carnal activities. His body has rotted, and even his ghost has rotted. The smell of him fills all the caverns. Yet, Bluebeard was very attractive to women in life, and he is still so in death.
"There was a little girl who went down into the caverns to play every day. Her mother had told her not to play with skeletons unless she was sure they were dead; but one day the little girl forgot that advice. The most rotten of all the skeletons, the one that still had some rotting flesh on it, called to her:

*"Give up your soul, give up your life.
Come rot with me and be my wife."*

" 'Oh all right,' the little girl said. So she was the wife of Bluebeard for one hundred hours in the caverns. When she came out, the stench on her was so strong that the people drove her out into the waste places. She gave birth to a little boy that same night, but he was rotten and stenchy and had only half of the flesh on his bones. She ran away and left him, but he ran after her and there was no escaping him. She still runs, and the rotting little boy still runs after her. People see them sometimes on the moors in the evenings.
"That is the story. That is the end of the story. That is the way it has always been told."

"As with most of the Tarshish storyteller's stories, this one has a lot of truth in it. I've seen them myself in the evenings, the two ghostly runners."
"Thorn, Thorn," Kate Blithespirit admonished her.

"Thy tongue will rot and fall out if you tell such things. But I have a strong interest in this Bluebeard now. I feel him, I feel him!"

There were provisions of a sort in the caverns. The sea biscuits were dead (sea biscuits are always the first things to go bad), no more than sea casks full of dust. The sweet water had long since evaporated from its barrels. But the Cueva Rica Rum was still alive and rampant in its glass casks, and the Mock-Madeira Wine was lively and sassy in its old nine-quart bottles. The flesh of the Thousand-Year Turtles from Far Tortugas was still edible, and there were more than a thousand cases of it. We could stay down in the treasure caves for as long a time as we wished. And spading a meter into the tamped floor of the caverns would bring a lapping pool and fountain from the ocean. The sweet-water oceans of Klepsis are good to drink. We could stay down there at least until we figured out the tangled affairs that were taking place up on the surface.

There was a wax museum figure of an "ancient scholar" sitting at an antique desk (probably of the third-generation-of-Klepsis period) in a sort of nook of the main arcade, a nook from which one could see the entire main arcade and the entrances to all the side passages. This "ancient scholar" might also be a collector's item, if we went into the business of collectibles. And yet, it wasn't very well done. It was too much a cliché piece. Ancient scholars don't really look like that, except in stage versions of them. But then we all felt a faint whisper of horror when we saw that the ancient scholar was beginning to move and was probably alive.

"Who are you? *What* are you?" Gold Coast asked. The man was beginning to unkink his mind and body. "I was wondering what unreal sort of wax you were made out of, wax that no bee ever saw. I should know who you are. I believe that you are a staple character."

"I am the tax collector," the living figure said. "I was appointed by Rose Lunaria, the wife of Juda O'Grogan-Brannagan, to stay at this station. Juda, though the nominal ruler of Klepsis, was bullied by the eleven pirates, his brothers and his sister. But they did agree that, for his letting them cache their treasures on his domain, a tithe or a tenth of that treasure should be his. So, I was appointed to stay down here and assess the tithe on any treasure removed from here, with or without warrant. Since most of the treasure was amassed without warrant, I have not been too particular on that point."

"I have seen you before," Princess Thorn said. "*I* always thought you were wax. But if you were appointed by Rose Lunaria, then you have been down here for a very long time."

"Have I? What is the date and the year? I do have an automatic dater here somewhere, but I always forget which drawer of the desk I put it in."

"This is the twenty-ninth day of the Month of Arpad, for I have just heard the midnight bells ringing out the twenty-eighth day on the surface above us," Thorn told the tax collector. "And it is the two hundredth year of the planet Klepsis and the two thousand two hundredth year of the planet Gaea-Earth."

"Yes, I have been here more than a hundred years, then," the tax collector said, "and I can feel every one of those years in my bones. But I have slept most of the time, and one does not age as fast when sleeping as when one is awake and active. I have this arrangement with the dogs that they will wake me up when they themselves are activated by any intrusion. And they did wake me up, but it takes half an hour or so for me to look awake. The only duties I have here are to collect the tithe when anybody takes treasure out, to write out a receipt when anybody brings treasure in, and to order more nard every nine years."

"Nard? Is there nard?" Fairbridge Exendine the Penny Philosopher asked. "Oh, it must be inferior nard. There is the good smell of it, but it is mixed with a bad smell in the caverns. You must have impure nard."

"No, the nard is to mask the smell of Levi (Bluebeard the Pirate) O'Grogan-Brannagan, whose restless bones and rotting gouts of flesh are pretty hard to mask."

"Can you control the dogs?" Bartolomo Portuguese asked with a touch of greed. "Can you control them?"

"Yes, I can command and control the dogs," the tax collector said, "but how can I command and control you ruffians? Do any of you belong to the great O'Grogan-Brannagan family?"

"I am a member of it," Thorn said. "I am the Princess Tharrala Thorn."

"Just let me look in my copy of the *Handbook of the Prophecies of the Family*," the tax collector said while he turned the pages. "Yes, you are here, and with a red asterisk. They do not give those red asterisks loosely. You are the great-granddaughter of David Ravel the Elegant Interloper. You are the granddaughter of Cloud Ravel, the do-nothing ruler, and of his wife Brigid Hearn. You are the daughter of the Princess Placidia Ravel-Brannagan and of the adventurer Tarquin Thorn who was murdered by one or the other of your uncles. You yourself were repudiated by your reigning uncle Prince Henry the Pirate and were driven into the wilderness for a sin too unspeakable to name."

The laughter that followed this disclosure almost brought down the cavern.

"Oh, you *are* a wonderful and unspeakable person, Thorn," Terpsichore Callagy sang in glee. "Who does your publicity? That is a master stroke. I will give you no rest until you tell me what the unspeakable sin was. I was never so delighted with anyone in my life."

"You are *one of us* now," Kate Blithespirit the Amazon cried out in joy. "Before this, you seemed a little bit distant. Now you are our intimate. Tell us what the unspeakable sin was. Tell us, tell us!"

The tax collector seemed to be a little bit puzzled by the reaction to the matter-of-fact information that he had read out of the *Handbook of Prophecies of the Family*.

"Flash me the royal sign, demotic form, if you are indeed

the Princess Tharrala Thorn," he spoke in an official-edged voice.

Princess Thorn did flash him a sign of some sort, but it was too rapid to note in detail or to remember.

"Good, perfect," the tax collector said. "My assignment is always to serve *any* member of the family in any way. I am yours to command."

"Could *I* get a copy of that *Handbook of Prophecies?*" I asked this official. "It would be very handy for the work I am doing."

"Certainly," he said. "You're *in* the book, Duke Tyrone the Historian, so you are legally entitled to have a copy of it. I'll make you one."

I slept for two hours then. I had been busy all the day and up to this midnight. But it was a troubled sleep I had, much intruded on by cavern ghosts and specters. I heard the terrible voice of Bluebeard the Pirate:

> *"Give up your soul, give up your life.*
> *Come rot with me and be my wife."*

And I heard the voice of a little girl say "Oh, all right."

"No, no, no," I tried to say in my sleep. "He is rotting and he will rot you and your fruit also." But the words weren't voiced.

"Wake up," Thorn told me then. "You're having bad dreams, and besides, there is somebody here to talk to you." She had a wet, soggy, winy person with her.

"It is good to be with you again," this wettish person said. "It is good even to know such a distinguished historian." I had heard that soggy voice before, but where had I heard it?

"Oh, you heard it in the wine vat," the soggy man said. "I was in there being healed for a long time, for fifty years, but I am finally healed. And I have just reported to the most august ghost on Klepsis (though in person he is not august at all), and he told me to find you and bring you and

your consort to him. You were supposed to come and talk
to him later in the night, and he says that it *is* later in the
night now. And you were about to say, Duke Tyrone, that
you were an historian but not a distinguished historian.
Well, you had better *act* like a distinguished historian while
you are on Klepsis. It was just two days ago that the Most
August Ghost on Klepsis said to a person who was visiting
him, 'I am coming to the end of my days, even to the end of
my secondary or ghostly days. I will put my affairs and the
affairs of my planet in order, and for that I will need the
services of a combination wizard-philosopher-prophet-
politician; in short I will need the services of the most distinguished historian to be found. Get the most distinguished historian here to Klepsis and get him here within
two days. Heads will roll else!' So, for the peace of the
ghostly realm, you *must* be distinguished. No doubt the distinguished historian *is* on the way here, but he must find
himself preempted. Fake it, man, fake it.''

"Oh, I've married the wrong man,'' Thorn giggled.
"Well, I'll not trade you off now, my love. We will ride it
out. You will fake it, and I will help you fake it. No, you
really don't look much like a combination wizard-
philosopher-prophet-politician, but we'll do what we can
do.''

"Soggy man, I believe that I have information on *you*
here in the *Handbook of the Prophecies of the Family,*'' the
tax collector and general-purpose official said. "I will just
read it—''

"You will just read it silently to yourself,'' the soggy man
said. "But, for the present, you will not pass that information along to anyone else.''

Thorn and myself and the soggy man went out of the
treasure caverns by the shaft entrance at the far or east end
of the main arcade, the shaft that had been dug out by Gold
Coast O'Mally and his friends just that night. We went to
keep our appointment in the walk-in tomb with the Most
August Ghost on Klepsis.

SEVENTH CANTO

Conversations in a Walk-in Tomb

"Ghosts wear out, you know. And a canny ghost must look to the future after he has faded away. He may want to leave something of himself," the old man said. "I have talked such things over with this Green Robe of the order of Saint Klingensmith. And I used to talk such things over with the Seneschal Fidelis here, until he was whipped to death and stabbed to death (so they thought) by the servants of Cloud Ravel. In derision he was then thrown into the vat of healing wine and told to heal himself. But the derision was misplaced, for the wine did heal him (though it took fifty years) and he came out of the vat, healed, tonight. So now I can talk things over with him again.

"And I also intend to talk things over with you, Duke Tyrone the Historian, the most distinguished of all historians! Do you know, another man came to my tomb tonight, only a little while after you were married to Princess Thorn here, and he said that *he* was that most distinguished historian and that I had sent for him two days ago. He is now buried in the potter's field below O'Grogan's Mountain at its extreme west or hinder end."

"I wish that I could have talked to him," I said sincerely. "We historians can often gain good information from each other."

"Oh, you'll have no difficulty raising his ghost," Brannagan's Ghost said easily. "Within a period of seven days after death, ghosts may easily be raised by ordinary methods. But after a seven-day interval it requires extraordinary methods. And I have also, to continue my discourse, talked these things over with Princess Tharrala Thorn before she was driven into the wilderness for her unspeakable sin. And now that she is back, I will talk these things over with her again. By the way, Duke Tyrone, that other man who came after you had been here, the other historian, he *did* seem more distinguished than you. Do not let a doubt creep into my mind about you now. Convince me that you are distinguished. Do something distinguished or say something distinguished every several minutes.

"And now, look into my coffin here, Duke Tyrone the Historian. You are the only one here present who has not looked into it before. Am I not a ruddy and handsome man as I lie there! The ruddy look, the flaming orange-yellow-red look when it crops up in the family, is from me. The black-hair and olive-skin look when it crops up is from Januarius O'Grogan first, and from David Ravel the Elegant Interloper in the second place. These two sorts of blood do war in the family a bit, but that is of small account. Now, Duke Tyrone, what do you see about my dead and preserved body in its glass coffin that is not quite as the legends have it?"

"The legends have it that you were a peg-legged man; and that, because of this, you set up inducements to get peg-legged persons to come to Klepsis and settle. Your reported words were, 'Give me enough peg-legged Irishmen and I can rule the universe.' And you *are* a peg-legged ghost. But your preserved body is arranged to make it seem that it is whole."

"Yes, that's right. Now let me switch on the coffin X rays," Brannagan's Ghost said. And he switched the machine on. All the bones of that preserved body were shown clearly, and all the bones were present and in good appearance in both the legs of the body.

"Then you were *not* a peg-leg," I said. "Why the deception?"

"If there was a deception, it was on me. I thought that I was a peg-leg. I was damned sure of it. I remember losing my leg, and nearly losing my life at the same time, quite clearly. It cannot be doubted. And I *am* a peg-legged ghost. This is one of the things that I want to discuss when we consider all aspects of reality. Do you notice anything else about my body that's not in accord with the legends, Duke Tyrone?"

"Only that you always wore a magnifying monocle in your eye, and that as a ghost you wear it now, but as a dead body you do not."

"Oh, there is only one monocle between us in these latter years. The other one was lost somewhere along the way. Most of the time I-the-ghost wear it for practical purposes (I like to see things in distance, and I like to see them in detail). But sometimes he-the-body seems uneasy in his death until he has it, so I put it in his eye for a while. The Seneschal Fidelis here, this soggy and winy man who came cured out of the big wine vat tonight, he has always said that I am not a ghost but rather a *forgotten twin*."

"Yes," said the soggy man. "True ghosts do not have weight. Brannagan's Royal Ghost here *does* have weight. It is not sufficient weight, but it is weight nevertheless. The most likely case is that he is indeed a forgotten twin, and that he is still a live person. It is true that he has suffered an unprecedented weight loss, and that he is more than two hundred years old. But the next most likely explanation would be clear and away out of bounds."

"Where did you all get the idea that a ghost is weightless?" Brannagan's Ghost argued his case, spreading out his hands and appealing to all of us. "I was a heavy man. I weighed twenty stone in life, and that without my left leg. I now weigh about one pound in my ghostliness. If a ghost is the residue of a big and weighty person, he may not be entirely weightless. All ghosts are not of the same sort anyhow. And for the benefit of you who came in late, in the last hundred years, a stone was fourteen pounds or about six and a half kilograms."

"Do something distinguished or say something distinguished, my love," Thorn whispered to me. "You owe him that much."

"What is the real problem, Royal Ghost?" I asked Brannagan's residue. "What is it that you want to find out?" Oh, possibly that wasn't distinguished, but it was to the point.

"I want to find out what is reality and what is not reality. That is why you are here, Duke Tyrone the Historian, to make discernments among these things. History is what is real—that is my own definition. And raw history is whatever is burgeoning into reality. But that which is not history at all will not be real at all. The situation here on Klepsis is complicated by three factors. The first of them is that we have an abundance of hallucinatory plants beyond that of any other world. Berries, root-plants, green-leaf vegetables, bush fruits, grapes, melons, and mushrooms especially are hallucinatory. These plants grow on most other worlds, but not to the extent or with the strength that they grow on Klepsis.

"Gaea-Earth is the only planet that did not have the hallucinatory plants originally. On Astrobe and on Camiroi they have been completely eradicated now. But most other worlds have them yet, and on Klepsis we have them more than anywhere else.

"It is for this reason that no person who has lived on Klepsis for any great length of time is entirely sane. The animals and the birds (with one exception) and the insects and sea creatures are not sane either. They are goofy. This is a goofy world.

"I was a remarkably sane man on the several worlds I dwelt on before I came to Klepsis. And I was again sane during a seven-year exile, a marooning that I suffered on a desert island of a desert asteroid; there was much to drive a man insane during those seven years, but I remained sane. But on Klepsis I have not been.

"Sometimes I believe that sanity is overrated, that we are not lacking a dimension on Klepsis, but that we have an added dimension. I haven't much good to say for prehistory, though I created two hundred years of it here, apparently; it is pure insanity. But I believe I might find good things to say for meta-history, for the beyond-history. We may have a little of it here.

"We have built many large buildings on Klepsis, but in the case of every one of them there is lingering doubt as to whether they were built indeed. There has been doubt as to their reality. In several cases it is now known that the buildings were completely hallucinatory, and yet their existence was accepted by tens of thousands of persons for several decades. People were born in them and lived in them and died in them.

"There is even some slight doubt as to the reality of Ravel-Brannagan Castle. (It really should be 'Brannagan Castle' only. David Ravel the Elegant Interloper built only the three north wings of it, and he added the one hundred cupolas which make it look a little cheesy.) About two percent of the people who used to come here from other planets could not see the Castle at all. And, not being able to see it, they would walk right through its location and not be discommoded by its walls or ramparts at all. This was a distressing situation. To nullify it, and following the advice of my advisers, I instituted the 'My God What Grapes!' countermove. That is to say, we offered the luscious and highly hallucinatory 'Summertime Grapes' (they were native to Klepsis, but they were named for my wife Margaret Summertime) at every point of entry on Klepsis, at every customhouse, and we edicted them to be offered in every private home that offered regional hospitality. So off-planet visitors were inducted quickly into our native patterns of hallucination, and the embarrassing anomalies were done away with. We also receive secondary hallucination from our beasts and birds. Indeed, some of the earlier names for Klepsis were 'Crazy Deer Planet' and 'Drunken Bird Planet' and 'Dancing Fish Planet.' Oh, we do have a goofy world here.

"As to mass hallucination, or as to mass resistance to hallucination, the general rule we now follow on Klepsis is that if ninety percent of the people see a thing, then that thing is to be regarded as real. This is known either as the Pragmatic Sanction or as the Categorical Imperative, I forget which. But difficulties remain, and that is why I need an historian.

"The second complicating factor here on Klepsis is that, in the early days when I feared that I could never get enough people to populate my planet, I called for phantoms from everywhere to come and give it the appearance of being populated. And the phantoms did come from everywhere. There were deep-space phantoms, there were planetary and asteroid phantoms, there were unbodied phantoms and anthropoid phantoms. And there were some of the phylum that is incomparably evil.

"Later, when it seemed that I *would* have a fair number of people to inhabit my world after all, I told the phantoms that they were dismissed. But many of them refused to be dismissed. They used various devices to become documented, the most usual of which was being born to a human mother. There was a sudden wave of human pregnancies that were completely unexpected. And the things were born with adult intelligence, safe from suspicion, and devious in their ways. And they used dozens of other tricks. They remain here yet, large numbers of them in full and visible phantom form, others of them blinking on and off, being sometimes visible and sometimes invisible, and still others of them entering into local creatures such as parley birds or Malcomb's coneys, rendering such creatures absolutely goofy. Those in human form hold high places and are of great influence. They will be hard to get rid of."

A small, brilliantly colored, and rather determined bird flew into the walk-in tomb. It flew right through Brannagan's Ghost. That was all right. It flew right through Seneschal Fidelis, the soggy man. That was almost all right, too. But then the bird flew right through me. That was not all right, not all right at all. The bird flew out of the walk-in tomb again. It flew out through a wall and not through the door.

"It is a Banner Bird," Brannagan's Ghost said. "Did it not look like a bright and flaunty banner though? This is the species that worries me and engenders doubt in me. It is the only native species of any sort on Klepsis that will not eat any of the hallucinatory plants, that will not take them in any form, that will not eat anything that has taken them. Ergo, it is the only sane and nonhallucinating creature on Klepsis. Since it does *not* hallucinate, it does see through things that are pure hallucinations. It does see through them, and it does fly through them too.

"But where does that leave us? If *we* are hallucinations, whose hallucinations are we? And can pure hallucinations have consciousness of their own, as we seem to have, or as I seem to have? But there is no use in hanging too much importance on this. The Banner Bird is not accounted very intelligent even by other birds.

"The difficulties remain. Every person or creature of any sort on Klepsis, except only the Banner Bird, suffers from hallucinations. And at least one third of the persons on Klepsis, many of them in high station, are phantoms.

"There is a third difficulty, and it is myself. Until I go, other things cannot come, things that most other planets have. If this is a backward world, then it is mostly myself who have kept it backward. Oh, I am right in a lot of the aspects of the problem. I am right in preaching the Joys of Illiteracy, although I am unfortunately literate myself. Besides having a peg leg, I walk with a paper crutch, as does almost everybody in officialdom. I am right in my recommendations to keep intuition as the guiding force, and that the pompous thing Reason must be kept on a tight bridle. I am right in insisting that a genuine Klepsis is better than an imitation Camiroi. But did you know that Klepsis Clubs are an *in* thing on Camiroi now among the young people? They dress in the pirate costumes of Klepsis of a hundred years ago. They phantomize at their meetings. They have imported the 'My God What Grapes' grapes, and they hallucinate, and thus bring back what had once been stamped out on Camiroi.

"While I still stir and walk and talk, even in my ghost form, then Klepsis is kept in its time of legend and *pre*history. But when I can no longer walk and talk, even as a ghost, then the history of Klepsis can begin. My fear is that the earlier chapters of Klepsis may be inferior history. But I am very curious as to what our history will be, and there is no way I can know it. It cannot begin while I am here, for I am unhistorical and an obstacle to history. As an underling once said to a superintendent, 'You ought to be here sometimes when you're not here, and see what happens when you're gone.' I am impatient that you solve this problem for us, Distinguished Historian and Duke Tyrone. Is there anybody else in your party who might speculate fruitfully on things like this?"

"There is one of us, named Fairbridge Exendine, from the Trader Planet Emporion, who is known as the Penny Philosopher."

"Then, enlist him in our cause and in our discussions, Historian. And we will discuss for a while, but not for a long while. Very soon I will insist on clear decisions and clear definitions. And if I do not get them, I will initiate clear action. One of the ever-green underground classics of all the planets is the *Big Brannagan Book of Tortures*, scribed by myself. Ah, there is a lot of meat to be found in that book, mangled meat mostly."

"Many-times grandfather, you would not really invoke merciless cruelty," Princess Thorn jibed him. "I know that you would not."

"Unspeakable favorite of mine, I would. What is wrong with merciless torture if there is a loophole in it? While there is some doubt about reality being reality, then there is some doubt about torture being torture. And there is some doubt about cruelty being cruelty. I might take refuge in that doubt."

"Many-times grandfather, you no longer have the living followers, and you no longer have the *power,* to impose torture on anyone," Thorn tortured Brannagan's Ghost at its most sensitive point.

"Want to bet, pet? You should see the ghost of brave David Ravel cringe when in the presence of me. He is afraid of me, and he loses his elegance in his fear. I still have powers more subtle than you know about. I am still the root from which this planet grows."

"I wonder whether you are not a double root, August Ghost," I said. "I would like to know more about the 'forgotten twin' phenomenon."

"That's a two-Bandicoot evocation and tale, is it not, Green Robe?" the old ghost asked.

"Probably three. You'd have to evoke several ghosts, probably including some of your own early ghosts. But I always enjoy these trips back, and it may inspire the historian here with some of the mystery of Klepsis."

"What are *you*—the devious Jesuit behind the throne?" I asked the always merry-looking cleric.

"There is no throne in Klepsis, Historian. And I am no Jesuit. I am a member of the Green Robe Order of Saint Klingensmith. We're the good guys. We wear the green hats. Dripping man, go get the Penny Philosopher. Brannagan's Ghost wants him to be present also."

"Yes," said the dripping Seneschal (how long would that man drip, anyhow?), and he went out, but not by the narrow entrance into the walk-in tomb by which we had entered. He went out by a sudden opening in the floor of the tomb. So then, the tomb of Christopher Brannagan, and the den of Brannagan's Ghost, had an underground connection with the treasure caverns.

The Green Robe lit a very thick and long Bandicoot hallucinatory cigar and gave it to Brannagan's Ghost. The August Ghost smoked deeply, then began to blow the smoke out in strange sculptured forms that were burlesques of each of us there. He blew an excellent caricature which was of the flaming orange-yellow-red brotherhood.

"By the way, Historian, this Green Robe is a thrice grandnephew of mine," Brannagan's Ghost said. But the smoke-caricature seemed to have a certain depth that the fleshed Green Robe lacked.

Brannagan's Ghost, smoking deeply, blew a caricature of the soppy Seneschal who had just left us on the errand. And this burlesque was of a rather dry and incisive and perhaps profound man, not quite in accord with the man himself, who had not yet recovered from his sogginess and winyness.

Brannagan's Ghost blew a reproduction of my Princess Thorn. The smoke of these Bandicoot cigars carries a flame-glow while it coils and uncoils. The reproduction was of a much younger Princess Thorn (though she was still quite young), of the little-girl Princess who used to visit the cranky old ghost in his tomb.

"Many-times Grandfather Ghost," Thorn said now. "You were my best friend in the world then, after the mechanical dog in the Castle, but you do me great wrong in this representation. I was never as malevolent as that."

"You were," the old ghost growled. "Yes, you were."

The smoke showed that Thorn had been a very pretty little girl. I looked at Thorn and I noticed for the first time that she was very pretty in her present self. Well, of course she was, but it was not the first or second or tenth thing that anybody noticed about her. With her, it was only a trifle. But the flame-smoke younger Princess Thorn did have real malevolence in her. When she was exiled into the wilderness for her unspeakable sin, there must have been real and shattering sin involved.

Brannagan's Ghost next blew a smoky takeoff of me. There was derision in it. There was humor. There was irony. But all these things were from Brannagan's Ghost, not from me. The smoky takeoff of me showed a person a little too weak for my liking.

"Please, my love," Thorn whispered to me, quite obviously feeling that I should be able to give a better account of myself even in smoke. "Look somewhat distinguished, act somewhat distinguished, say something distinguished, even *think* something distinguished. My many-times grandfather's ghost has not known you before this evening and night, and all the impressions that he has of you are from this ongoing night. Please tip the balance a little bit. I don't want you to come through as a simpleton. Appear distinguished. Function distinguished. Let your blood-flow and your brainwaves be distinguished. Let your adrenaline flow with power and distinction. Breathe distinguished. Do this for me."

I tried it. I thought distinguished, and I sat distinguished (on a stone outcrop of the tomb). I tried to let my blood-flow be distinguished, to let my vibrations be distinguished. I tried to breathe distinguished. But of all my efforts, my breathing was the only one I had any control over.

I'm afraid, though, that I merely inflated myself and puffed myself out with air. I pouted my chest out, and my smoke image did the same. It was funny and grotesque when it puffed itself, like the frog of the pond. Brannagan's Ghost laughed. The Green Robe laughed. I myself laughed, but it must have been an ambiguous laugh. I had never felt less distinguished in my life. And Thorn was crying softly.

Then, up through the floor of the walk-in tomb, there came the soggy Seneschal Fidelis along with Fairbridge Exendine, the Penny Philosopher from the Trader Planet Emporion. Brannagan's Ghost brightened to see Exendine. (He had not brightened up either time he had seen me.) He blew away the takeoff of myself and then drew heavily on the Bandicoot stogie for new smoke.

Then the ghost spoke rather heavily (rather ghostishly, I should say) around the smoke that was curing in his mouth and gullet and lungs.

"You people, even those who know me best, do not realize the power or the scope of the images (nay, of the real beings) that I can evoke," he spoke. "This power is almost without limit. Once I even attempted to evoke God the Father, to have him come to me in ghost. He did not come, but He sent one of His angels. 'Be quiet,' the angel told me. 'You are an exasperation. There are not nearly enough quiet hours in your days.' This advice was good, so I then began to have many more quiet hours in my days. But according to the formula for invocation as I worked it out by myself, I should have been able to call up *anybody*. Or rather, I should have been able to call up anybody living, and that includes God the Father. Indeed I may have done so. I believe that God the Father sometimes goes around in disguise, as did the Sultan Haroun Al-Raschid on Gaea-Earth; and the Father Himself may have come to me disguised as one of His angels. But I can evoke all humans, alive or dead, whom I have ever known. I may evoke some of them now to settle a question that has been bothering me for these several centuries.

"There was a trial held on me, you know. It was called by the person whom I loved more than any except my wife in the world, and it was found against me. It was a 'Commission in Lunacy,' and I did not accept its findings. I wonder whether I will accept them now? I have an overwhelming suspicion that they were correct.

"And I had other powers, and perhaps I still have tatters of them. I had, of course, the power of bi-location, as many great men do have. This may be connected, Duke Tyrone Historian, with the forgotten-twin syndrome. Indeed, one of the findings of the commission was that I was a forgotten twin. This was one of the findings that I did not accept.

"And I also had the power of introspection to a degree

that I have never heard of any other person having. Listen, I have taken voyages by ship (both the ship and the crew and myself being diminished a million or more times) into all the interior passages of myself, through all the valves of my heart and through all the wheezing and roaring tunnels of my lungs, through my genes and through my spleen, and especially through the great straits and caves of my brain. I take these voyages less frequently than I used to, but I have just decided to take one tonight. And all of you here will go with me, as diminished crew on my diminished ship. That was always one of my pleasures—introspection. This introspection or 'looking-at-self-from-within' I can do with these voyages, and few others can do it that way.

"I will invoke and convoke that old commission again. And I will go voyaging again. I do not know which I will do first, or whether I will do both of them at the same time."

Another person came into the tomb. Or perhaps he solidified there and did not come in through any of its entrances except that named "apparition." I knew, with such apperception I have as an historian, that this was the person that Brannagan's Ghost had just spoken of as 'the person I have loved more than any except my wife.' It was a man bigger in many ways than Brannagan himself, and more compassionate in all ways.

EIGHTH CANTO

A Commission in Lunacy

"And now, Duke Tyrone Historian, you have not given me any indication at all of the insight an historian should have," Brannagan's Ghost was speaking to me. "Tell us now, who is this man who has just appeared?"

"Oh, Januarius O'Grogan," I said in as offhand a manner as I could manage. This man had to loom big in the Klepsis story, and from such scraps of Klepsis history as I had been able to pick up that evening and night, only O'Grogan had a stature comparable to Brannagan.

"You are right," Brannagan's Ghost said. "You may not be entirely hopeless."

"Christopher Begorra Brannagan," the O'Grogan Apparition chided. "Is it for the business of that same old Commission in Lunacy that you are calling up us dead people again? The trouble, Chris, is that I am not usually bothered by lunacy unless I'm with you. It's catching, you know. It's the most dangerous and most mortal of all the epidemic diseases. Well, there are inoculations against it, and I believe that I've availed myself of them."

"Yes, it is for the same Commission, Januarius. It must be settled now. But I have never been convinced that lunacy is all that bad. I often have good words to say about it. I do not remember at the moment whether I ever committed to paper my minor masterwork, *The Pleasures of Lunacy*, but if I haven't done so, I should."

"I told you at the time, Chris, that you should allow all the proceedings of the Commission to be on tape, but you would not allow it to be done. Tapes do not forget nor falsely remember. Ghosts do. And ghosts do not like to be bothered by amateur evokers, amateurs even after two hundred years of practice. Oh, some of the ghosts, those who abide in a worse place than this, are grateful for a little surcease from their torments while they testify. Others, like myself, who abide in the better place, may resent having to come back to this dingy world. I'd resent it myself except that I enjoy being with you, for the love that I bear you. You certainly don't intend to have a complete reconstruction of the Commission proceedings, do you now, Chris?"

"No, Januarius, I was always a skipper, and I'll skip and choose here. But perhaps I'll balance that out by having some parts of it repeated again and again."

Januarius O'Grogan, dead about a hundred fifty years, appeared to be about thirty years old. I had not yet learned to make the slight mental jog to bring the years of Klepsis and of Gaea-Earth into accord, so my estimates of apparent ages of persons was very rough. I believe that he appeared to be about the age he was when the Commission in Lunacy was convoked. He was of the age that he had been when the things being recreated took place. So would they all be. And now half a dozen other persons began to take on an appearance and shape and substance there in the walk-in tomb.

"Why not have the whole thing in the courtroom where it was originally held?" I suggested. "I believe that Brannagan's Royal Ghost could as easily convoke buildings and rooms as he can convoke people. And as historian, I would very much like to be present in an authentic courtroom of this planet Klepsis a little less than two hundred years ago."

"No, Historian, there was no courtroom on Klepsis in

the early days. What need would peaceful pirates such as ourselves have of a courtroom? There were no courts of law then, for the reason that there was no law on Klepsis then. My father-in-law, Christopher Brannagan here, who had run Klepsis pretty much unchallenged until the time of the Commission, believed that law (like literacy) was an evil and a snare."

Januarius O'Grogan was not at all of the flaming orange-yellow-red descent, as was Brannagan, as was Tharrala Thorn. Januarius was one of the fountainheads of the black-haired and olive-skinned strain in the family. But his ghost carried his years better than did Brannagan's.

"There were no courtrooms on Klepsis then," the spacious Januarius went on. "The hearings on the lunacy case were held in this very place, in this cultish cave as it was then. It has since been regularized, by a few blocks of limestone, into this walk-in tomb and monument of Christopher Brannagan. So, we are met in the original place of the Commission. And even in the old days it had several purposes. It was one of the secret entrances to the treasure cavern. We were already dazzled by that gold."

"But was there already gold here before it was brought here by the Eleven High Pirates of Klepsis, they who were your own sons and daughter?"

"Yes, Historian, yes," Januarius told me. "It was primordial gold. I have even heard that the minted gold was here first, and that the cavern was formed around it by geological processes. It was primeval gold. And my own flighty children, for all the shiploads of it that they brought here, did not increase the amount of it by more than five percent."

"But who did put the first gold here then, Royal O'Grogan?" I asked. The sketchy ideas I had formed of the middle history of Klepsis were scattered by O'Grogan's statements. "The Great Brannagan and his followers were the first humans to come to Klepsis, and there are no stories of early Brannagan gold, nor of early O'Grogan gold, for that matter."

"It was the dragons who first put it here, Historian," the greatest of the O'Grogans told me in his intricate voice. "The old Klepsis dragons (they were of the species *Draco Rufus*) mined and minted it here for many thousands of years, apparently. They had quite a number of mints here on Klepsis. Examine for yourself the titles and images and mottoes that are on most of the gold coins down in the treasure caverns. You will find that almost all of that gold is of dragon mintage."

"Please, my love," Princess Thorn whispered in my ear. "You will have to learn to catch them on the fly. Don't let them bounce and dribble. This greatest of the O'Grogans is a great kidder."

"You, renowned Januarius O'Grogan, are a crooked-faced kidder," I said, to put Thorn's advice into effect immediately. I pretended that I could see right through him without the aid of Princess Thorn, who was now officially marrow of my marrow.

"Nay, no kidder, man," the O'Grogan told me. "I am a liar pure and simple. This cult-cave, this walk-in monument, was also, long ago, the lodgehouse of the Royal Kangaroos Liars Association, a fraternal group. Thrice was I named Liar of the Year by them. We met here twice a month and told high lies and boozed and ate. Indeed, the Commission in Lunacy itself was held under the Sign of the Kangaroo. There was no other sign to hold it under."

A fork-tongued, two-faced liar and pirate was this famed Januarius O'Grogan, and at the same time he was one of the most pleasant and personable men that I have ever encountered. Indeed the Sign of the Kangaroo was still prevalent in the cave or tomb, spreads and dazzles of primitive and leaping art and calligraphy. And under the same sign the review of the Commission would now be held.

But had O'Grogan in fact lied when he told about the dragon gold? Or had he only lied in saying that he lied? I had seen the Sign of the Dragon on several of the gold coins in the cavern. The Klepsis kangaroo is not related to that of Gaea-Earth. It is really a variety of Drexel's dragon, a

man-sized hopper. Were the Klepsis kangaroos the same as
the Klepsis *Draco Rufus* dragons? Well, a kangaroo lodge
would still be a kangaroo lodge, and a kangaroo court
would still be a kangaroo court very like those found in the
boondocks areas of Gaea-Earth.

"*Why* the reconvening of the hearings now anyhow,
Christopher?" O'Grogan asked his father-in-law,
Brannagan. "It's been fifty years since you had the last
replaying of the mummery. I thought that you were past
such things."

"I feel that my years, even my second set of years, are
coming to an end," Great Brannagan's Ghost said. "And,
Januarius, beloved pup, this will *not* be a replay. This time
I want originality and invention and examinations and arguments. This time, of course, I want a different conclu-
sion to be arrived at, though of course I do not want a di-
rected verdict. This time I want to get to the reality of the
matter. And I'll get to it too, no matter how much I have to
shake up the cast of participants.

"Let all of you now take oaths to delve into the reality of
the matter. I am in the hands of all of you. But be warned of
this: though I am in the hands of all of you, if you displease
me in this your final verdict, I'm likely to bite off the hands
of all of you right to the wrist."

I couldn't help it then. I knew that O'Grogan was a kidder, but I had to go and find out something. Quietly, when
none of them was looking at me, I went down through the
hidden door in the floor of the tomb and then through the
underground windings into the treasure cavern. And, very
quietly there also—for I could hardly explain what was on
my mind—I took gold coins from about twenty different
chests that had been opened; about a hundred coins in all.

"How are things going, Duke and Historian?" Terpsichore asked me as she came up on me quietly. I realized
that I would not have to explain anything to any of them.
We were ourselves a sort of convenanted band now and we
all trusted one another.

"It is very smoky up there, Terpsichore," I said, "and

very spooky. It's all full of ghosts."

"So is it here," she said a bit fearfully. "Not all of the chests are full of gold and gemstones. Some of them are full of bones. We know them by the groaning. We open one from which a groaning comes, and we find it full of bones, the bones of eight or ten persons all jammed together, broken and unbroken. The bones talk a little bit in their several voices, but they are incoherent. But I have discovered my own treasure house here. It isn't the gold, though much of it is made out of gold. Long John Duke of Tyrone, there is art here above my fondest imaginings, art from every world, and also dragon art."

"How about the dragons themselves?" I asked in an attempt at a light-hearted voice.

"Bartolomo Portuguese and Sebastian Jamaica saw a dragon cub. They tried to catch it, but they couldn't."

"It's well they didn't. Convince them that they should leave the things alone if they see more of them. The mother dragons are likely to take mortal retribution on anyone who chases their cubs."

I went back out through the twisted maze passages and up through the floor of the walk-in tomb again. One of the nondescript evoked ghosts was giving testimony.

"I will read into the transcript a space verifax of a deposition by Dame Delfina Brannagan, the mother of Christopher Brannagan, as to her son, which verifax has just been received from Gaea-Earth in response to my questions sent to her. She writes quite a good hand for a ninety-eight-year-old lady, and she writes thus:

" 'My son, Christopher Begorra Brannagan, was of single birth. Had I had twins, I would have been the first to know it, would I not? Or at least I would have been the second one to know it, after the attending doctor. And I had the word of the doctor that I had given birth to a single child. Christopher was not a twin, though he was big enough for two. He was a singleton, as the birth certificate signed by the attending doctor indicates.' Well, that is what Dame Delfina writes. It seems to be conclusive."

"It sure would seem so," Brannagan's Ghost declared, "but I've been bothered by something there ever since I heard it for the first time. It is almost the only conclusive evidence on my side that I am not a twin; the only document stating implicitly that I am not a part of that dreadful 'forgotten twin' phenomenon. In that phenomenon, one of the twins is very often insane and so is inclined to break all the laws of physics and nature. On the other hand, though it would probably go against me, I'd like to know what else my mother wrote. She never wrote just a short spate and then stopped. She was garrulous in tongue and in pen."

"But that's all of it," said the nondescript ghost. "See, that is the end of the paper."

"And what is on the reverse side of the paper?" Brannagan's Ghost demanded.

"It is illegal on all the worlds to write on the reverse side of a paper."

"I know it is, but my mother had a lot of illegal habits. Now, turn the space verifax over and read to the kangaroo court what is written on the other side of the paper. You neglected to do this at the original Commission hearing and I did not catch the neglect till I thought about it in a lonesome place many months later."

"Oh yes, there are writings on the other side. She writes:

" 'My husband, Barlow Brannagan, wanted to get a second opinion on it, so he asked the apprentice doctor about it. The apprentice doctor said to him that *there might have been* a second birth but that it had "gone vague" immediately. The apprentice doctor said that he had told the attending doctor about it, but this person had said "Forget it. It can only be a 'forgotten twin.' With all the popular pieces like *Forgotten Twins, Are They an Alien Invasion of Our World?* it seems to me that we should ignore it. 'Forgotten twins' can only bring discredit to everybody involved. If a 'forgotten twin' does turn up in this case, we want to be able to say 'He didn't turn up here,' " so the attending doctor had answered the apprentice doctor and dismissed the case. The apprentice doctor stated further that he saw the second-born person or phenomenon standing in the door-way of the room a little while later, and that then this small person or phenomenon had simply walked away. This was in the days when it was still argued whether there was such a thing as a forgotten twin or a what-is-it, and when less than a dozen of them had been reported in medical history. My own opinion is that I did not give birth to a second son, but that I may have given birth to a what-is-it. It was three weeks after my giving birth that I saw the what-is-it again. He could walk and talk well then. More than that, he could climb into our third-story window to the room where Christopher was. Christopher and the what-is-it were already close friends then, as they would always be, but Christopher was very far behind the what-is-it in development. The what-is-it was frightfully precocious, too much so in some directions. It had already been stated by researchers that, if there were any such thing as a lost twin or what-is-it, it would always be erratic and irresponsible and insane, even though it would be personable and quite intelligent. It may have been so with ours, for he was the flightiest and at the same time the most advanced child that I had ever seen. By the time that he was four months old he was studying my husband's engineering books and was asking questions about them, to some of which questions my husband could only answer, "I'll look it up, I'll look it up somewhere, I'll try to find the answer."

" 'I named the lost twin or what-is-it Chrysanthus Bygosh Brannagan, which was the only name I could think of that went well with Christopher Begorra Brannagan, the name of our regular son. Chrysanthus Bygosh was with us all the time after that, visible and lively, when only members of our own family were there. But when strangers (to him) came, Chrysanthus would often go vague or invisible. As the years went by—'

"That is the end of what Dame Delfina Brannagan wrote."

"There has to be another sheet to it," Brannagan's Ghost maintained. "Get on the vector transmission and trace it all the way back to Gaea-Earth if necessary. Get the further sheets of the space verifax, and have the clerk who failed to transmit them fired. Have his ears cropped too, if that can be done."

"It has been nearly two hundred years, Former Ruler Brannagan, since the verifax was received and first introduced into the evidence," the nondescript evocation said. "The clerk who failed to transmit it is probably long since dead."

I looked at the gold coins which I had taken from the chests in the cavern, perhaps a hundred coins in all. I made a pile of them on a stone outcrop of Brannagan's tomb, and I transferred each of them to another pile after I had examined it. The noble face of Brannagan himself was on two of the coins. The face of Januarius O'Grogan was on two of them. There were three gold twenty-guilder pieces from Gaea-Earth. There were six pirate-head coins from the Pirate-Emirate Asteroids. There were nine coins of San Simeon gold from Gaea-Earth (there used to be a ballad song about that gold bubble and how it burst). There were five of the Enrique d'Or gold coins from Golden Astrobe. There were twenty-one coins that I couldn't identify, though the faces on them were human faces and the wording on them was in Roman letters. And the rest of the coins, fifty-six of them, had depictions of proud dragons on them. Had there indeed been whole dynasties of dragons on Klepsis who were intelligent enough to mint coins? The pictures were clearly of a dozen different dragons, and they all seemed to be royal dragons. These were not merely popular pictures. They were of strong dragon personages, each of them of strong and unique character.

Did dragons still live in the dark and enchanted underground of Klepsis? Could any human person read the dragon writing that was on the coins?

"Yes, there is a Chair of Dragon Studies at the Imperial University of Klepsis," the excellent Princess Thorn whispered to me, taking up my thoughts as she often did. "No, the Imperial University is not at all well known. It is located in three dim and dusty rooms up in the attics of Ravel-Brannagan Castle. I attended it once when I was a youngster, and there were then two other students. I do not know whether the student body is larger or smaller now. I don't know how many 'Castle Kids' there are now. But Flobert Traxley, 'The Man Who Talks to Dragons,' still chairs the dragon studies. I learned that just this evening. He can read the inscriptions on the coins.''

"I will now take the bull by the ears," said a ghost who was not at all nondescript. "I'll present a flaming bill of particulars here. I am Joshua Thorn, for those of you who remember me not. I'll not stick to the script of the original Commission hearings either. I've thought of additional things to say during my ghostly decades. Bat-brained Brannagan, the prisoner in the docket, must be toppled retrospectively to the time of the original trial; this for the salvation of the World Klepsis. Let us not say that it is impossible. There has been much good work done lately in the field of retroactive sequencing. I doubt whether you other ghosts have kept up with it."

"Brannagan is no prisoner, and there is no docket here," O'Grogan said.

"The man Brannagan is of a rabid insanity, and he has a haunt attached to him," Joshua Thorn spoke in a kind of roar. "His insanity is virulent. There is nothing harmless or comic about it. He has a one-legged haunt that is a shape-changer and a size-changer. This haunt knows almost everything, in books and out of them, but he used his information disgracefully for the harm and retardation of the World. And Brannagan himself is a total dolt. The haunt cannot be killed directly, but Brannagan can be killed. If we kill Brannagan today, which I heartily recommend, then I believe that the haunt will wither and die, as having no home to return to."

"Is this flaming orange-head of a man, this Joshua Thorn, an ancestor of yours?" I asked Princess Thorn.

"Probably a collateral ancestor. I don't believe that he lived long enough to settle down and establish a family. I don't know whether that part of it will be reenacted here or not, but angry Brannagan killed insolent and accusing Joshua Thorn right in the middle of this improbable courtroom. And it was for that murder that Brannagan, saved from execution, was deprived of his office of Director of the World Named Klepsis and was marooned and left to die on the most desolate island of the most desolate asteroid in the universe. It was the O'Grogan who saved him from execution and had him marooned instead. It was also the O'Grogan who succeeded him as Director of the World Named Klepsis. It is a little hard to follow things here unless you already know what happened."

"As an example of the insanity of this smirking madman Brannagan, he maintains that the worlds have not begun yet, and that all of us are imaginary nonbeings," Joshua Thorn was continuing his railing. "He says that he has some ideas as to whose imagination it is that we all nonexist in. He suggests, not too subtly, that it is his *own* imagination that we are all in and that if he is killed, then we will all blank out and be never-has-beens. Just for the hell of it, let's kill him right now and see whether it works that way!"

"I second that suggestion," another of the evoked ghosts spoke. "Let's get rid of him right now. Don't let him answer. He'd talk the ears off a mockingbird or the warts off a hog. Kill him now!"

"You and Joshua Thorn try it, man!" Brannagan's Ghost barked back, "and add two more to your side to even it out if you wish. I can take any four of you. Well, rule out one man here, and then I can take any other four of you. There is nothing wrong or forbidden about my speculations, and they are most likely true. Nonexistence does *not* have to prove its nonexistence. It is existence that *does* have to prove its existence. And it's never done that.

"People are simply too sketchy to be real. And they are too sketchy to be imagined directly by the Almighty. If they were imagined directly by the Almighty, *then they would be real*. But rather they are imagined by a lesser being, by a demiurge, or by an ultimate human. You people cringe when I imply that all persons might be imagined by myself, but I believe myself to be the most likely person for it that I've ever met. I have traveled everywhere. I have seen and known a hundred thousand superior men, each of whom has risen from and been the best of a hundred thousand. But I have a spaciousness and a scope that none of the others has. I am the only one who has true consciousness, the only one who can substantially look at myself. My own mind is solid and not merely sketched out. And I reach peaks where I have physical and mental and psychic speed unmatched."

"You have a haunt that has the speed, yes, and the intelligence, a very much twisted intelligence," ranted one of the accusers. "But a haunt is a devil, and we'll no longer be ruled by a devil on Klepsis. You yourself are not swift and you are not solid and you are not intelligent. You are a super-active moron, that's what you are, and they are the worst kind. There is no such person who contains all others in his imagination. If there were such, he would be nothing like you. Your insanity has gone out of bounds. If there is no halting you this side of the grave, then it must be to the grave with you!"

"It is because people are so sketchy that they cannot be anything except imaginary," Brannagan's Ghost went on again as if he had not heard the railers. "You have seen comic artists and caricaturists who can suggest a face and a person with no more than several broken lines on a paper. Human persons are like that, mere suggestions made out of long and short broken lines. Most humans cannot hold one millionth of their brain content in their conscious mind at one time. So then, that brain content is largely imaginary, or it is a group-shared thing to be dipped into. It is the ink pot from which the lines are drawn. You, Joshua Thorn, are done with only seven comic lines, and you have no solidity at all. You're one of the easiest things I ever did. I made you so sketchy because my imagination was tired when I made you.

"And time is too sketchy to be real time. If we do not live

in real time, then we do not live at all. We know only the narrowest of strips, the present. By a little arrangement that I have devised here for the pleasure of my soul, we are in two presents at once, and they are a little less than two hundred years apart. But even in the purported histories that are assembled on other planets (but not yet on Klepsis) there is only a set of dots to indicate the flow of time. Most of the extent of time is not touched at all. And the extent and flow of time are only two of the ten thousand aspects of time. I am the only one who understands this, for which reason all of you are imaginings of my mind, and I am not an imagining of the mind of any of you."

Brannagan's Ghost was curiously at his ease now, for he had faced the opposition and found it to be lightweight and sketchy. And Brannagan the un-ghost, the preserved dead man in the transparent glass coffin, was heard to chuckle and seen to move in diaphragm and throat and mouth. Oh, they were right: Brannagan was twinned. But they were wrong to think that they could outlaw the what-is-it one of the twins. That was Brannagan's Ghost, he who could climb through third-story windows when he was three weeks old, and could read his father's engineering books when he was four months old.

Joshua Thorn and several other blaze-heads railed at him and gave witness and false witness against him. Then Brannagan's Ghost took a short leave from them and came to Princess Tharrala and myself. The railers seemed to believe that he was still in confrontation with them, however, and they railed at the spot where he had stood a moment before. This Brannagan person really did have the power of bi-location. He really did have the power of going vague. He did have the power of projecting illusions. He really was twinned, and then sometimes he was twinned again.

"What they are really arguing about is what is in my mind," Brannagan's Ghost said to Thorn and myself. "They are arguing about the proposition that to kill me might be to extinguish themselves also. They are arguing about whether I am running a big bluff. Well, I really don't know what is in my mind any more than you two do, for I haven't literally looked into it for a long time. But I *can* go and look into my mind, and they can't go and look into theirs. I think I'll do it. Ah, and I think I'll go on a sea voyage, on my last sea voyage ever. Princess Tharrala and Duke Tyrone, I intend to take a sea voyage on the ship *The Dina O'Grogan* before morning light. I want you two to come with me on it. I want the last crew of the ship to come with me, the crew of the little voyage of yesterday afternoon, such of them as are still alive. I want Prince Franco the Outcast to come. I want the Princess Angela Ravel-Brannagan to come, but not her husband Prince Henry. I want Flobert Traxley, the Man Who Talks to Dragons, to come. Where we are going there may be dragons. I want the other historian, buried in the potter's field just west of O'Grogan's Mountain an hour ago, to be dug up and reanimated and brought along on the voyage. (I suspect, Duke Tyrone, that he *is* really *the* distinguished historian whom I requisitioned, and that you are not; but I accepted you immediately, on sight, and I'll not own myself wrong.) I want Doctor Luke Gilmartin to come. And I will tell the Seneschal Fidelis to come. And the Green Robe. That is about enough of you to give witness to what is in my mind. What is in my mind and what *was* in my mind are all the same, for I regard this last two hundred years as an illusion, as an imagining of my own, just as I sometimes regard all the people in the worlds as imaginings of my own. Hey, they really are belaboring their points! Joshua Thorn and his gang, I mean. They don't believe that my mind is big enough to hold the superior fauna of even a very few worlds. They don't believe that I will probably be *the first one awake*. They don't even believe in the awakening."

One of Brannagan's attackers had turned to withering scorn in an attack on a thesis which Brannagan had never actually proposed but had only hinted that he might propose. And meanwhile, Brannagan's Ghost had rejoined himself. Are ghosts more easily split than are live people?

"All the rolling spheres are in your noggin, are they,

bland-brained Brannagan?'' one of the jackals was snapping at Lion-Ghost Brannagan. "And they are nowhere else except in your head? The billions of people on Gaea-Earth and on Astrobe, and the millions of people on each of the other planets, they are all in your mind, and only in your mind, are they? What? Is your mind bigger on the inside than on the outside then? From the outside it isn't very impressive."

"Aye, it is much bigger on the inside," Brannagan's Ghost spoke with a sort of vocal grin. "Several persons here have *been* in my brain, and they have some idea of the scope of it. And a few others will visit it this night, and they will declare that it is the wonder of the worlds."

"We had better be on our way, my love," the Princess Thorn said to me. "You yourself have never resurrected a dead man, and I've had only doubtful experience at it myself. It may take a few minutes to do it. And we don't want to miss the mysterious night voyage on *The Dina O'Grogan.*"

We went out from the walk-in tomb by the ground-level slotted doorway of weathered limestone.

"Oh!" the Princess Tharrala Thorn cried as if she had suffered a sudden hurt. *"There is one star too many in the sky!* Who is it? Has it already happened? And what does it mean?"

"I have no idea what it means, good Thorn," I said.

"You an historian! And you do not even know what it means when there is one star too many in the sky! You see, my love, 'historian' carries a different connotation here on Klepsis that has never had an historian of its own. Oh, my poor loud-mouth ancestor, done to death again! People rate you too highly here, Long John, my love. They rate you as a seer and a prophet and a sage. But even a journeyman historian should know what it means when there is one star too many in the sky."

NINTH CANTO

The Introspections of Brannagan

or

One Star Too Many in the Sky

"Tell me, extraordinary Princess, what *does* it mean when there is one star too many in the sky?" I asked my droll wife.

"It means that somebody has just been murdered. The 'Star Too Many' is the murder crying to the sky for vengeance. It does not matter, for the first moment, whether the murder is justified or not. The murdered blood cries out first, and the questions are asked later. And if that murder is *not* justified, the crying-out blood will continue to manifest itself on high. The One Star Too Many will remain in the sky, even shining alone and bright in the daytime sky, for three days and three nights, or until the murder is avenged, whichever is first.

"But if the murder *is* justified, the One Star Too Many will fade from the sky within a quarter of an hour. I am afraid that the present case is the murder of my collateral ancestor by Brannagan (which we must have just missed), and that it is justified. It was justified the first time it happened. And this is still the first time, for Brannagan makes it so."

"You are faking it, droll Princess," I said. "You cannot notice *one* extra star in the sky, or one hundred."

"Oh, but I can. We all can on Klepsis. You could too, if you'd only study our Klepsis sky. Your Gaea-Earth has spoiled you with its over-plus of stars. On a good night you can see about six thousand different stars with your bare eyes on Gaea-Earth. But on Klepsis, because of our much brighter night skies, we can see only between thirty-five and sixty-five different stars in the sky, depending on the hour and the season. No more than that with the bare eyes. And we know each star by name just as well as we know the names of the different members of our own family. We *do* notice when there is one star too many in the sky. But with the crowded arrangements that you have in the sky of Gaea-Earth, how are unjustified murders ever punished?"

We went around O'Grogan's Mountain, through the little thicketed hills that surrounded it, and we came to the small potter's field at the west end of the mountain.

"What is the name of the historian?" I asked suddenly. "What name will I look for on the tombstone? There have surely been several burials here tonight, with the executions and all, and with the gunfire at the gala. Which grave, which grave?"

"We will try the latest one, my love. The Brannagan said that it was about an hour since he'd had the fellow killed, and all of the executions and most of the riot victims were two or three hours ago. It will be the grave of the most recent burial, my love."

"And how will I know which one is the most recent?"

"You really don't know? By the sight of it, of course, and by the smell of it. How do historians nose out history anyhow if they have such weak noses? Oh, you shock me, an historian who can't even tell by the sight and the smell of it which heap of dirt was shoveled last! It is this one, my love. And here is the 'municipal shovel' that you can use. It is dull and it is bent, but it will be better than nothing. We forgot to bring a good shovel. Dig him out, Duke Tyrone my love."

With the battered 'municipal shovel' I began to dig for the distinguished historian. There is always a 'municipal shovel' in a potter's field.

"Is this not just another imagining of Brannagan's Ghost, that we will be able to bring the historian back to life?" I asked.

"Why, of course not. Trust me. We are always able to bring a victim back to life if he's not been dead more than an hour or two, and if he's been properly executed. Of course, we cannot do it if he's been barbarously executed. But with Brannagan's Ghost that is not the case. Almost all of his executions are proper and seemly. All that it takes to bring such a person back to life is strong faith and Dog Latin and the pulling out of the five nails—the death-nail in the heart and the other four nails from the four corners of the coffin lid."

To you people across the parsecs and the decades, if this *Annals of Klepsis* should deservedly have taken its place among the great "Histories of Worlds" and if it should come to your hands, pay particular attention to this part. There may come a time when you yourself may wish to raise a person from the dead, perhaps a loved member of your family, or a person of stranger attachment.

This is the way it is done:

The excellent Princess Tharrala Thorn recited the first part of the ritual with total faith:

> "Strive with death in manner urgent.
> *Omni mortui resurgent.*

"There, that verse took the nail out of his heart, the most cruel of the death-nails."

At the same moment, the municipal shovel in my hands banged into the cheap plastic coffin in which the eminent historian was buried. And also at the same time there was an answering bang from inside the coffin, and a muffled shout.

"Saints preserve us! He's alive in there!" I cried with a touch of terror.

"He *becomes* alive now, good husband. That canticle that I recited took the death-nail out of his heart. Then these four more that I shall recite will take the four nails out of the lid of his coffin and permit him to arise."

"There are no nails. It's a plastic coffin," I said.

"They are symbolic nails, my love," Thorn told me. And then she recited another verse of the ritual:

> "Lave in fountain and in spa too.
> *Surge, nunc, et ambula tu!*

"There, that took one nail out of the lid of his coffin," Thorn said.

"Ah, he's stirring, he's cursing, and the life is careening through all of his vessels again! I wouldn't have believed it!" I cried as I tried to clear the dirt from the coffin; and, due to my ineptitude, it tumbled back into the hole almost as fast as I shoveled it out. And the Thorn of my Heart was again intoning in her wonderful voice:

> "Pray thee pleading, pray thee urgy!
> *Home, dico tibi, surge!*

"There, that's two nails out of the lid of his coffin."

I was making slow progress at clearing the dirt, and the man in the coffin was impatient. The eminent historian was raising a ruckus in his box. And the incomparable Princess Thorn continued to draw the symbolic nails out of the lid of the coffin with her enchanting voice:

> "From the grave an easy exit.
> *Ecce! Homo resurrexit.*

"There, that's three nails out of his coffin lid."

I began to get the lid off the coffin then, which was difficult because I was standing on it. And Thorn gave me the final power to do it.

"Grant us this, and grant yet more us!
Lazare, O veni foras!

"That's all four of the nails out of the lid of his coffin. Oh, help him to stand up, my love, and let's get him out of this horrible hole."

"It's the most barbarous mismanagement I have ever heard of!" the furious and eminent historian was sputtering and railing as he came out of his grave. "What can one expect on a barbarous planet like Klepsis? I say 'Kill a man, or let him live, *but do not bury him alive!*' That is the ultimate barbarity. There is nothing more horrifying than waking up alive in a coffin in a grave."

"How did they do it?" I asked. "I'm a stranger on Klepsis myself. I just arrived here last evening."

"They did it with *elaionheliotropionmekon*," the historian spat furiously, "with the oil of the dread sunflower poppy. I'll never forget that taste. They had to force it down my gullet this time. They use it as knock-out drops in the Barrio district of Astrobe City on Astrobe, and I was a victim of it a few times when I was doing historical research in the bars and taverns of that district. It throws one into a cataleptic trance. In the Barrio they stack up the cataleptic persons, laying four of them out one way, then four of them crossways on them, then four of them the first way again, till it is as high as a person can reach. They pile up their most troublesome customers so and leave them there until their trance wears off. But they don't bury them alive when they're in a cataleptic trance. That's reserved for this barbarous planet. That crusty old man intended to do it too, to have me buried alive. He knew exactly what he was doing. I wonder whether any of the other persons buried here are recent enough to dig up?"

"No, they were all done in by more barbarous executions, or by bloody gunning fights at the gala. They weren't done in by the dread poppy juice."

"Oh, then they're dead forever."

"No, no, no, Eminent Historian," Thorn declared. "I believe in the Resurrection and the Life. I believe that all the dead shall arise on the first day."

"You mean on the last day," the historian commented.

"No, I mean on the first day," Thorn insisted.

"I am Titus Livius Morrison-Bryce the Historian," the man said. "You two have saved my life on this strange planet, so I thank you."

"I am Duke Tyrone, also an historian," I said, "and this is my wife of several hours, the Princess Tharrala Thorn-Ravel-Brannagan."

"You are the false and incompetent historian who preempted me," Titus Livius spoke at me in near hostility. "Well, there is no time for enmity now. Let's go, let's go— well, somewhere, anywhere out of this cursed place."

"You were the one I intended to marry, Titus Livius," Princess Thorn said, "but then something went wrong, or maybe something went right. My, but you are a crabby man! I got my historians mixed up as I didn't know there would be more than one of them."

"Being buried alive is enough to make anyone crabby for a little while. But I am not so always. Let's get out of here!"

"There is a shortcut," said Prince Franco, appearing suddenly, as only he could. "We will go *under* O'Grogan's Mountain, not around it. We will go down through this grave that looks like all the other graves and is not. And we'll go into the caverns and rouse out the crew. And then we'll go to that gallant ship *The Dina O'Grogan*."

The One Star Too Many had faded from the sky. The murder, probably that of Princess Thorn's collateral ancestor Joshua Thorn by Brannagan's Ghost, had been justified. Of course, Brannagan would still be punished for the murder, but not by the sky.

We went down into the caverns through an entrance that was camouflaged as a grave. There was sufficient light in the caverns. It was like bright moonlight. There were no chests of gold or gemstones in this part of the caverns, but there were thousands of gold pieces loose on the floor.

"There are very many entrances to these caverns, and very many passages in them, so that a stranger in them might be lost completely," Prince Franco said. "An adventurer drawn to the caverns by the stories of great treasure to be found in them might wander for several days before coming onto the gold. Then, after taking all that he could carry, he would mark his path away from it by dropping a gold coin every few feet so that he could quickly find his way to the treasure when he came back for more of it. But almost always he would take a wrong turning and run into a blank wall almost exactly when he had dropped his last gold coin. So he would follow his trail back to the treasure again and take all the coins he could carry once more. He would select a different path this time in trying to find his way out of the caverns, but he would mark his new path in the same way, by dropping gold coins. And again he would come up against a blank wall at the same time that he had dropped his last coin. So, he would continue getting lost and dropping gold coins until he died of exhaustion. Many adventurers come into the caverns and they scatter big quantities of gold on the different paths, but they are not able to carry much gold out of the caverns.

"There are quite a few entrances into the caverns from the Castle. One of them even comes out of the bottom of the big healing wine vat. Well, gold is a great healer for many ailments. There are several entrances winding down through the caves of O'Grogan's Mountain under which we now travel. And there are several entrances coming from the waterfront area. If one knows the way, one can sail right into the caverns in a fairly large ship. At least two hundred persons have access to the caverns and know all about them, and every one of them considers all the treasures to belong to himself."

We turned a corner in the caverns then, and we came onto the full blaze of gold.

"By the holy muse, Clio, I have never seen anything like this," the historian Morrison-Bryce cried with joy. "Much barbarism can be forgiven a world that has such treasures as this. I would give my life to own all of this for just one second."

"You are too prodigal of your life, Other Historian," Prince Franco said to the eminent person. "Every person

who comes into the caverns does own all of this for many
seconds, as you own all of it now; and he comes back to it
again and again. I first owned it all when I was a boy of five.
And when I think large thoughts about it, I am still a boy of
five.

"Ho, there is the crew! We sail on the good ship *The
Dina O'Grogan* almost immediately. Board you the ship at
once and ready her for one of the most exciting and mysti-
fying voyages ever. It will be dream stuff and ocean stuff
mixed together, and it may well be the most dumbfounding
night in the lives of any of you. Board the ship and make
ready."

"We are treasure-cave owners and no longer ocean sailors," Andrew Gold Coast O'Mally lilted in a voice that was
drunk on tincture of gold. "We are on honeymoon now
with the treasure thing. Come again in another moon,
twenty-nine nights from now, and we may be ready to go
on the dream-stuff-and-ocean-stuff-mixed-together voyage. This is already the most dumbfounding night of our
lives."

"Go you free or go you in chains, but you will all go on
The Dina O'Grogan tonight," Prince Franco threatened.

"You are better than most of them, Prince Franco, but
we will not go on your orders, not tonight."

"Will you go on *my* orders?" the Princess Angela
Gilmartin-Ravel-Brannagan asked in a steely whisper as
she entered the caverns from one of the Castle entrances.

"Not even for you, Angie Princess, but you come closer," Kate Blithespirit the Amazon said. "We will not be
willing to do anything except gaze at our gold for a long,
long time."

"Will you go on *my* orders?" my Princess Tharrala
Thorn asked.

"No, not even on your orders, one-of-us girl, but we are
coming closer all the time," the green-eyed Sparaticus
spoke.

"On whose orders will you sail, then?" my Thorn asked
it.

"On the orders of only one person on all Klepsis," Jerome Whitewater answered. "Only on the orders of Brannagan himself."

"Brannagan will be on the voyage, but he will not be in charge of the voyage," Thorn said. "He will not be in command."

"If Brannagan is on the ship, we will *put* him in command," Sebastian Jamaica let it be known. "We sail, we sail, we sail!"

And all of us gave the same cry, "We sail, we sail, we sail!" We swept through the water-level caverns and into the roiling water, and we swam to *The Dina O'Grogan*. Hektor Lafcadio climbed the main mast and whispered the news to the ship that she was going on the most dumbfounding voyage ever, and with her first master on board, he who had built her and named her *The Beloved Harpy* two generations before her later namesake, the woman Dina O'Grogan, was born.

"I know it, I know it," the ship spoke like winds in her own rigging. "Parley birds have already been here and told me."

Persons and personages arrived on *The Dina O'Grogan* then. The O'Grogan himself came. Jerome Whitewater had not been thinking clearly when he said that the crew would sail only under the orders of one man, the Brannagan. Every member of the crew would as readily sail under the command of the O'Grogan. And it was seen at once that the O'Grogan was in command. This great son-in-law of the Brannagan had always been the number-one man of the Brannagan party.

Flobert Traxley, the man who talked to dragons, came on board. Doctor Luke Gilmartin came on board. There was some confusion. In all of the six generations of Klepsis, there had always been a Doctor Gilmartin who was official Doctor of the Realm, and all these Doctors Gilmartin had looked remarkably alike. Well, this man was either the father of the grandfather or of the great-grandfather, or of some earlier grandfather of the Princess Angela Gilmartin-

Ravel-Brannagan. She knew who he was, but did anyone else?

Seneschal Fidelis came on board. The Green Robe of the Order of Saint Klingensmith came. Then nine strongmen came and they were dragging the Brannagan (it was really Brannagan's Ghost) in cruel chains. They chained him, with his hands and arms behind him, to the main mast of *The Dina O'Grogan*, his own earliest ship on Klepsis.

"Never mind," said Sebastian Jamaica in his whisper that was like a sandy reef barely scraping the bottom of a ship. "Let us get under way. Let us sail nine sea miles. Then we will put the Brannagan in charge, or we will know why not."

We sailed with a scram of ghosts in command. Oh, they were old and outstanding ghosts, but where except on Klepsis could such a thing happen?

"It seems a puny ship and a weak undertaking, all of it, under a vagary of minds that aren't even there any more," I said. "Well, nothing can happen to us on a calm ocean at night."

"There is always the opportunity of enlargement of the voyage," the Penny Philosopher Fairbridge Exendine told me. "The old pirate ships of Klepsis and Tarshish did sometimes, in the middle of a slow ocean voyage, skip to the oceans of other planets while scarcely losing a puff of the wind in their sails. They called it 'Crossing the Ocean of Hiatus,' and that crossing took hardly a minute to accomplish. They also called it 'Sailing Through the Bushes.' "

Ah, Fairbridge, Fairbridge, the only 'penny philosopher' I ever knew who was worth a farthing.

Those wraiths with Klepsis roots were not ghosts at all. They were Extended Spirits. This phrase had been coined by a person known as Quasimodo who had been as near to being an executive officer as Brannagan ever had when he ruled the Planet Klepsis.

With the highly intelligent and infinitely compassionate Extended Spirit, the O'Grogan, in command, we sailed.

But in common parlance, O'Grogan was a ghost. With a crazy-as-a-sea-coot, laughing, flame-headed giant Extended Spirit, the Brannagan, as clanking prisoner, chained to the main mast, we sailed. And Brannagan was a ghost with a real wooden leg. Brannagan's Ghost did make a ruckus of it.

The person at the tiller was a ghost or an Extended Spirit (one with a short tailpiece at the back of his seaman's trousers); and the lookout up in the crow's nest was a ghost also. We sailed on the sweet-water ocean like a song, and Brannagan's Ghost-in-Chains was singing an old Gaea ballad:

> "He built a bonny ship and bold
> To sail the saltless sea.
> The mast is beaten pirate gold,
> The sails are cramoisie."

Yes, yes, the sails did look to be cramoisie, or crimson, by the light of the two moons. There was a curious little humpbacked dwarf into everything on the ship, and he seemed to be a person of consequence.

"He is Quasimodo," Thorn said, "but how can that be? He is here as a young and grotesque man. But he is the 'sleeper' at the Castle, old and grotesque. He is not dead. Can this be a youth-ghost of an old man who still lives?"

And Brannagan's Ghost continued to sing in his beautiful, booming voice:

> "A murder-man be chained to mast—
> (Lo! Lightning in the sky)—
> On Desolation Isle'll be cast,
> Marooned and left to die."

I had never heard the Brannagan sing before, but he had a rich and wonderful voice that set the whole sky and the forty-seven stars in it to ringing.

"Oh, queer his doom and droll his crime,
(Oh, be you ware and wey!)
For he has died in former time,
And you will die today."

A shout had gone up, "Stowaway, stowaway, spy, spy, spy!" And a rather imposing-looking man had been dragged out of the ratlines. He was dressed as a shabby seaman, but the shabby dress did not become him.

But the Brannagan still sang:

"My tale is tall, my writ the sky,
My tongue is double-jointed.
Oh, if I wake, you all will die!
I am the Lord's Anointed."

Hektor Lafcadio brought a schooner of rum to Brannagan, but Brannagan refused it. "I have rum of which you know not," he said. "Oh, hark the song of the barnacle geese:

"I whittled from my lost leg's bone
A whistle for my daughter.
My eight-valved heart is bleeding stone,
My brain it is saltwater."

"There really *is* a legend of the Margaret Whistle, that of the Brannagan's daughter, Margaret O'Grogan, that will blow louder than all the trumpets on the First Day," the Penny Philosopher Fairbridge Exendine told me. "And the Tarshish storyteller has based one of his stories upon it."

And Brannagan (well, of course he was Brannagan's Ghost, but he was so essentially the original Brannagan now, chained and high-spirited and defiant) sang another stanza:

"The Beta Sun's a squeaky ball
In badly need of oiling.

In one place only all folks all
Inside of me are roiling."

Brannagan's Great Ghost was drunk (on a rum that we
knew not of) but he seemed to feel no guilt for the murder
of Joshua Thorn, that railing enemy of his. Oh, it is all running like a two-track cinema, with the tracks two hundred
years apart, but we are resolved not to let it confuse us. The
Commission in Lunacy had found Brannagan to be a lunatic, and he had been forced to disgorge Klepsis from his
rule. It had been a 'coup of just a moment' when his world
was taken from him. He had killed the harassing Joshua
Thorn with one blow of his ruddy hand, and he had been
sentenced to be marooned on the most desolate island of
the most desolate asteroid of the universe.

"Oh, they are only a mime of ghosts," I said. "With
them it is all two hundred years ago."

"With all of us here it is two hundred years ago,"
Fairbridge the Penny Philosopher said, "because time never began on Klepsis. It is still legend here, and in legend all
persons are contemporaries. Hercules was contemporary
with the revolt of the Titans on Gaea-Earth, and he was
also contemporary with Pericles of Athens."

"The stowaway and spy is Grand Marshal Golconde of
the Paravata Defense League," said Titus Livius the Eminent Historian who knew faces and facts of all the planets.
"He can be stowed away here for only one reason—to find
out how the ships of Klepsis and of Tarshish are jumped
from one planet to another. He arrived on the same transport that brought me in here tonight. He must have had a
scan that told him that a ship was jumping on Klepsis tonight, and none have jumped here for many years. The
Paravata Defense League has scans that go a few hours into
the future, but they do them little good. They run into every sort of paradox when they try to avoid the futures. But
Golconde is entirely too intelligent ever to understand how
the shipjumping is done, and so are all the other ladies and
gentlemen of the PDL. I did a study on the PDL once for

the FHP Press. I was almost too intelligent to understand how it was done myself, but fortunately I have a goofy spot in my brain."

And bumptious Brannagan still sang his ballad verses:

> "My eye is clear, my beard is curled.
> I fear not man nor wooman.
> And if we jump to other world,
> We jump by short-tailed human."

So sang Brannagan's Indomitable Ghost in its clanking chains.

"Oh, Brannagan's Ghost has just told Grand Marshal Golconde and all other persons present how the planet-jumping of ships is done," Titus Livius said sourly. In spite of the barbarity of his greeting and his being buried alive, he had now become a partisan of Klepsis. "Yes, Brannagan told it in verse, but I hope that Golconde is still too intelligent to catch on."

There were several of the crewmen, both the ghostly ones and the modern fleshed ones who had tailpieces at the back of their trousers. Presumably, one or more of them were short-tailed humans from Tarshish. But could these quasi-people really jump not only themselves but whole ships from one world to another? I was very nearly too intelligent to understand it myself.

They, the mime of ghosts (it was the O'Grogan or the O'Grogan Ghost who told me this now as I walked over to talk to him) had decided to kill the Brannagan for the murder of Joshua Thorn, but they had hesitated as they worried over Brannagan's jibe that all of them were no more than imaginings in the great Brannagan mind; if Brannagan died it would be as if the rest of them were not, and had never, been.

"If we kill him, maybe *we'll* disappear," one of them had whimpered at that Commission of Lunacy hearing.

"We'll test it by stages," that loving son-in-law of Brannagan, Januarius O'Grogan, had proposed. "We'll half-kill the abomination first, and then we'll see whether half of us disappear." They were twelve good men and true pronouncing the doom on Brannagan. They made a garrote to strangle him and they put it around his neck. They would half-kill him first. Then, if all went well, they would kill him altogether.

They did half-kill him. Then the six good men and true looked at each other in a sort of bleak panic. Yes, half of them, the other six of them had disappeared, and they would no more be found ever. They had also disappeared from memory, for the six survivors could not recall the faces or names of those who were undone.

"I believe that I suffered brain damage from that grueling half hour of strangulation," Brannagan's Ghost told me now. "After that time, my great mind has had islands of fog in it."

"We'll travel that road no further," O'Grogan had said when the half-death of Brannagan had resulted in the obliteration of six good men from the kangaroo party. It was then that they decided to maroon the Brannagan, and now (or *then*, for time had not yet begun on Klepsis, so the two-hundred-year interval could be considered or ignored at will) they were still about the business of the marooning.

"We *did* maroon him," the O'Grogan Ghost told me (for in my role as historian I was checking them all out), "in such an obscure place that even God does not have it listed. There was no way that he could have been located. There was surely no way that he could have been rescued. But, seven years later, he came back to Klepsis just as he had always been, except that his peg leg was of ivory horn instead of wood. What I believe is that his other person, his what-is-it, his lost twin, had rescued him. No one else could have located him, but Brannagan and his what-is-it were essentially of one mind.

"And I believed, or half-believed, that we *were* all imaginings in the lunatic mind of Brannagan. The reason that I only half-believed it was that Brannagan, on his return from his exile and marooning, told me that he had rid

himself of a cosmic onus and had loaded it onto another
person.

"So, according to one of the versions that Brannagan
(and later, Brannagan's Ghost) maintained, it is a sleeping
person in Ravel-Brannagan Castle who now holds all
things and all persons (including Brannagan) as imaginings
in his mind. Care is taken that this sleeping and dreaming
person does not wake, and also that he does not die. 'I like
it better this way,' Brannagan told me. 'The responsibility
of it all was beginning to weigh on me.' Ah, Historian
Tyrone, I believe that we ghosts, the scraggly company of
us, will soon break up, some of us going to our damnation
and some of us going to our beatification."

So O'Grogan's Ghost told me. But did O'Grogan's
Ghost also have a double-jointed tongue? It was when
O'Grogan's Ghost was in this pensive mood that Titus
Livius the Historian and Fairbridge Exendine the Penny
Philosopher came to him with a suggestion for disposing of
the stowaway and spy, Grand Marshal Golconde of the
Paravata Defense League.

"The Paravata Defense League would be warlike if only
it had something to be warlike with," Titus Livius the Historian said. "If they have the secret of planet-jumping they
will be making raids everywhere with their spaceships. A
ship could raid and return to its home base almost before it
started."

"All right, you two do as you suggest, then," O'Grogan
agreed. "Use the leaky lifeboat for it, though. It is of no
use to *The Dina O'Grogan,* but it will only have to hold together for about six seconds. And use the aft
mind-stripper."

Titus and Fairbridge took the most obscure of the three
short-tailed humans, put him in the leaky lifeboat, took the
Grand Marshal, ran him through the mind-stripper (they
have these only on unscientific worlds like Klepsis), put
him in the lifeboat too, lowered it into the saltless sea, and
pushed it off.

The short-tailed human grinned and waved, and then the

lifeboat with its two occupants disappeared completely from Klepsis World.

"In six seconds it will appear in the luxury lodge of the Paravata Defense League, in a fishpond in their great meeting hall, a small and sinking lifeboat with the Grand Marshal Golconde, totally insane, in it. And with the other occupant a little sideshow monster. What will they think?" said Titus Livius Morrison-Bryce the Eminent Historian.

"I am worried," Doctor Gilmartin told me. He was a living man and not a ghost, a grandfather or great-uncle of the reigning Princess Angela. Alive he was, but he had come to look a little like a ghost, from associating with them so much, especially with Brannagan's Ghost.

"When Brannagan's Ghost gets tired of the fun of being a prisoner in chains, he is likely to do some wild thing. He can raise sea-tempests, you know, violent ones that could easily destroy a ship of this size. He is not God, but he knows many of the little God-tricks. He can say to the winds and the waves, 'Rise and roar,' and they will do it. And then he can say, 'Be calm again,' and they will be calm."

"Have you seen him raise tempests, or have others told you of this?" I asked the doctor.

"Others have told me of it, but they are such ones as I believe. Of course, since the epiphany of the Doomsday Equation we can think in no other context than that of the equation."

"What is the Doomsday Equation?" I asked.

"You are an historian and you do not know the Doomsday Equation? Its revealing is certainly the most important historical event of the century, just as it is the most important philosophical and eschatological event."

We had been moving on a clear night ocean, but now strange floes (not of ice) were suddenly floating in it. And with the floes there came a queasiness, a lightness, a giddiness. There had been a change in everything, but either it was not a rapid change, or it was so subtle that it took us a while to realize that it had happened. But we were lighter now; there was no question of that. And the air pressure was much less. The ghosts realized it first (they are as sensitive as canaries to ambient changes), especially the lookout ghosts in the crow's nest.

"Jump ahoy! Jump ahoy!" he cried down from the low sky (a low overcast was part of the change). "Sea's gone strange, sky's gone strange. Jump ahoy!"

"I believe that we are breathing pure oxygen now, and not enough of it," Doctor Luke Gilmartin said.

"First Engineer, report to the Instruments Room," somebody yelled over the ship's speaker in a light-hearted voice, even a kidding voice. "World gravity is on the fritz, down to a tenth. First Engineer, come and repair world's gravity."

Almost everybody laughed at this, but the gravity was surely only a fraction of normal. The ship rode very much lighter and higher in the water, and it bounced and skipped dangerously.

"What is it, what is it?" the Eminent Historian Titus Livius Morrison-Bryce asked me.

"Let's just go see," I said. I got a bucket and a rope. I dunked the bucket into the ocean and pulled it up again. "Taste it, Titus," I said, and he did.

"It's salt water," he announced in a moment, "and all the seas and oceans of Klepsis are fresh water. It baffles the brain, but I say that we are no longer on Klepsis."

"It's the jump, the biological planetary jump, the short-tailed jump," said Fairbridge Exendine the Penny Philosopher from the Trader Planet Emporion. "It is a biological change as much as a change in convoluted space. Plants and animals, and the lower animals more than the upper, do migrate from planet to planet and to asteroids. Usually when humans arrive at a new world they will find that plants and animals of the Gaea-Astrobe-Camiroi families have already been there for about a thousand years. They feel impelled to 'get the planet ready.' But some of the higher animals may have been on the new world for only

about fifty years. Some of the older elephants and mules on
Klepsis (there is real evidence of this) have even been born
on other worlds and have migrated to Klepsis without human aid. Plants and animals do not have spaceships. They
jump through the hiatus, they jump through the bush, they
jump through the jungle. And when humans do make the
planetary jumps, (they do it very rarely, and usually are either illuminati or pirate groups) there is a very strange sym-
biosis or parasitism as a side effect. They pick up green me-
mentos on their jump. For instance—"

Fairbridge Exendine pulled up his seaman's sweater.
Green leaves and fronds were growing from his belly.

"I always thought that was a tall story, Fairbridge," Titus the Historian said. "How do you do it?"

"I do not do it. It is done to me, just as it is done to you. I
went along on a jump from planet to planet, or probably
from planet to asteroid. I feel much lighter, but I've been in
no-weight space a lot and it doesn't bother me. I smell salt
spray, and there are green mosses and spoors growing on
my body. That's the way it was done to me. How was it
done to you, Titus?"

"To me? Let me see," Titus said. Titus was dressed more
formally than was the Penny Philosopher, so it took him
longer. But when he finally bared his belly, yes, green
leaves and fronds were growing on it. So were they on
mine.

"If we jumped, so did the ship," Titus said. "That makes
it a spaceship, I suppose. But regular spaceships don't pick
up green goop. Maybe it's because they go too slow, or
don't go through a biotic medium."

"Yes, when I dipped the bucket, I noticed—" I began.
We all went to the rail and examined the side of the ship.
The whole hull of the ship was bosky, bushy, green-leafed
and green-fronded and even green-boughed. And the stuff
on the ship was a meter thick.

"There is no great mystery about it," Bartolomo Portuguese said. "Of course, I've jumped before. The Penny
Philosopher says that it is usually members of either the il-

luminati or the pirate groups who make the jumps, and I'm
a member of both. Moreover, I'm a short-tail. It is only a
quick parasitical growth that fastens on us as we go through
it on a jump. We couldn't jump without picking up some of
it. Jump space is fantastically populated—with botany. My
God, what botany! The interstellar dust that some astrono-
mers write about is interstellar botany. You will find that
many old pirates cultivate and affect this green growth on
themselves.

"The pirate ships have always been great jumpers—the
pirate ships of Tarshish and Klepsis especially. They would
coast along in their own poor backwaters, and then in an instant they would be in the richer waters of another planet
and bearing down on unsuspecting prey. They would rob
and scuttle. And then, when they had a shipload of wealth,
they would go away again by the hiatus road. If an armada
should get on the trail of one of them and be about to over-
haul it, the ship would disappear from that world completely and appear on its own world, or on some other world.
The eleven great pirate ships of Klepsis (of which this is
one) made such jumps routinely. And *The Dina O'Grogan*
on which we ride made more such jumps than any of them,
for the ship's captain, Dina O'Grogan herself, was the
most fearless of the eleven great pirate-captains. Moreover, she was a short-tail, though that was secret. She made
the space-bustle popular for a while with ladies of the pirate families. Her brothers admitted that she was the most
fearless. My own grandfather sailed on this *Dina O'Grogan*
many times in the great age of piracy. I myself am of the
sixth generation of pirates," said Bartolomo Portuguese.

"Where is Quasimodo?" chained-to-the-mast
Brannagan's Ghost howled loudly, and his happy voice
suddenly had blade-steel in it. "Why is he not with me? I
need his advice."

"Christopher, you know that Quasimodo is still alive,"
the O'Grogan called across to Brannagan's Ghost. "He is
alive, but in restricted sleep. He cannot come to you as
flesh, and he cannot come to you as ghost. You know such

things, Christopher. Collect your wits, please, and do not be calling out like the lunatic you have been proclaimed."

"Oh, what are you talking about, Januarius?" Christopher Brannagan's Ghost called back, in happy spirits again. "Here is Quasimodo now. He was just about other business for a few moments."

So O'Grogan, and possibly the other ghosts of the kangaroo court, could not see Quasimodo. But some of us living ones could see him plainly, now and then, as he came and went. But there was an elusive element about the little hunchback. Was he really the "sleeper" back in the Castle?

And now we were in the hot doldrums of whatever world we were on.

"Somebody knows where we are and where we are going," the Historian Titus said. "This is not a random buffeting of the elements. This would be an intolerable place, for as much as half a day. A person would die in this within half a day. The O'Grogan here knows where we are and where we go."

"On one level I know, yes," O'Grogan's Ghost agreed. "I only hope that I know enough of our navigation to get us back to Klepsis."

"These strange doings are partly to my liking," Titus Livius Morrison-Bryce the Historian said with pleasure. "With historians at least it is always good fishing in muddy waters. I was summoned to Klepsis to advise a leading man who had once been the autocrat and ruler of that world. It happened that he was no longer a leading man but a lunatic ghost instead. He mistreated me, and among other things he had me buried alive. And yet I believe that all things I encounter in the Klepsis context will go in my favor. They will add spice as well as substance to my work. I have decided, since I am already here (though, for the moment, the 'here' does not seem to be Klepsis) to write a total history of the planet. What have *you* decided to do, Duke Tyrone, you who attempted for a while to preempt my place?"

"I have also decided to write a total history of Klepsis," I said. "That was my original idea of coming here. When I heard that it was a 'planet without a history' I decided to write a history of it. Nobody summoned me to come."

"My own work will be titled, simply and professionally, *The Annals of Klepsis*. What will your work be titled, Duke Tyrone, if indeed it ever does come into being?"

"My own work will also be called, simply and professionally, *Annals of Klepsis*," I said.

"The difficulty about writing the history is that there are parallel lines two hundred years apart, and they are meeting constantly," Titus said. "Klepsis really has not had any history, we know. It has had something else entirely. Oh, I love these 'My God What Grapes!' grapes. It was thoughtful of somebody to provide them."

"Brannagan's Ghost spoke to me in much the same way earlier in the night," I said. "He told me, and I quote: 'While I still stir and walk and talk, even in my ghost form, then Klepsis will remain in its time of legend and *pre*history. But when I can no longer walk and talk, even as a ghost, then the history of Klepsis may begin. My fear is that the earlier chapters of it may be inferior history.' "

"Interesting, interesting," said Titus. "But the earlier chapters of it will be inferior history only if written by an inferior historian. I'm happy that I'm not such. And Brannagan will not be able to walk and talk, even in ghost form, for very long. His marooning is a form of execution. I can't say that I'm sorry. As an historian I am totally objective, but as a man I am a little bit subjective about the fact that he consigned me to be buried in my coffin and to wake up screaming in it."

Flobert Traxley, the man who talked to dragons, joined us. It had been getting hotter and stuffier and harder to breathe by the minute.

"It will not be safe for the Brannagan to be marooned anywhere on this planet," Flobert said. "This is really one of the Dragons' Asteroids, and dragons on their asteroids immediately and completely eat every human they come upon."

"Well, that is part of Brannagan's sentence," the

O'Grogan said. "We didn't intend him to live more than a day or two at most. Damn, I hope it's sufficiently removed here. It's not even in our part of the galaxy. I believe that the things and the creatures *here* will become the imaginings of his mind and will take our places there. *They*, not we, will perish when he dies. I believe that we will have gone clear out of his mind and out of the zone of destruction. I'll not worry about Brannagan, though I love him like a brother, the insufferable monster!"

"I wasn't worrying about Brannagan. I was worrying about the rest of the universe," said Flobert Traxley.

"Island Ahoy!" sang out the ghost-lookout in the crow's nest. "Damnedest island I ever saw, Ahoy!"

"If I know my dragons, something very strange and unpleasant is going to happen when the dragons eat Brannagan's Brain," Flobert still worried.

"Iron-Mountain Island Ahoy!" the lookout called down to us. It became hotter and hotter. And then, quite suddenly, too suddenly, we were right alongside a bitterly hot, mountainous iron island that seemed to be composed entirely of sheer cliffs.

Seamen from the top of the main mast threw grapples to the iron cliffs, and one grapple took hold. A line was run up from the top of the main mast to where the grapple had bit into the iron cliff.

"Brannagan," said the O'Grogan in a sad but reasonable voice. "Do us a favor. You who can climb like a Squallton's squirrel, run up the mast and up the line to the cliff. We'd have a devil of a time getting you up there if you refused to go."

"Oh, I'll go readily enough," the Brannagan said. Men came to release Brannagan from his chains. But, with a clattering laugh, to show that he could have done it any time he wished, he broke the iron chains by sheer strength and was up the mainmast and up the line from it and onto the iron cliff, going like a Skokumchuck Planet squirrel.

And Quasimodo, the humpbacked dwarf, who had a lot of physical giantism mixed with his dwarfism (a funny-

shaped person he!), was up the mast and line and onto the
iron cliff right after the Brannagan.

"Fare thee ill, Brannagan," the O'Grogan called up to
him. "Thou'lt be alone for the short time you have left to
live here. Even Quasimodo will not be with you. But then a
disposed ruler doesn't very much need an executive officer
for his final moments alone. Fare thee ill, old fraud."

O'Grogan and the other ghosts of the kangaroo court really couldn't see Quasimodo. And that dwarf was really in
a very paradoxical position.

"Fare thee well, all of you," the Brannagan called down.
"I am going to do a thing five minutes after you leave me
marooned in this terrible place, but I will only be doing it in
fun. I say that in advance so that none of you will perish
from fright. I am going to scare all of you speechless, wit-
less, liverless, breathless, hopeless. I am going to show you
how easily I *could* destroy you. And then I am going to let
you go. I will do this out of the goodness of my heart."

We pulled away from that scorching-hot iron island as
quickly as we could. We tried all directions until we felt the
wind in our faces.

"Brannagan will soon perish," Flobert Traxley said sadly. "He had no water and no food, and he has no shelter
from the terrible heat and glare. He will die of exposure
and thirst, or he will be killed and eaten by dragons."

"I'll bet it goes the other way," said the Green Robe of
the order of Saint Klingensmith. "The Brannagan will
know how to kill a banquet-sized dragon. And Quasimodo
will know how to make a banquet out of it."

Then we ourselves made a resolve not to die of the heat
and weirdness, but to come back to our better place.

"We will jump soon," the O'Grogan said, "very soon. I do
not know the second of any jump but I do know the minute. This is the minute."

We jumped almost immediately. We came into nearly
total quiet, but there was a shrieking uneasiness on every-

thing. We were on an ocean like none that we had ever seen. It was red and ocher in color, and it had a pushing flow to it as if it were being pumped. The ocean was strange, yes, and the sky. The sky! There wasn't any sky; that was one reason for our shrieking uneasiness. We were totally enclosed. We were cut off from the sky by a rather low firmament, a *steroma*, an overhanging solidity.

"We have misjumped," said Bartolomo Portuguese, who knew about planet-jumping. "We are on neither Tarshish nor Klepsis. We are not on any of the commonly recognized planets. I have sailed on all of them, and none of them have ocean-scapes like this. This is a world impossible and totally wrong."

"It is impossible, of course," said old Doctor Luke Gilmartin, "so I won't even tell you what this new world so comically resembles."

Our ship was sailing down a rushing torrent. Then our ship was rushing *up* a torrent, pumped almost vertically into—into whatever was up.

Utter fascination, utter fear, and the threat of utter extinction! It was depressing and deadly. There was not a blade of vegetation that we could recognize as such, and yet there were solidities all around us. There was no good way to tell the land from the water, for both of them seemed soft and soppy and semi-fluid. The mountains, the folding mountains over our heads, were of tan and gray and rose and dull slate color. They were the color of total despondency.

And, oh, the people in that dim and dingy world: sad, empty-eyed, without hope, shaking with fear. Yes, there were people here, sinking and screaming into the land, and walking quakingly on the water. There were at least ten thousand people on that one promontory, and there were hundreds of other simultaneously crowded capes and heads. There were hopeless meadows and despondent sloughs and apathy valleys; and they were all populated by people who were somehow straited and incomplete.

"This is the Doomsday Equation put into audio-visual form," Doctor Gilmartin said. "The name of this three-D panorama is 'The Introspections of Brannagan.' But Brannagan isn't introspecting Brannagan; *we* are introspecting Brannagan."

"I am sure that we can see only a small portion of it from here, but what it looks like to me—" Flobert Traxley, the man who talked to dragons, tried to explain something, and then he fell silent. His face was twitching.

"I am sure this is only one aspect of it," the Historian Titus Livius was saying, "like the tail of an elephant. But a man who really understands the tail end of things, might reconstruct—Oh God, what might he not reconstruct! No, no!"

"I am sure that this is only a limited sampling of it," Terpsichore Callagy was saying in a fearful voice, "but to one who has the artist's eye and mind, as I have, the pattern is evident. Of course we are in the middle of—"

"No, no, don't say it," the Greek-god-made-out-of-stone, Hektor Lafcadio, cried out. "It must be something else we are in. It cannot be what it seems to be. Do not say it!"

"Of course we are in the middle of a giant human brain," Terpsichore finished her bit. "Giant? Yes, giant. Many kilometers is every dimension of it."

"Och, Brannagan's Brain!" O'Grogan shuddered the words out. "He was always an impossible and irresponsible man. I loved him more than any man on our world, but he was clearly an oaf and a slob, a wooden-legged slob. Ah, but he was always a brainy man! He really does hold all of us in his brain now. Oh, how can we hide from a person in his own brain?"

"Let us not panic," Doctor Luke Gilmartin said easily. "If this is really the Introspection of Brannagan that we are experiencing, then it is a happening worth living. As Brannagan's Ghost's physician and doctor, I have been into, though not in, Brannagan's brain a few times before, extracting bullets from it and such routine things as that. I think I recognize a place in it now. I'll just climb up there and let you know. In just a minute I'll call down to you whether it is Brannagan's brain or not."

It seemed to be easy but messy, rather malodorous, climbing. But old Doctor Gilmartin was entirely professional as he carried on his investigation. He climbed high, two hundred meters or so. He prowled about a spot there for a while. And then he called down in a glad but faint (from his great distance away) voice:

"Triumph, scientific triumph! I have made absolute identification from a spot that I know well. Yes, this is Brannagan's brain. Oh, it is big! From down there you can have no idea of the size of it. Immense, immense!

"Ah, and the interior valleys and cities that I can see from this height! Millions and millions and millions of people in them. I really believe that all the people of all the worlds are there. They're not very happy people, though. They're a little bit like people who have never been awakened, or have never been born."

"Trapped in Brannagan's brain! Then, we are all lost!" the O'Grogan moaned.

But there was a movement that was a little less than a movement. Those of us who were paying attention knew immediately that we had begun another jump. The big human brain that had contained us vanished completely, and that left Doctor Gilmartin up in the air. He fell to the foredeck of *The Dina O'Grogan* like a plummet and was killed and curdled into an unsavory mass.

"Let the rule be: 'Do not ever climb so high on the cliffs of imagination that the fall from the top will kill you,' " the Penny Philosopher Fairbridge Exendine said.

"A good line," the historian Titus approved, and he wrote it down in his pocket notebook.

Like big thunder, we heard the happy, clattering laughter of Brannagan then, worlds away from us. He'd been having a little fun with one of his Projecting Tricks. He had always been full of them. Did you know that Brannagan had been a stage magician when he was a young man, on his first trip to Astrobe?

We completed our planetary jump, and we came to . . .

TENTH CANTO

The Possibility of Worms

For want of a nail the shoe is lost,
For want of the shoe the horse is lost,
For want of the horse the rider is lost,
For want of the rider the battle is lost,
For want of the battle the kingdom is lost,
For want of the kingdom the world is lost,
For want of the world the cosmos is lost,
And all for the loss of the Horseshoe Nail.
                              —Nescio Unde

We completed our jump and came home to the little dock at the base of the hill below Ravel-Brannagan Castle. I went to hurl the leader rope for the tie-up hawser, but I saw that we were already made fast to dockside.

Very little damage was done to us on our outlandish trips, and what damage was done was easily undone. Doctor Gilmartin, our only casualty (unless we put Brannagan and Quasimodo in that category) soon proved to be no casualty at all. The old doctor rose from the deck and seemed to pull himself together. He was neither dead nor impaired, he said, but he was stiff and muscle-tired from the high climb.

"It was all a matter of proportion," old Doctor

Gilmartin said. "Sure, it was more than a two-hundred-meter climb up that brain cliff, more than a furlong. But at the same time it was much less than a millimeter. And a fall of a millimeter isn't going to kill me, not if I keep things in proportion."

There were crowds of people around the dock and around everywhere. They were not remnants of last night's gala people. They were newly arrived people, many of them media people. How did I know that they were media people? I had asked my Princess Thorn.

"They are media people," she had said. "How can you be an historian and not know media people when you see them? And some of them are scientific people. From the way they are running around, it seems that they are all wanting places to stay. And they all want Instanto lines to Gaea-Earth and to Astrobe and to Camiroi. They all want conference rooms, and they all say that they are anchor-people. They all want something. What do you want, my love?"

"I want to go on my honeymoon, Thorn, now that we have been almost everywhere else this busy night. I want to go now, when the morning is almost here, and the white dawn has already touched the top of O'Grogan's Mountain."

"How sweet and how poetical! With whom would you go on honeymoon, my love?"

"With you, of course, Thorn. With no one else, ever!"

"But that would be vulgar. I'm married to you. Oh, don't look so bedashed, Long John Tong Tyrone. I was just being quippy. How can you be an historian and not know quips when you see them? I think that second-rate history is almost entirely quips.

"Oh, some of the media people are asking about the five royal, intelligent, golden bears who disappeared so myste-riously from Astrobe, disappeared right from in front of the eyes of fifty people there. They blocked all possible ways they might get off Astrobe, and yet they have been re-ported here on Klepsis. They sound a little bit like that nice bear family that was sitting next to us last night on

O'Grogan's Mountain. Well, where shall we go on our honeymoon? Around the Castle landing here, around this part of Klepsis, the rich people go to Kaye Spencer's Hay Meadow, and the poor people go to Hogan's Haystack."

"We are rich, Thorn. We are among the numerous co-owners of the greatest treasure in the universe. Neither the Hay Meadow nor the Haystack sounds very private, but we will go to the richer of them, the Hay Meadow. What is that oaf of a dockmaster saying? That we never left dock at all last night?"

"No, Duke Tyrone, of course you did not. Are you still kidders after morning has begun to appear? I have had to explain it to the Penny Philosopher and to several others that you did not leave dock last night," the dockmaster was saying good-naturedly. "I even had to explain it to the Outcast Prince. Do you really believe that you left? At first I believed that you were carrying part of last night's play-acting over to this morning. This is the first time since I've worked here that *The Dina O'Grogan* has been host ship for the Shipboard Theatre. Indeed, there was a mix-up to-night. The people of the ship *The Polled Unicorn* believed that their ship was scheduled for it, and they were a little bit perturbed by the situation. But when they saw what good theatre you people on *The Dina O'Grogan* put on, they were appeased. I liked it best when Brannagan's Ghost was chained to the main mast and sang those rousing ballads. Then I liked the part where you 'space-jumped' to the asteroid and all of you had green leaves growing out of your bellies when you got there. Who wrote that part of the skit anyhow? It was rich. And I liked the part where the tall, inflatable cliff collapsed and the funny doctor fell all the way down to the deck and was killed. And I liked the part where you pretended to forget to untie from the dock and you set your sails for voyaging. If there had been much wind last night, you might have wrecked the dock. It isn't built very well, you know. I liked the part where you pretended that you were out on the stormy sea when you were still in calm tie-up. How did you make the ship bounce around like that anyhow? That was good theatre too, comic theatre. I tell you that the audience on shore was the biggest we've ever had for Shipboard Theatre. Even the slopes of O'Grogan's Mountain were full of people watching you. It was classic."

"I wonder whether the bears watched us?" Thorn asked.

"Of course they did. The five bears from Astrobe. They space-jumped from there, you know. Animals can do it easier than people can. I bet they never saw a show as good as yours on Astrobe. You were classic, classic."

"Classic indeed, dockmaster," Thorn said. "What bait brings all the land fish from other planets to Klepsis this morning?"

"It's just the End of the World. Or maybe it is only the rumor of the End of the World, though everybody is pretty sure that it will happen this morning. The world is supposed to end on Klepsis slightly before it does on other places, and it will be big news. It's all known as the Doomsday Equation."

"Oh, Science-Crisis-Catastrophe Theatre."

"Yes, something like that, Princess Thorn."

"You two can't be taking off now," Historian Titus protested to Thorn and myself. "You also are an historian, Duke Tyrone, and the stuff that history is made of is thick around this region this morning. There will be more than a hundred important historical and scientific symposia held around here, if they can find places to hold them all. I would like you and Thorn to attend those that I cannot attend. Nobody knows who is in charge of the arrangements here. It may be Prince Henry the Pirate, but he is not to be wakened this early in the morning. Besides, there's a rumor that Prince Henry fell in a coup last night and is the only one who doesn't know about it."

"Oh, I can do the 'Prince Henry the Pirate' role much better than Prince Henry can do it," Prince Franco the Outcast chortled. "I love to be in charge of arrangements. What is it, people, special tickets that you want to something, special treatment? Nothing easier. We'll just slip into the Castle and run off all the 'special permission' tickets you want. There are at least three hundred conference rooms in the Castle itself, and you people can bunk almost anywhere. If nobody else is in charge of the arrangements and hospitality, then I will be in charge. Begone, Thorn and Long John, you'll not be needed here.''

"Well, was there a coup last night?" Titus the Historian asked Princess Angela. "Who rules the realm now?''

"There was a coup, yes," Princess Angela said. "So far, we have told only a very few people about it, but it is in effect. And *I* rule the realm now.''

Thorn and I went to Kaye Spencer's Hay Meadow, and I was glad to see that it was an hotel (I had been told the day before that there were none of them on Klepsis) rather than an actual hay meadow. Scientific and media persons were waving thousand-thaler bills and demanding rooms. One of them used a cute approach.

"You say that you have no rooms at all in reserve?" he asked the desk captain archly. "What if (where's that list of local nobility?), what if Princess Tharrala Thorn should come looking for a room? Would you have a room for her?''

"Indeed we would," the desk captain said. "If the Princess Thorn should come, we'd have a suite for her.''

"Well, she's not coming," he of the cute approach said. "Let *me* have that suite.''

"But I *am* coming," Princess Thorn spoke in her ringing voice. "We are coming, and we are here. What suite do you have for us?''

"Well, what about the Princess Thorn Honeymoon Suite? Lord knows we've kept it waiting long enough for you, all through the years of your disappearance and exile.''

"Yes, that will be fine. That will be wonderful," my Princess Thorn said.

"Let's go over to Hogan's Haystack and try the same line," he of the cute approach said to his two traveling girlfriends. "This time, when I tell them that the Princess Thorn isn't coming, I'll be telling the truth.''

"Is Hogan's Haystack another hotel?" I asked.

"No, there are no hotels on Klepsis," the desk captain told me. "There are only such houses as this one that we open to our friends out of the hospitality of our hearts. Hogan's Haystack is the second-best such house around here, and Hogan has the second-best heart in the neighborhood."

There really were top scientific people (not all of them human) who had gathered on Klepsis by white dawn that morning, and they continued to arrive all through the morning hours. And there were really top media people. They were overdue. Klepsis had many things of interest and mystery that should have been examined long ago. Then, why did all these people come today and not before, and why did they come in such clots and bunches? Because they were sheep and they flocked like sheep.

It was not even certain when the end of the world would come. The Horseshoe Nail, that third focus of the construct, might not die until *tomorrow* morning.

As to the honeymoon itself, both Thorn and myself were inexperienced in the thing. But each of us had read a book (a different book) on it, so we did know something about it.

"I wish that I had married that Titus the Historian instead of you," Thorn said, "because he is so much more eminent than you are. On the other hand, I'm glad that I married you instead of him because I've come to like you so much. But on the third hand, I wish I'd married him instead of you because he's so much more personable than you are."

"Three hands are not allowed, Thorn," I said. "There are no three-handed persons anywhere."

"Yes there are," she happily contradicted me. "All the pickpockets on the Trader Planet Apateon are born with three hands. Really they are, my love. It's in a proverb."

As both Thorn and I were of loving heart and healthy body, things went famously with us, and it was the happiest two hours I ever spent in my life. It was perfect down to

Thorn's final or frosting-on-the-cake proposal. And that one astonished me.

"Oh, Thorn, that can't possibly be in the instruction book," I said.

"No, but it's going to be in the appendix of the next edition of the book," she argued. "Come ahead and try it. Don't be so fainthearted."

Thorn and I had a few slight interruptions during the morning. A green-and-orange bird came into the room out of the sound ventilator. All well-appointed buildings on Klepsis have sound ventilators as well as fresh-air and heating ducts. They have them so that the sound may circulate and will not become stale. Well, what is the matter with that? Sound really does have a tendency to become stale on Klepsis if not properly circulated and ventilated.

"I come from Titus Livius Morrison-Bryce the Historian," the parley bird spoke. (Titus had learned the mechanics of communication on Klepsis quickly, as a competent historian should.) "He begs me to inform you that one of the most important of all the symposia on Klepsis during this terminal emergency will be going on in the room just below yours. He begs that you should leave the sound duct open (in fact I have jimmied it open) so that you can hear and record this symposium. He begs that you understand the importance of it, made up as it is of leading scientists and philosophers and systems inventors and cosmological speculatives and end-of-the-world buffs. He begs that you will consider this deeply and then tell me whether you will do this or not. Please give me a yes or a no answer. I have a better record of accurate transmission on yes and no answers than on more complicated responses."

"The answer is no," I said. "We are completely occupied with personal matters."

"The answer is yes," Thorn said. "Oh yes, my love, I want to hear all these famous people. My attention actually increases when it is split among several different things. I have an awful amount of attention to spread around. I am always able to do several things well at one time; and listening to a symposium won't interfere with our other activities.

"The answer is yes," Thorn told the parley bird, and the bird went away with that answer.

"Plenty of the 'My God What Grapes!' grapes for them," someone was speaking to someone else in the room below us. "And plenty of ice water. And pencils and pens, hundreds of pencils and pens. And a piece of paper, perhaps even two pieces of paper. That's what to set out for people when they hold a symposium."

"We will get all these things for the important visitors at once, at once," another person in the room below us said.

"Oh, oh, oh!" Thorn cried beside me, and she pulled the bellpull for instant service. "How could I have forgotten to order things like that?"

The waiter came into our room instantly.

"Heaps, oodles, pounds, kilograms, bunches of the 'My God What Grapes!' grapes," she ordered. "There cannot be too much of those wonderful things. And ice water. Well, that's what the people in the room under us are getting. I never did know what people do with all the ice water they order. It's like doctors when they come to deliver a baby always wanting a lot of hot water. 'What's it for, all the hot water that the doctors always order?' I asked my mother once long ago. 'It's to make instant soup out of,' my mother said. 'Doctors are the biggest instant soup eaters in the world.' And pencils and pens, waiter, hundreds of pencils and pens. And a piece of paper, perhaps even two pieces of paper. Why do you laugh, my love? That's what the people for the symposium underneath us are getting, and we're as good as they are."

"Indeed we are, Thorn," I said. I had the waiter bring the names of those who were attending the meeting under us. I recognized the names of all those great scientists and also the persons in ancillary fields, and I recognized the voices of most of them as they began to arrive. All of them had been on the air on all the planets in the various "New

Breakthroughs In Science" specials made on Gaea-Earth and Astrobe and Camiroi, and I have always been a sucker for the "New Breakthroughs In Science" specials.

Oh, now I heard the birdlike but heavy voice of the Asteroid Pythagoras (the only bird that rumbles). This Pythagoras has as a brother, the Asteroid Midas, possibly the richest creature in the universe, who has a pinion on every planet. And the Asteroid Pythagoras was surely one of the most intelligent and informed creatures in the entire cosmos, with a distal feather in every brain-bust. The Pythagoras was an ostrichlike bird with the addition of the great wings of the *gigantiornis* and the functional hands of the *cheirornin*. The Pythagoras did not come to any except the most weighty meetings, because of not being invited to the lesser ones. It just wasn't worth the risk, for the Asteroid Pythagoras was but borderline socially acceptable.

When crossed in argument, the giant bird would go after the eyes of the opponent with its terrible beak. The informal League of Blind Scientists was made up of learned persons who had lost their vision in fateful encounters with the Pythagoras.

Very soon I heard the voice of Oliver Roundhead, one of the top brains of Astrobe; Decimus Gormley from World Abounding (there was a peculiarity about Gormley that people didn't always realize immediately); Aloysius (The Brain Crying in the Wilderness) Shiplap from Gaea-Earth; Sidonia Sopher from Far Tarshish; Alex Braveheart from Camiroi; Becky Breaksticks from Dahae.

"Why are there no worms in grapes?" Becky was raising her pewter-toned voice from the moment of her entry. "Take all the grapes away. There are worms in apples, in pears, in plums, in sultana fruit, in Dahae dates, and in quigs. Waiter, waiter, bring me fruit that has the possibility of worms. I'll not be restricted in my options or possibilities. And I don't want any of these 'My God What Grapes!' grapes in this room at all. They offend my sense of fairness. Out with them, out!"

"*In* with them, *in!* I like them. Be quiet woman," the Asteroid Pythagoras bird screamed-rumbled.

"Male pig-bird, *you* be quiet!" Becky flamed angrily. "Male pig-bird!"

"Watch your eyes, Becky!" Alex Braveheart warned. "It can be very, very, fast."

"Why am I the only female here?" Becky demanded. "Throw out that damned bird and bring in another female in the interests of equity."

"Why am I the only nonhuman here?" the Pythagoras screech-rumbled. "Throw out that damned Becky-the-Mouth and bring in another nonhuman."

"Becky," I heard Oliver Roundhead whisper, "the Asteroid Pythagoras *is* a female bird. Know your symposium members."

"Oliver," I heard Becky whisper shrilly, "Decimus Gormley *is* a nonhuman. Know your symposium members, you and that damned bird too."

"Titus the Historian will be proud of us," I told Thorn, "for recording such thoughty discussions from such brainy scientists. And they have hardly begun yet."

"There is the possibility that the damning construct and the damning equation, the Doomsday Equation, may contain one element that hasn't been taken into account," Alex Braveheart was speaking in his beautiful baritone (all the more respected scientists have beautiful baritones), "and I refer to the mysterious and malevolent planet of Tarshish. Is it possible that Tarshish is located within our construct? If it is, it changes everything. It even takes the 'Doomsday' out of the equation; it proves the equation in error and in need of updating. But also, if it is in our construct, why had nobody seen it in our construct? I feel that Far Tarshish is not far at all. But how to find out? Why has its gravity not affected the construct if it is in it? The fact is that nobody knows where Tarshish is."

"I do," Sidonia Sopher said. "I come from Tarshish. I am a citizen of that orb. I arrived from there only an hour ago."

"Well then, give us the astronomical location and bearings and orbit and mass and density and magnetic index of Tarshish, and we'll get to work on something really momentous."

"I cannot. I cannot give you any of these things. I do not know any of them. The data of Tarshish are not like the data of other worlds. They aren't subject to detailed description. And Tarshish has always been ruled by an anti-scientific clique; and these things are not permitted to be known."

"Well, can you tell us whether Tarshish is located within our construct?"

"No, I cannot."

"Is it possible that you do not understand the mathematics and astronomy of the problem, Sidonia?"

"Oh, I understand the mathematics and astronomy of the problem. I'm as good at mathematics and astronomy as anybody in this room. But I do not understand them in the Tarshish context. Tarshish is not amenable to mathematics and astronomy. And you, you others, there are certain things that *you* do not understand. Do you understand how a planet may not be a planet in every sense?"

"Waiter, there is a worm in my apple!" Becky Breaksticks was railing loudly. "This is abominable. If we were on Dahae, heads would roll!"

"It was madam herself who asked me to bring worm fruits," the waiter was excusing himself.

"No, no, no! I asked for the *possibility of worms*. I certainly did not ask for the *actuality* of worms. Because I demand that all options be open to me does not mean that I will accept all options."

"How did you come here from Tarshish, Sidonia?" Alex Braveheart asked.

"There are two classes of people who may come from Tarshish to Klepsis or to any other world. The poor and the rich. I am classified as rich, for the line between the two is very low. Of the poor, it is said that they walk, but I do not believe that the poor people of Tarshish travel at all. I came by irregular flight. Regular, scheduled flights have never been allowed to or from Tarshish. Those who take flight from Tarshish are blindfolded, so to speak (they have certain optic nerves pinched off for a while) and are deafened temporarily (by small and casual surgery). They are also brain-pierced to inhibit their sense of direction and their perception of elapsed time and their ability to think logically. Then they are sedated, and so they fly, programmed with after-flight apprehensions and taboos, in an outlaw ship of no registry.

"They arrive on Klepsis (even irregular flights are allowed to Klepsis only and not directly to any other world) listless and incurious. And it is only after an hour or more here that they look at their papers and find them to be the papers of a completely falsified flight. My papers show falsely that I came from the planet Analos to Klepsis, and they make no mention of Tarshish. It is puzzling, even to a Tarshish person, and probably much more to you."

"Such a faked trip probably cost a fortune," Alex Braveheart guessed.

"No, Alex, it didn't. It costs less than a good meal. That also is puzzling."

"If we put you in deep trance, do you suppose that you could figure out where Tarshish is, Sidonia?"

"My after-flight apprehensions tell me that I'd die if I were put into deep trance, so I probably would. But we'll try it if you believe it important."

"A little later, perhaps, Sidonia. Far Tarshish is the name of it in legends and tales. But what if it is really 'Near' Tarshish, so near that it falls inside our construct of the presently accepted four suns and seventeen humanly inhabited planets?"

"What if? What if, Alex?" Decimus Gormley of World Abounding or Aphthonia asked with easy irony. "If Tarshish belongs to our construct, then of course the Doomsday Equation for our construct is proved wrong, in the light of Tarshish's presence. As it happens, the Doomsday Equation, while not completely wrong, is incomplete. I have completed it. I will unroll the completed and corrected equation now. Gorge your eyes and your mind on it!

It will take a while, but my version is absolutely complete, elegant, and correct."

There was a silence in the room below us for an hour or so. That amended equation must have had deep stuff in it to take so long to digest.

"Do you think that I should go down and help them with it?" Thorn asked me. "I'm pretty smart. I'm an Intuitive, and it doesn't sound as if any one of them is. And besides, I learned middle mathematics at the Castle School from Flobert Traxley, the Man Who Talks to Dragons. I learned dragonry from him too. I know the smell of dragon mathematics, and I can smell it now, up the sound shaft."

"No, Thorn," I told her gently. "In mathematics, those people are completely out of your class."

"Then we had better do a little bit of reclassifying. I don't believe that they are completely out of my class at all."

"Decimus, your equation does *not* provide for the planets of our construct to survive as *humanly* inhabited planets," Alex Braveheart was heard to say in the room below after an hour or so had passed.

"No, it doesn't," Decimus Gormley, that nonhuman person from World Abounding, said with obvious pleasure. "Is that part important to you? It just is not possible for the planets to survive as humanly inhabited planets. But it *does* provide for the planets of our construct to survive as *dragonly inhabited* planets."

After that, I heard no word or sound from the room below for several minutes. Then I heard the rusty voice of Aloysius Shiplap singing softly:

> "Oh, me mother was a dragon
> And meself do breathe the fire,
> But I do not take it kindly
> That my friends should all expire."

"Come, my love, rise and go with me to visit an old, old friend," Thorn said to me about noon.

ELEVENTH CANTO

Greater Love Has No Man

There were knots of people gathered around thirty-three of the thirty-five tall gate doors of Ravel-Brannagan Castle. But these knots of people were all standing back about twenty meters from the Castle gates themselves. Between the knots of the people and the Castle gates there was, in each of the thirty-three cases, a hasty gibbet made out of pot-metal, set up and in business. On each of these hasty gibbets there was a man or a woman hanged by the neck. This was a way that Prince Henry the Pirate had of telling the people, the visitors especially, that they must not press too closely on the Castle while they were waiting to be invited in. One could feel the seething resentment in the knots of stand-back people.

"It is things like this that give Klepsis the name of being a barbarous planet," Thorn said bitterly. "It is things like this that make Uncle Henry *be* Uncle Henry. This is all bad for our fame and reputation."

Twenty-eight of these hanging persons had been declared officially dead by the Dead-Man's Reeve, a minor official who made the rounds of the Castle and the hanging persons, ringing a hand-bell as he walked, crying out the words and warning, "Polite Waiting is the Best: Do Not Be Pushy!" and drawing blood from the left great toe of the hanging persons. If the blood from the toe (the furthest member from the hanged neck) was clotted, that person was declared to be dead. If the blood flowed freely, the person was declared to be either doubtful or still dying. Five of the hanging persons were still officially either doubtful or still dying. One of them had a peg leg, and no test blood could be taken from it, although he was clearly dead. One of the other four was still conscious and was talking in a horribly constricted voice:

"Do not give up!" the hanging man tortured his words out. "If there were not some way of negating the Doomsday, this Doomsday Prince Henry would not be so adamant in forbidding us to see what is both the point and the person of the Doomsday Equation. Do not be deterred. In our very hanging there is hope."

Then that person gave a horrible croaking, and he died. And soon after that, the Dead-Man's Reeve declared all the hanging persons dead, and he went home to his noon-day meal.

The two Castle doors that had neither gibbets nor knots of people in front of them were those two close-together doors, the Sleeper's Door and the Wine Door. The Sleeper's Courtyard in front of the two of them was so filled with old bushes and trash and weeds and spiderwebs that the Sleeper's Door could not be seen at all from any distance, much less approached. The Wine Door could be approached and entered, by a narrow path, but nobody going past on the cobbled walks would suspect that it was there at all.

Princess Thorn and I entered the Castle by the Wine Door.

"I know this old Castle like the rats in its walls," Princess Thorn said to me. "I have been through every rat-run in this building when I was successively a little girl, a lass, and a woman. Oh, I can talk to the rats in the walls just as Flobert Traxley can talk to the dragons. The Sleeper's Room is really on the lower level of the *En-Arche* Bell Tower, but only a person who knows the Castle from inside its walls would ever know that. There are no windows in the Sleeper's Room, one chimney only, and it is believed that there is only one door to the room. We start this way, my love, because we are devious. We go up the little chimney in this alcove. Yes, isn't it filthy though! It takes me back to when I was a little girl and was dirty all the time. Speak to me, my rats! Advise me when the way is clear!"

The rats advised us that the way was clear. We came off from the chimney and were between two walls, both of them of coursed stone. Thorn was a thicker person than myself, and I thought that I could follow her any way that she would go. I barely could. We came to close places.

"Think fiddlefish, think eel, think snake, think all things narrow," Thorn encouraged me. And by narrow thought and by narrow contouring we came through the striated places.

"We are there," Thorn said. "What is all that trash in my way? That one for you, my love, and this one for me. Look through the eyes and talk through the mouth, but do the first more than the second for a while."

"What is it? What am I looking through and what am I talking through?" I asked her.

"You, my love, are looking through the death mask of Juda O'Grogan-Brannagan, and I through the death mask of his wife Rose Lunaria. This was called the Death Mask Room before it was called the Sleeper's Room. The alarms of Prince Henry sound only if somebody unauthorized enters the Sleeper's Room, but we do not enter it. We only look into it and talk into it. One hundred one death masks of the family are built as plaques into the walls here. I notice that stone workers are making a plaque for the one hundred second death mask now. It is no good questioning them. Two of them are always mutes, and the third will answer only two persons: the one whose death mask is about to be mounted and the new regent of the family, or else the heir of the one whose death mask is being set here. Most of the masks are of the eleven high pirates of Klepsis and of their unruly and felonious offspring.

"Many of the haunts come to their own death masks now and then, and this makes this room one of the most haunted in the entire Castle. But I used to look through Rose's mask when I was a girl in the Castle. And, as to Juda, he was the only gentle man ever in the entire family. He'll not give you away. Sometimes his haunt comes here and sings, 'Rosa, Rosa, Rosa,' very softly, but mostly it sings it up in its own watchtower where he strikes the bell with the little hammer for musical accompaniment. Quasimodo, my old, old friend, do you know who this is?"

"Yes. It is the Thorn, the Thorn, the Red Thorn of Klepsis, she who committed the unmentionable sin and would never settle my curiosity as to what it was," the most grotesque voice that I have ever heard in my life spoke from an old heaped-up bed in the Sleeper's Room.

Thorn and I were not alone in our visit. I noticed that several of the death masks on the walls had living and moving eyes in them.

"Quasimodo, my old, old friend, are you asleep or awake?" Thorn asked.

"I am asleep. By law I must sleep always and never awake. It is kind, though dangerous, for you to come to visit me, Thorn." It was a very deep animal voice, but twisted and muted and talking out of its fleshy smothering with great effort. I had heard the youth-ghost of this person speak on *The Dina O'Grogan* the night before, but this voice-grown-old was much more weird.

"Quasimodo, my old friend from my childhood," Thorn was talking to him. "You have a new code name since I visited you here last. You are the 'Horseshoe Nail' now. For want of you will the cosmos be lost?"

"So I have heard. I hope not. I'd rather save it."

"Are you blind now?"

"Yes, blinded. I cannot open my eyes and I cannot move. Who can say that I'm not asleep? They have made me the substance of a riddle. If I wake up, then all the persons in the universe will vanish, for they were all imaginings in my dreams only. And if I die, then all the per-

sons in the universe will similarly vanish, since there is no
way that they can live in my dead brain. I don't know where
the Doomsday people got their facts. A thing like this has
never happened before. Why should I cause it to happen
now?"

"Quasimodo, my unusual friend," Thorn still quizzed
him, "*are* all the people of all the worlds only imaginings in
your mind?"

"I don't think so. My mind has become pretty barren
ground lately. But, yes, all of them are in my mind in complete detail, the billions of people on Gaea-Earth and on
Camiroi and on Astrobe, the millions and hundreds of millions of people on the other fourteen inhabited planets. I
know every hair on the head of every one of them, every
pore in the skin of every one of them, every bacterium in
the entrails of each one of them. I know every cell in every
body of them, I know every thought in every brain of them.
This is so. I do not imagine these things about my
imaginings. They are clear and troublesome facts. But that
is not what you asked me. You asked whether they were
only so many imaginings in my mind, and I don't think so.
Are the images in a mirror *only* images in that mirror, or
may they not have primary forms outside of the mirror
also? For a reflection, may there not be something to be
reflected?"

I was able to make out the face and body of Quasimodo
then. Oh, of course he was ugly. He had grown two hundred years old in his ugliness. He was a humpbacked and
ugly dwarf, with a giant inside him threatening always to
break out. Because of this ugly appearance, Christopher
Brannagan had bought the little monster at a slave market
those two hundred years ago. Then the Brannagan had discovered that the twisted dwarf had a giant mind, the most
spacious and balanced mind ever to be met with. And so
Quasimodo had become the nearest thing to an executive
that Brannagan ever had during the decades when he was
autocrat of the Planet Klepsis.

The rats chittered a warning to their friend Princess

Thorn, so all three of us were silent.

Prince Henry the Pirate came into the Sleeper's Room with a dozen of his thugs and a giant tracking-and-smelling-out dog. He looked angrily at the stoneworkers preparing a plaque for a death mask.

"Whose death mask will that be?" Prince Henry demanded hoarsely.

Two of the stoneworkers were mutes, but the third one answered, "Yours."

"There will be no death mask for me any day soon!" the Prince swore. "Stop the work on it at once."

"We may not," said the speaker—one of the stoneworkers. "We are under preternatural compulsion to do this work for the newest death mask."

Prince Henry turned to his thugs and to the big dog.

"Find the traitors, death-dog and death-men," he ordered them. "In the death masks on the wall, death-dog. Tell us which ones are served by traitors. They'll not come out of the walls, for the narrow ways are now everywhere guarded. And we'll have them here."

The big dog (Kynegos was its name, I learned later—Kynegos the Hunter) went to plaque after plaque of the death masks. He growled viciously at one, and two of the thugs pulled the death mask off the wall, and two others pulled the unfortunate person out of the wall. It was a media person, that was clear, either from Gaea-Earth or from Astrobe, of a species sometimes called 'documentary reporter.' And into a spiked iron collar that person was locked, to be taken out and killed in just a while. Another and another spying person was pulled out of the walls when found by the dog Kynegos. This was indeed a death-dog. It came to the death mask of Juda through the eyes of which I looked into the dog's eyes, and I was gripped by total fear.

I heard his growl muscles tighten, but he did not growl. Neither did he break into happy greeting as he wished to do when he recognized Thorn next to me. He showed remarkable restraint, for a dog—for anybody. He moved on to the next plaque, and to the next. He growled again at another

mask, and one more investigating media person or
investigating scientist was pulled out of the wall and
clamped into an iron collar. In all, nine of them were pulled
out of the walls, fitted with the spiked iron collars, and
taken out to be killed, either quietly or with great show.
And their only crime was trying to investigate, and perhaps
prevent, the end of the worlds.

Oh, the fine minds and the fine persons of the nine who
were to be destroyed! But what of the twenty-five billion
persons, most of them fine persons of fine minds also, who
might be destroyed on Doomsday Morning, who *would* all
be destroyed if the Doomsday Equation should prove correct and should be effected?

Prince Henry the Pirate and his bravos left with their victims, and in a few moments the rats in the walls chittered
their all clear to their friend Thorn. We resumed our
questioning.

"Quasimodo, my friend," Thorn said, "do you believe
that things are moving towards a crisis with you?"

"I believe that I will die very soon, yes. I can feel the vi-
tality running out of me as from a leaking bucket, and that
bucket is about empty. Perhaps I'll die this night, or sometime before morning. This is night, isn't it?"

"No, it is only a little bit after noon," Thorn said. "Do
you want the Green Robe to come to you?"

"Oh, he was here, about an hour ago. And he gave me
the sacraments of the dying, but he said that he preferred to
call them the 'sacraments of the living.' So do I."

"Do you feel that, when you go, you will take millions
and billions with you?" Thorn asked.

"If I do, it sure will be crowded on what they call 'the
narrow way,' the contorted path out of this world. No, I
don't feel that it will be so. But as to thinking it out, I can
no longer think, and once I considered myself a great
thinker. My mind is shot. Do the billions of people who live
in my mind know that things are getting very much worse? I
believe that there are defects in the Doomsday Equation,
but my mind has lost much of its mathematics. It is a bird-

brained business, literally. We may be saved, though, by a multiplicity that the Doomsday Equation does not know about. I am not alone in this curious state.

"There are two other persons in the universe whose minds also contain all things and all persons in the universe, including myself and each other of them. My own mind does have firm and total knowledge of every person and most things of the worlds, of the inmost thoughts of all the people, of the inmost thoughts of the animals, of the awkward green and brown thoughts of the plants. And my mind also has firm and total knowledge of the minds and persons of the other two entities who also have firm and total knowledge of it all. The Doomsday Equation does not know about these other two persons."

One other person, a second other person, a third other person, a fourth other person, had come through the space between the walls somehow and had found seeing and listening spots at four of the death masks. Did they know that each other were there? Did they know that we were there?

"Quasimodo my friend," said Thorn, talking carefully now, for she knew that several unknown (but probably sympathetic) persons, besides myself and Quasimodo, were listening, "would it not be possible that these two other persons are also imaginings of your mind, and that their detailed knowing of all persons in the universe is also an imagining of your mind? The Doomsday Equation, after all, *did* identify you with the tertiary focus of our construct. It did not identify them."

"It would be possible, yes, but barely possible," the malformed humpbacked dwarf said. Quasimodo himself was a paradox, an anomaly, a beautiful personality (though now much eroded with the approach of death) in an ugly, or at least a grotesque, body. "There is another possibility—that I have been dead these two hundred years and am in purgatory and suffering the deliriums of purgatory, and all of you persons are indeed no more than the imaginings of one of the other poor souls. This really answers more of the questions than does any other possibility."

"But in that case, we would be nothing at all, and the worlds would be nothing at all," I protested. "That is hopelessness itself."

"No, no, no," the poor suffering dwarf contradicted. "That does not follow at all. There may well be beautiful universe after beautiful universe, valid and bountiful and blessed. These universes may be populated with countless suns and planets, and with innumerable humans and other species living spacious and happy lives in more intricate detail than anything we can even think of—happy, enchanted, moving towards the Beatific Vision. But all those fortunate universes upon universes and all their happy and transcendent people *would not have any point of contact with any of you, not anywhere, not ever.* You would all be totally nonexistent and without the possibility of existence; and so would I who dreamed you be without existence of any sort."

"That is the most dismal possibility of all of them," I protested.

"What, would you not like there to be hundreds of billions of brilliantly happy people just because you could never have any part of their brilliant happiness?"

"No, I don't believe that I would," I said. "How is that selfish of me? If I have no being or attributes, then I cannot have selfishness either."

The rats were chattering urgent warnings, their most puzzled warnings, their we-don't-know-what-it-is-but-something-bad-is-about-to-happen warnings.

There were metallic noises between the walls, noises of metal coming together with other metal.

"Oh, oh, it's got me!" a voice wailed.

"Oh, leggo, leggo," another voice howled.

"Not with a bang but with a steel spring!" a third voice spoke in agony.

"Oooooooohhh." That horrible sound seemed to come from myself. "I am caught in steel springs at my ankles, my wrists, my throat. There is no breaking this steel grip. I'm caught, I'm caught!"

A fiend had rigged these torture traps, but how had he gotten into place behind the death masks without activating them? Or how could they have been set and sprung later? Oh, the setting of triplex bear traps is an art in itself. The fiend, whoever he was—and he had to be Prince Henry—was playing me like a keyboard, with a terrible tightening of the steel bonds, first at the ankles, and I could feel the bones crunch. Then the pressure on my ankles lessened, but it set in horribly at my wrists till I believed that my hands would be severed from my arms. Then, slackening at my wrists for a little, it intensified at my neck, so that I was being strangled as surely as if I were being hanged on one of those hasty gibbets. Then, when the strangling pressure lessened on my throat, I babbled a little childish verse, for my strangling had addled my wits:

> *"Bleed my toe and bleed my head.*
> *Dead-Man's Reeve, pronounce me dead."*

At that, the silvery laughter of Princess Thorn rang through the Sleeper's Room as well as the rat galleries between the walls:

"Oh, bless you for that, my love. I was feeling a little low myself, what with the intense pains and all. If you can still make comic verses under torture, then I'll not give up either. We'll fight loose yet, but how? Awuuu—"

Thorn ended with a strangling note as her throat bonds were tightened again to strangle her. But she was an indomitable woman.

"How shall we be loosed? Oh, let me count the ways!" came the voice of one of our fellow prisoners, and I immediately recognized it as that of Bancroft Romal, the Voice of Up-Beat Science from Gaea-Earth. "If mathematics doesn't work, there's always magic."

"The dragons haven't any word for 'magic,' " Thorn spoke in a bruised sort of voice, her throat bonds being released a little. "Isn't that odd of them?"

"Whence do you have that information, Princess Thorn?" Bancroft asked in his up-beat but pain-racked voice. "I collect curious facts like that, but I haven't at the moment the means to jot it down."

"I have the information from Flobert Traxley, the Man Who Talks to Dragons. He was one of my instructors in Castle School right here in this Castle. I studied middle mathematics and stoics and dragonry from him."

"I wish *I'd* studied stoics from somebody. I need it now. Oh, oh, oh!" another of the betrapped fellows was moaning in her pain (she was a female). "How will we get out of this? There is a palace revolution, or a Castle revolution going on at the moment. It's been going on for twelve hours. But how will that help us? Palace revolutions aren't magic. We have the word, but we haven't the magic."

" 'Comes like magic in a pint bottle,' " a third of our fellows quoted in pain. "Anybody got a drink?"

"He comes like magic in a much larger bottle than that!" Bancroft Romal spoke with a lilt of hope. "I've heard recordings of the footfalls of all the great rulers of the planets. His are unmistakable, *push kluk, push kluk, push kluk*. There are no other footfalls quite like his in the universe."

The rats began to chatter with their "somebody's coming, somebody's coming" warning. Then—well I didn't believe it either but I heard it—all those rats in the walls fell silent. Then, flop, flop, flop, they fell flat and began that very soft rat snoring of deep sleep.

"Who is he who commands the winds and the waves and the rats also?" Thorn asked rhetorically. "But can he command steel traps too? He is my many-times grandfather, and he comes, he comes!"

And with his *push kluk, push kluk, push kluk* footfalls (the real leg and the wooden leg) Brannagan's Ghost came into the room. He didn't come through the door. He came through the wall very near the door, but he left the wall undamaged where he came through. "Damn!" he said, "I missed that door again. I'm coming closer though."

"Many-times grandfather, get us loose from this," Thorn cried.

" 'A redder berry on the thorn.' Tell me, many-times granddaughter Princess Thorn, what *was* your red unspeakable sin? It's one of the few riddles that I haven't unriddled yet. You'd be surprised at the folks who speculate about it in the ghostly realm. 'What sin could possibly be unspeakable?' they say. 'What evil could be beyond evil?' Get you loose, you ask? Sure I can get you loose. I'm still the King of the Castle, and it's still my favorite game. This seems like no more than a half-Bandicoot job to me. I should have a stub here somewhere. *Epetheta*, be thou opened!"

Brannagan's Ghost pulled half a Bandicoot cigar from one of his ghostly pockets, stuffed it in his mouth, said, "Hello, Quasimodo," and bent over that blind and dying dwarf. And Quasimodo raised an ill hand with a lighted fusee in it, lit the half-cigar for Brannagan's Ghost, then gave the wan hand the 'magician's flip,' and showed the hand empty of fusee. "Hello, Brannagan," the dying dwarf said. "Get me loose from this too. Death I don't mind, but this bestial dying is killing me."

From the half of a Bandicott cigar, Brannagan's Ghost blew those smoke clouds which were high art to him, those transcendent burlesques. He blew caricatures of all of us, and I recognized two other of our fellow prisoners of the traps from their portraits in smoke. They were Isadora Ragsley, that mistress of particle explication from the planet Paravata; and Clarence Pinnacle, the pioneer in eschatological algebra, from Analos. Smoke caricature is a fragile art, but out of a real master's mouth it is astonishing.

(A fifth person caught in a trap had apparently died.)

"Fun is fun, many-times grandfather, but when will you get us loose from this, from this, ah, from, from—" Thorn began by demanding peremptorily, and then trailed off in confusion.

"Oh, your shackles have already been removed," Brannagan's Ghost spoke grandly. "Tell the rats they can wake up now. Almost everything in this Castle is amenable to me. And come into the room. It's drafty between the walls there. There's a door from the between-the-walls run into this Sleeper's Room here. It's right under Issachar O'Grogan-Brannagan's death mask there."

We all came into the room, and then we held high confab.

"Old tainted patriarch," Bancroft Romal began in his friendly way—

"Watch him, Bancroft, he can charm the birds out of the trees," Isadora Ragsley said about old Brannagan.

"But there are no trees on Klepsis," Clarence Pinnacle answered.

"Old discredited tyrant, what is your own strong view?" Bancroft asked. "Will the worlds all end today or some day soon? And will Klepsis be the first one of them to end?"

"I have no idea," Brannagan's Ghost answered. "It is not given to me to know the day nor the hour. But the Doomsday Equation is sound, as far as it goes. What it predicts will happen. What it seems to predict will seem to happen."

"Did you once hold all the persons of the universe as imaginings in your mind?" Clarence asked.

"Oh, absolutely. I always knew that I held millions and billions of them in my mind, but I hadn't realized that it came to the totality. Then I received a request from the Planetary Board (this was when I had been the Tyrant and Autocrat of Klepsis for only a short time) for census figures on Klepsis. 'This will be a mess,' I said. 'I don't have time to go around and count everybody on Klepsis. And if I appoint someone else to do it, we will no longer have a one-man government here.' Then I thought, 'I'll just run them all through my mind and count them as I do it. I believe that I know them all and if I pay attention I'll not miss a one of them.' I did so, and I came up with a total human population of 3,005,928 for Klepsis. 'While I'm at it,' I said, 'I might just as well give them the populations of the other sixteen planets also.' I did it. The other planets went ahead and took their own counts at great expense, but when they were compared with mine, the members of the Planetary

Board said that mine were a little bit over. But they were not. The official counts were a little bit under. The official counters of the other sixteen planets missed a few persons, but try and tell them that."

"How do you account for your receiving this power when nobody else has ever received it?"

"Why do you say that nobody else has ever received it, Clarence Pinnacle? Probably many persons have received it. But it's true that it comes to only a small minority. In my own case it came to me because of my towering ego and conceit, my arrogance, my outlandish presumption, my roominess, my intellectual capacity, my boundless curiosity. It came to me because I reached out my hands and my mind and took it. I swept all people into me.

"And then I transferred it all to Quasimodo here. He was taking so much work off my hands that I thought he might as well take this too. I couldn't have transferred it to just any other person, but I believe I could have transferred the thing to the special person in ten billion."

"The qualities of Quasimodo do not seem to be the qualities of yourself, Old Unicorn," Bancroft said. "What qualities do you believe that he had to make him receptive to the power?"

"Total compassion, total goodness, total aptitude for all things, and the wish to serve all his fellow creatures—a good bag of talents. No, they are pretty much opposite to my own talents, but they work well."

"Do you believe that this holding of all persons in your mind means that you hold them as imaginary creatures in your mind only, and that they are not real persons?"

"Oh, in most cases, yes, but not in all. There are probably several dozen valid persons in the universe at all times. The rest are imaginary."

"Do you believe that the worlds will end when Quasimodo dies, because of the fact that the worlds are only imaginings in his mind?"

"No. I believe that the worlds will end when he dies, but they'll end for another reason entirely. The fact of the point and the person being identical and being the third focus of the construct that is the humanly inhabited universe has little to do with that person being an omniscient, a know-all. The mathematics of the Doomsday Equation, besides being the most elegant mathematics of any equation ever, are clear on that point. It would not matter whether the person who was the point did not even know the names of the members of his own family: when he died, the universe would die also. It would seem that real elegance would dictate that the person who was the point should be an idiot or a halfwit, but this requirement is served equally in Quasimodo's being deformed and abridged in body.

"Once a kinetic three-dimensional ellipse has learned to live with itself, it cannot change fundamentally. If the third focus dies, then the universe and all the people in it will die also. Hang on as long as you can, Quasimodo."

"No. I'm ready to go now. Somebody tell me the way out, tell me the way out."

"Isn't there any way to break the premise of the construct and the equation, Autocrat Brannagan?" Isadora Ragsley asked.

"Several ways, lass, but all of them seem a little bit impractical. One of them is to move an exterior planet into the construct. But planet-moving isn't easily done. There is one man who has the equipment to do it, so he believes, and he is avid to try it. Come to think of it, that man arrived on Klepsis this morning. Arrived, yes, and with four hundred shiploads of equipment. But the betting is seven-to-five against him being able to do it.

"No, omniscience in the person-who-is-the-point isn't required. The Doomsday Equation is most clear on that. The omniscience is only a hook to catch the imagination of the rabble, and I'd rather it weren't caught."

"What do you know about the 'what-is-its' or the 'lost twins'?" Clarence Pinnacle asked.

"Almost nothing. It has been said that *I* am such, but I never believed it. I have always been a single personality, with the gift of bi-location it's true; with the gift of astral projection, it's true; with the gift of planetary jumping, it's true; with the gift of projecting giant illusions, it's true. Several of you here were inside the giant brain that I projected last night, one that was very well done and was quite a few kilometers in each direction, but it was still no more than an illusion.

"I look at my own body and bones every day as they lie in their transparent glass coffin, and yet I do not believe that there is any real difference between Brannagan the dead man who lies there and Brannagan the Ghost who walks and talks. No twin am I. But there may be such twins.

"Prince Henry the Pirate and Prince Franco the Outcast may be such twins. Or they may be a single person as I am. Or they may be (but I doubt this very much) two distinct persons. You can find out which is the case almost immediately, though, by close observation. A Castle revolution has just gone into its final phase here. Princess Angela Gilmartin-Ravel-O'Grogan-Brannagan has just toppled her husband Prince Henry the Pirate. She'll, of course, have him whipped to death at the tail of the magnificent donkey until he is dead. She believes in observing all the old customs. If you can do so, observe Prince Franco the Outcast while this is going on. If great welts rise on his back for every whip stroke that Prince Henry receives, then they are the same and a single person. If only small welts arise, then they are twins, a primary and a what-is-it. If no welts at all rise, then they are two distinct persons."

"What was the business of the steel traps in the walls that came alive, as it were, and almost did us to death?" Isadora Ragsley asked.

"All old castles have sleeping traps of one sort or another. Before this was the Room of the Death Masks, still more before it was the Sleeper's Room, this was the Room of the Covenant, the room where the eleven high covenanted pirates met at long intervals. And they were spied on by some of the slickest spies in the universe. The spies would come inside the walls and spy through the eyes of the 'idol masks,' those of false gods that the pirates had collected on their travels and set as decorations in these walls. It was the lass Dina O'Grogan herself who had the traps built by the finest trap-builder of the worlds. They are under voice control and mind control by anybody who has real authority here. Prince Henry had them under only hazardous authority and control, for his whole reign was quite hazardous. They are really an anachronism now, a sort of souvenir of the old days.''

A little while later, after we had had many more of our questions answered, and had been told that many more of them were unanswerable, Brannagan's Ghost summoned his own gang into the Sleeper's Room: the Green Robe, the Seneschal Fidelis (the dripping man), Doctor Luke Gilmartin, and Flobert Traxley (though Brannagan had no real need of this latter; Brannagan could talk to dragons himself). They'd keep the rabble out of there and not let them bother Quasimodo in his dying.

"And you five others here, you of a slightly more beloved rabble, you leave this room also," Brannagan's Ghost told us. So Princess Thorn and I, and our three companions of the traps, left the Sleeper's Room.

There had indeed been a palace revolution in the Castle.

It had really been decided during the sharp gunfighting of the night before when the bravos of Princess Angela had nearly wiped out the bravos of Prince Henry the Pirate. But there had been a lot of details to work out after that, and Princess Angela had been working them out slowly and methodically.

Prince Henry had kept his own dozen guards, and they had even been arresting traitors and dragging them out to be executed all the early part of that day. The executions, however, had not taken place.

"My myopic husband has always had trouble reading the handwriting on the wall," the Princess Angela was reported to have said. But now the workers were taking down the long bell pull rope from the Henry Bell Tower. If

Prince Henry ever rang the bell in his tower again, he'd ring it as a ghost, and ghosts do not need bell pulls. Other workmen had begun construction on the Angela Bell Tower. And a magnificent donkey of royal mien had been tethered, with tethers of steel, on one of the execution knolls. The handwriting on the wall was getting bigger.

Then Prince Henry was arrested during a particularly arrogant outburst, was handcuffed, and was brought to the tail of the donkey. The handcuffs of the toppled Prince were then knotted into the tail of the magnificent donkey who came from World Abounding. Oh, they do have some prize animals on World Abounding!

Princess Angela ("Call me Queen. I do not do this wrenching thing to remain a Princess," she said), Queen Angela of Klepsis looked harassed and angry and even a little bit evil in her triumph.

"I will give the people of Klepsis an honest but flamboyant rule," she said. "The people deserve the royal touch in their royalty. I shall ride on a hippopotamus. It is a great waste to have a herd of royal hippopotami and none of them ever ridden. I will wear scarlet gowns with fifty kilograms of gold woven into each of them, and that will be when I'm wearing old clothes. I will change the name of the eighth month of the year to Angela. It's such a pretty name! And that is only a start. I will go elegant always. I will call tomorrow (my coronation day) The First Day of the Worlds."

"Empress Angela," an exuberant and young billionaire named Malabu Worldwinger from World Abounding addressed her. "Would you, as Empress, sign these purely routine landing and takeoff permits? Oh, they will become collector's items, the first official signing of the Empress. The permits are for four hundred shiploads of heavy equipment. Actually they have already landed, but I'm told that I need a permit for such a large armada. I am Malabu Worldwinger, but many persons call me Malabu Worldmover because my business is moving worlds. I intend to move the Planet Tarshish into a new orbit."

"If Tarshish moves, can Klepsis long stand still?" the Empress Angela asked. "I didn't even know that Tarshish has an *old* orbit. The 'If Tarshish moves' thing is a sort of proverb from the old times. Its meaning isn't known. All right, I'll sign the permits. But don't let every world-mover think I'll sign their permits just for the asking. I like to be called Empress. I hereby declare myself to *be* the Empress Angela indeed. I hereby declare that every deck of cards hereforth made on Klepsis shall have an empress in each suit, the empress card to be worth a king and an ace together."

"Far Tarshish is a hidden planet that I will have to locate before I can move it to a new orbit," Malabu commented. "Do *you* know where Far Tarshish is located, Empress Angela?"

"You'll know when you get there. It's the only place that is even more bush than Klepsis."

Prince Henry at the donkey's tail looked frightened, but also somehow resolute.

"Why, Angela, why?" he asked as she came to the knoll of the execution.

"You ask why, Henry? The Princess Thorn sinned an unspeakable sin once, and nobody knows what it is. I wonder whether I, as Empress, can compel her to tell me? But you have sinned unspeakably hundreds of times, and I do know what most of those sins are. For your vile and cruel executions, for your traffic in slaves, for your commissioned piracies (your ancestors and mine at least performed their piracies themselves), for your frauds, for your outright robberies, for your rapes and sadisms and perversions, for your tortures; and most of all for your incredible vulgarities, for these things I replace you and obliterate you."

"Surely there is something good in me."

"You have a brother who is more good than bad. He is the closest thing to good in you."

"Have you no forgiveness?"

"Seventy times seven times I have forgiven you, and as to your offences against me I would forgive them forever.

But for your offences against others, against whole populations, I can no longer forgive you, nor is it my place to do so."

"Imprison me then, Angela, but do not kill me. There really *is* a hidden thing that will change the matter when it comes to light."

"The hidden things around you are better not brought to light, Henry. Do you want a Green Robe before you go? Your sins *do* need shriving."

"Yes, I want that, but not at a donkey's tail."

"There is no other way. You are tethered to the donkey, and you will die tethered to it."

"But this is a highly intelligent donkey, Angela. He will hear and understand all the black sins that I confess. Yes, and he'll *tell* them too. This donkey can speak more than one hundred words, and he can make several hundred sign-language signs. I'll not have him listening while I confess."

"Attendants, bring two kilograms of medium-hot beeswax," the Empress Angela commanded. "Well, quickly, quickly! Does it take forever to bring as common a thing as beeswax?"

The beeswax was brought almost immediately, and one kilogram was poured into each ear of the intelligent donkey. Then the Green Robe came, and the Empress Angela withdrew a short distance.

"Did I not know it impossible in Prince Henry, I'd almost believe that there was a touch of intended humor in that last set-to," the Empress confided to one of her aides. "But with Prince Henry, of course, humor would be impossible."

I myself was learning the real tricks of the historian, tricks I had not learned when I majored in historiology in school. The magnifying monocle, and the ability to read mouth which I had been learning for the last few hours, these were invaluable historical tools. They gave me the content of almost all conversations and comments up to the middle distances.

Thorn and I and Bancroft and Isadora and Clarence had

been looking for Prince Franco everywhere. We called out
for him often, thinking that he might have gone vague but
might still be quite near. He would not likely miss something as interesting as the execution of his brother Prince
Henry.

Then we saw him, coming furtively out of the hard-to-
see Wine Door of the Castle. Coming furtively? Prince
Franco? How unlike him! We saw him coming out of this
unsuspected door of the Castle, and he seemed to be in a
great hurry to get somewhere. He looked very distraught,
but also excited, as though filled with a secret pleasure.
Well, his brother was about to be put to death, and perhaps
he still had some filial feeling for that monster.

"Wait, wait, hold, hold, Prince Franco!" Princess
Thorn called out, and Prince Franco waited, though for
a moment it actually looked as though he would run away
from her.

"Prince Franco," Isadora said. "We are investigating the
relationship of a twin and a 'lost twin,' and of a twin and a
what-is-it. We want to see how one will react to the other in
a moment of crisis. This is all very scientific, and we want
you to help us. We want to see whether welts will rise on
your back when your brother is whipped to death."

"You become too familiar," Prince Franco said. "You'll
not bare my back, but you *will* see how I react to Prince
Henry's death-flogging. Oh, you'll see, you'll see!" Somehow this didn't seem quite like the Prince Franco we knew.

As soon as the Green Robe of the order of Saint
Klingensmith had confessed Prince Henry, strongmen began to flog him with long whips. And there was no way they
could flog the man without flogging the magnificent donkey also. So the Prince would be kicked to pieces by that
big beast that could kick lions to pieces.

Prince Henry was almost broken in two by the first volley
of hammer-hooves. The whip would always set one of
those giant World Abounding donkeys to a kicking that
was absolutely lethal.

"Goodbye, Angela," Prince Henry spoke out of broken

lungs and broken throat, in the last words he would ever speak, "I always cared for you, Angela, but I couldn't tell you so. The circumstances wouldn't allow it."

"Henry," Empress Angela said, "this is so strange. You're not—"

Prince Henry's back and neck were broken by the next volley of hooves, and the two sorts of whiplashing almost took his head off.

But Prince Franco had gone into spasms of hilarity. There had never been such rotten laughter as his. He seemed to be out of his mind, and he giggled dirty doggerel:

> "Oh, Hank and Frank, the brothers rank!
> It's fact that both the brothers stank!"

Another volley of hooves from the giant donkey did take Prince Henry's head completely off.

"This is the joke beyond all others," Prince Franco chortled. (How could this be the Prince Franco whom we knew?) "Die, my fool brother, kicked to pieces by a donkey and broken by the long whips, die! Oh, do you realize how funny you look with the parts of you being kicked in every direction? I must run now, but even if they catch me, it'll be worth it to see you done to death like this."

And Prince Franco—How could this be our resourceful friend, Prince Franco?—was off at a high run towards the thickets north of O'Grogan's Mountain, running hard and still laughing like a madman.

"Oh! You're dead! How horrible!" Empress Angela cried out. "Oh, stop the flogging! Get him loose from the animal, what's left of him! Oh, dead man, you're not, you're not, you're not Prince Henry! You're, you're—Oh, oh, oh!"

"Stop that running Prince, whichever one he is!" one of the strongmen of the Empress called out with loud authority. "Stop him, stop him!"

"Why does Prince Franco have to run when he can simply go vague and be beyond any pursuit?" I asked stupidly.

"Because that isn't Prince Franco running. It's Prince Henry," Thorn cried. "And Prince Henry doesn't know how to go vague. Oh, catch him, catch him!"

"Oh, oh," the new Empress Angela was crying over the pieces of the kicked-to-death man. "You're not Prince Henry! You're Prince Franco! Why, why, why did you take his place? Why, why, why did you die for *him?*"

Three men covered with rock dust, two of them mutes and one of them voiced, came out of the Castle and began to make the death mask of the dead prince.

"Which name will we put on it, Empress?" the voiced one asked.

"I, I don't know. Let it go for a while. I'll think of something."

TWELFTH CANTO

Lords and Commons of This Realm

A few of us were listening to Malabu Worldwinger, the exuberant young billionaire from World Abounding.

"I can move anything," Malabu boomed in his omnipotent voice. "On Gaea-Earth, on the tomb of a Polish priest named Niklas Kopernik, there are the carved words: *He moved the Earth and made the Sun stand still.* When I was a boy I wished that I could have those words on my tomb also. Now I'll settle for a better epitaph, one that I've earned: *He could have moved them both.*

"I am in the business of moving worlds. Though so far I have moved nothing larger than a medium-sized asteroid, it has only been for lack of opportunity. But now it seems to be a mathematical necessity that Tarshish or some comparable planet be moved to a new orbit within the construct of the four suns and the seventeen humanly inhabited planets. Such a moving *may* alter the Doomsday Equation so that our construct will not collapse and perish when its third focus perishes. I welcome the challenge. I have the equipment to do the job. I can move any ordinary-size world to a new orbit, *if only I can find that world.*

"Tarshish is a world that is difficult to come to by ordinary means. Does anybody here know how to get to Far Tarshish, which may not be very far? Does anybody know

187

how to get four hundred shiploads of heavy equipment into tight orbit around this Tarshish? Does anybody know the mystery of Tarshish, *why* it is not counted among the humanly inhabited planets, since many persons, several of them in this room, live there?"

Almost everybody I knew on Klepsis was in this cavernous hall. We were in the Januarius O'Grogan Memorial Lecture Theatre of Science and Inquiry, a large hall down in the bowels ("We're actually in the ileum—the third and last region of the smaller gut," Thorn whispered to me in one of her informative asides) of Ravel-Brannagan Castle. We were there because the Empress Predilect ("Aunt Angela says that beats being an 'Empress Elect' any day, especially when she hasn't been elected by anybody except herself," Thorn gave me the further explication) Angela Gilmartin-Ravel-Brannagan had ordered all of us to be there.

The O'Grogan Memorial Theatre was built like a supper club, with two dozen or so twelve-person banquet tables readied for the banquet. Most of us were already seated at the tables. There were already heaps of the "My God What Grapes!" grapes on the tables which would insure happy hallucinations for all of us. There were very large piles and platters of roasted leftover whale. They'd be eating leftover whale for a week around the Castle. There was buckwheat bread and hippopotamus butter, Lobsters *a la Margaret Summertime*, Red Raider Rum, "Old Bubbly" (I liked this alcoholic drink, but I don't know what it's made of), shark meat, cork island ox, gamecock, ocean-cock, baked ibek hump, Tarshish blood-bread and sunflower-oil butter, blackbird bang-dish, onion delight, gang-plank potluck, Sheba McSherry salad.

Myself and Princess Thorn, Titus the Historian, Flobert Traxley the Man Who Talked to Dragons, Doctor Luke Gilmartin, Bancroft Romal, Isadora Ragsley, Clarence Pinnacle, Gold Coast O'Mally, Terpsichore Callagy, Kate Blithespirit the Amazon from Camiroi, and the worldmover Malabu were at one table.

At the table right next to us were our friends Jerome Whitewater, Bartolomo Portuguese, Hektor Lafcadio, Fairbridge Exendine, Sebastian Jamaica, the green-eyed Sparaticus; and the friends we knew only through the sound duct at Kaye Spencer's Hay Meadow—Oliver Roundhead of Astrobe, Decimus Gormley the nonhuman from World Abounding, Aloysius Shiplap from Gaea-Earth, Sidonia Sopher from Tarshish, Alex Braveheart from Camiroi, and Becky Breaksticks from Dahae.

The sixth of those great scientists through the sound duct, the asteroid Pythagoras, was not at this near table. She was at the Notables Table along with Brannagan's Ghost, the Head Green Robe of Saint Klingensmith, the Tarshish storyteller, and with Princess Placidia-Ravel-Brannagan-Thorn. Placidia was the sister of the newly executed Prince Franco and of the probably still-alive-and-plotting Prince Henry. She was also the mother of my Princess Tharrala Thorn-Tyrone, though she would not speak to her daughter because of the unspeakable sin, about which she knew nothing, however, not even the name of it.

The Trumpet Master of Klepsis was also at the Notables Table. He was the chief of the One Thousand Royal Trumpeters, which group really had only about one hundred blowing-and-working trumpeters. The other nine hundred Royal Trumpeter sinecures and prebends were held by non-horners and they were awarded for various services to the realm. The terms "Brass Slush Fund" and "Brass Feeding Trough" referred to these nine hundred.

The other six persons at the Notables Table were not known to me, though they were clearly notables. One at least of the six was a ghost. One at least was a nonhuman. And one of them was a 'beggarman either blind or crippled.' It was the law that a 'beggerman either blind or crippled' must sit at the Notables Table at every high banquet.

A touch of the droll was evinced at another nearby table where the five space-jumping tawny Intelligent Royal

Bears from Astrobe were seated with seven other entities even more droll than were they.

It was a little bit after the fall of the "twilight of night." There was no "dark of night" on Klepsis because one or the other of the more distant Centauri Suns—Sun Proxima or Sun Alpha—were always in the sky (I heard that this was a Proxima night), and at least one of the moons was always in the sky. The banquet was going apace, not being hampered by toastmasters or ceremony. There were about a hundred persons in the Januarius O'Grogan Memorial Lecture Theatre of Science and Inquiry.

Then the Empress Angela rode in on a hippopotamus with a slave in chains, looking fearful and unhappy and yet quietly dignified, tied to the tail of the behemothish beast. You could have heard a shipload of hardware drop, so quiet did it become for a moment. The Empress was in scarlet for mourning. She was not in mourning for her husband Prince Henry, who was probably still alive and plotting against her. She was not in mourning for her dead lover Prince Franco, for he had not been her lover though many people believed that he had been. She was not in mourning for her father who was long dead, nor for her mother who was still alive, nor for her children of which she had none. And those were the only relationships for which a woman could go into mourning on Klepsis. The Empress was clad in mourning-scarlet because she felt like mourning and because she looked so good in scarlet.

She slid off the hippopotamus very heavily. She did indeed have more than fifty kilograms of gold woven into her gown, and she also had a very heavy and rather barbaric golden crown on her head. All in all, the weight she was carrying in gold was more than the weight of a man. The barbaric golden crown had been that of Sheba McSherry, her grandmother-in-law.

The Empress then began to speak in a queer voice that was full of implied threats.

"Instead of warning you about my arriving on a hippopotamus, I will tell all of you an anecdote about my grandmother-in-law Sheba McSherry whose crown I now wear, whose crown is now mine. She once arrived at a banquet in this very hall mounted on a hippopotamus that was the grandmother of this hippopotamus of mine. The hippopotamus immediately disgraced herself. And the banqueters laughed. Sheba McSherry (may her soul be as turbulent in death as it was in life) immediately ordered that the hippopotamus hokey should be served as the final course of the banquet. And she immediately ordered that two score of headsmen with gleaming double-bladed beheader's axes should stand at waiting in this very banquet hall. At the close of the banquet she asked every diner with great solicitude how he liked that final course of the banquet. And every one of them said that he had never eaten anything like it. And yet I believe that it was overpraised.

"I am declaring tomorrow to be the 'First Day of Klepsis.' I am declaring the history of Klepsis to begin tomorrow with my coronation. My many-times grandfather Christopher Begorra Brannagan, onetime autocrat and tyrant of Klepsis, whose ghost is in this hall tonight, once stated: 'While I still stir, then we remain in our time of legend and prehistory on Klepsis. But when I can no longer walk, even as a ghost, then the history of Klepsis may begin.' Old Christopher, if you stir henceforth, stir quietly and be unobserved about it, for the time of legend and prehistory on Klepsis comes to an end. If you will still walk, then walk unseen, for the history of Klepsis will begin with white dawn tomorrow morning, and you will not stand in the way. The two historians present will please take note of this: the history of Klepsis begins at dawn tomorrow, and the annals you intend to write should also begin at that time.

"Oh, I'd have liked to be a legend myself. I believe I'd have made a good one. But I declare the time of legends to be over with and the time of life to begin. We will live now as people, and not as wraiths before our time.

"Clocks and watches have never caught on with us here

on Klepsis, though persons from Astrobe and Camiroi and
Gaea-Earth and World Abounding have carried them to
our world and have even tried to introduce their use here.
But they did not catch on here because clocks and watches
measure time, and time on Klepsis will not begin until tomorrow morning. I order now that twelve watches and
clocks be brought to Klepsis and offered for sale. I predict
that they will all be sold within a month, and that perhaps
others may be required.

"This slave that I have brought at the tail of my hippopotamus is the last slave who may ever be brought to
Klepsis. I bought him just this afternoon, and no others
may ever be bought or sold here. This slave is a master
mathematician from one of the worlds out of the back door
of Klepsis, from the Tarshish side of the universe. Since he
is a slave, he must solve such mathematical problems as are
given to him, or his well-being and life are forfeit. He must
solve the problem of the Doomsday Equation. He must
give us a more complete and more correct version of the
equation, a version from which the Doomsday Element has
been removed."

"There's another solution," said Isadora Ragsley from
Paravata, speaking confidentially and almost
conspiratorially to the other eleven of us at the table. "We
can destroy one of the planets of our construct to save the
rest. Do all of us here belong to WEAP? Oh, I see from
your look of incomprehension that one or two of you do
not. WEAP is 'Wholesome Excision of Ailing Planets.'
Any planet can be destroyed from any other planet, of
course, instantly and with negligible power consumption.
All WEAP members carry a 'trigger' upon them at all
times. The technology of it presents no problem at all. We
could destroy any one of the planets (any one except
Klepsis, that is) before the death of the person-who-is-the-
point on Klepsis, and so we would deform and nullify the
Doomsday Equation. We'd pull the fangs from it. Klepsis
cannot be destroyed, for it contains the third focus of the
construct, but the other sixteen planets are fair game. Let

us get one trusted person from each of the other sixteen planets and cut cards for it. Low card is the planet to be destroyed. This will change the construct and avoid its collapse and destruction."

"We'll do it," Bancroft Romal agreed with total enthusiasm. "We'll start assembling the sixteen persons immediately. I'll represent Gaea-Earth. Clarence here can stand for Analos. Isadora is Paravata. Kate Blithespirit is Camiroi; that's a good start right here. And the technology is so easy! It's quite difficult to move a planet to another orbit, but anybody can destroy a planet, instantly, and from any distance."

"We'll do it, we'll do it!" we all agreed.

"I do not wish that the first day of World Klepsis should be the last day also," the Empress Angela was continuing, "but that will be the case if we do not escape from the inexorable Doomsday Equation. Let me tell you something that has been kept a secret (Oh, I see from the look on your faces that it has been kept secret from hardly one percent of you): that when Quasimodo (code name the Horseshoe Nail) dies, the construct of our suns and humanly inhabited worlds will die also; that sad fact has been known for twenty years. The worlds will die because Quasimodo is identical with the point that is the third focus of our kinetic three-dimensional ellipse. And a kinetic three-dimensional ellipse cannot exist without its third focus. For the last twenty years there have been monitors on Quasimodo, and all his interior and exterior functions have been logged and transmitted to Astrobe where they are appraised to the smallest detail. Twenty years ago, the analysts on Astrobe named tomorrow as his death day. Really, those analysts are that good! And for twenty years the experts on Gaea-Earth and Analos and Camiroi and Astrobe have been seeking a solution for the dilemma of our system. Time runs out for our system or construct just when time begins for Klepsis. We are at the last minute of the last hour now.

"We want fast answers. We're almost at the point where we don't care whether they are good answers or not, just as long as they are fast. Slave, slave-master-mathematician, provide a fast answer at once, by my coronation hour tomorrow morning, or die! Oh, there are doubtful answers springing up all over the place; we must encourage them for what virtue might inhere in them. There is a man in this hall who believes that, by physically adding another item to the Doomsday Equation, the doom of the equation can be forestalled. Malabu Worldwinger, go at once and do what you think you can do! There are four hundred intuitive space-jumpers waiting beside your four hundred ships that are loaded with heavy world-moving equipment. They will take them and put them in close orbit around Tarshish, and at the same time around everything else that seems too closely related to Tarshish. If you can take the doom out of the equation by adding to it, do it. There is something about Tarshish that you don't understand at all, but we'll leave you in the dark about that. It may be that your project will succeed for all the wrong reasons.

"Several other persons present believe that they can do something about the Doomsday Equation. I say do it, then. The Asteroid Pythagoras believes that she can do something about this, but she comes to the whole business with tainted talons. Nevertheless, if you can do it, birdperson, do it! The woman Becky Breaksticks from Dahae believes that she has the solution to the problem. Effect that solution then, Becky.

"If time does begin for us here on Klepsis, for us who have had only pre-time before, the bell in the *En-Arche* Bell Tower of this Castle will ring of itself without bell rope and without hands. So it was when the rough material of the cosmos was made in the pre-time of the Big Bang, a bell hanging without stanchion in a void was rung without activation and without hands. Oh, there's real evidence of that. It's in all the latest astronomy books.

"When time begins on Klepsis tomorrow, several of the anomalies will be swept away, just as our legends and prehistory will be swept away. This business of having things that are separated by two hundred years happen simultaneously will no longer be accepted. I believe we'll all like the new ways better. After so many decades, it becomes a little bit childish to continue to live in legend.

"And now I will set up a government here on Klepsis. I do not believe that our world should continue to be a covenanted piracy. I believe that we should have a consulting legislature, so I hereby declare you one hundred one persons here present in this hall to be that legislature. Each of you will have one vote, and I will have three. Some of you are visitors to Klepsis, and that is the way I want it. You belong here now. You may not leave here ever, save only Malabu Worldwinger and others who may be leaving on short, special assignments for the saving of the universe. Let the trumpets blow in acknowledgment of our establishing a consulting legislature."

The trumpets did blow loud and clear. What trumpet master would not have his trumpeters standing by and ready when such a trail-breaking assembly was going on!

"Anybody can propose a law here!" the Empress announced. "Now. Right now. I give you time to propose one. One, two, three. That is a long enough count. Since you fail to do so, I will now propose several laws for Klepsis. You will approve them by ringing voice vote; or, if you wish to be tedious, there can be objections to them, and then we will vote by tally count."

This Angela, who had been the most beautiful woman on Klepsis only yesterday (and I looked at a gold coin from my pocket with her picture on it to verify how she had looked), was not beautiful nor even pretty now. She was in a sort of travail, and she had to give up something for it.

"It is hard for a people to move from prehistory into history, and from legend into the approved tedium of a current world, especially a rock-headed people such as we have been on Klepsis," she was saying in a measured way. "We were the dregs of space on Klepsis, the marooned and the transplaneted and the escaped. We were mostly of the criminal class, and we set up a pirate royalty here. It was a little bit like dogs setting up a royalty. Many of you here are of Piratical Klepsis from birth. Others of you have come here with cloudy pasts. I recommend that all persons have patience with all other persons, and that killings and maimings be kept to a bare minimum during our period of transition. Who votes yes?"

About a dozen people called out "Yes."

"And who votes no?"

Nobody voted no.

"It is the law then," our new Empress said. "We will call it the 'General Purpose Tolerance Law.' If anybody has a pencil and a piece of paper, let'm write it down. It will be the first governmental document on our world. Old Brannagan's Ghost over there used to scribble things on paper sometimes, but this is not the same thing. Whoever writes it down will be the Speaker of the House, the second highest office on Klepsis, after that of Empress."

"I have pencil and paper. I write it down. I will be the Speaker of the House in perpetuity," Becky Breaksticks spoke firmly and suddenly in a quick power grab.

"Here's another law," the Empress Angela said. "Oh rats, these things are too heavy! I'd as well be carrying the hippopotamus on my shoulders."

My Princess Thorn went to her aunt the Empress (who was only one year older than herself), took the heavy golden barbaric Sheba McSherry crown off her head, set it on a table loaded with leftover whale, took two dozen strings of gold ornaments off the shoulders of the Empress and laid them on the same table, then brought a big chair for the tired Empress to sit on. That stuff had been very, very heavy.

"Let it be a law that each of the roughly three million persons on Klepsis shall be co-owner of all the treasures in the treasure caverns. This being so, the gold will be of no particular value among ourselves, and all transactions will be carried out by barter and by the new flintstone coins to be made at the Ballydehob Flint Quarry, each such flintstone coin to have the picture of the Empress Angela on it," the Empress spoke in her new enacting voice. "I believe that persons will be less avid and greedy for flintstone coins than for gold coins. And we enact that nobody shall take the worthless gold out of the caverns except by special permission of the Master of the Caverns who shall have absolute control of them and everything in them. See, by such a simple law as that we can be unburdened of our wealth. Who votes yes?"

About twenty persons voted yes.

"Who votes no?"

Nobody voted no.

"It is the law, then. Write it down, Speaker of the House Becky Breaksticks. Now we need a willing person to serve as Absolute Master of the Treasure Caverns with Plenipontentiary Powers."

"I will serve in that post," Becky Breaksticks said.

"Now we need to have a little law and order," the Empress said. "If anybody exhibits uncitizenly conduct, let the Master of the Dungeons put that person in the Castle Dungeon that is named the Whispering Room. But let the Master of the Dungeons be a little circumspect about this because the Whispering Room will hold only one hundred persons. Who votes yes?"

Three or four persons voted yes.

"Who votes no?"

Nobody voted no.

"It is the law," the Empress said. "Write it down, Speaker of the House Becky. Now we need a strong-minded volunteer to serve as Master of the Dungeons, one who can make up her mind quickly and firmly as to who should be thrown into the dungeon and who should not be, one who would not be swayed by the screaming and carrying on of those caught in uncitizenly conduct. The Master of the Dungeons will have absolute power in enforcing her decisions."

"I will serve in that post," Becky Breaksticks said.

"Now we come to the problem of the renegade Prince Henry who has escaped to the border backlands and is no doubt trying to gather malcontent people to attack us. He may even have gotten hold of a boat and gotten to Tarshish. Let it be enacted that if he comes to attack us with a force of ruffians, we will shoot the tails off all of them with large-and medium-bore weapons. Who votes yes?''

About fifty persons voted yes.

"Who votes no?"

Nobody voted no.

"It is the law," the Empress said. "Write it down, Becky. Now, I believe that we should enact a Freedom of Information Law to show that all of us are in favor of both freedom and information. Let the Freedom of Information Law be enacted, and pursuant to it, let the Princess Thorn-Tyrone, my dubious niece, be compelled to tell us what her unspeakable sin was, since we are all curious about it, and since it is *information* that we should be allowed to make *free* of in accord with this law. Who votes yes?"

There was some tittering, but nobody voted yes.

"I vote *my* three votes yes," the Empress said. "Who votes no?"

Three persons, myself, Thorn, and Terpsichore Callagy, voted no.

"Oh, a good law has just failed to pass," the Empress lamented. "Maybe we haven't chosen the perfect form of government yet. Let us go for another one. Let it be enacted that the peg-legs no longer be accorded special treatment on Klepsis, unless they lost their legs accidentally. If they had a leg taken off to take advantage of the regulations on Klepsis, then let them *not* be allowed to take advantage of the regulations on Klepsis. Who votes yes?"

About a dozen persons voted yes.

"Who votes no?"

Four of us, myself, Andrew Gold Coast O'Mally, and two other persons, all of us peg-legs, voted no.

"That's a regrettable thing," the Empress said. "I like it best when the laws are unanimous. I say, If you can't have unanimity, forget it! This law does not pass because of the objections of four measly peg-legged persons. Well, we have set up a government, and that's something. But if it lasts less than a day (due to our world lasting less than a day after time begins with us) what have we gained? Quasimodo will die tomorrow if he doesn't die tonight. And all the worlds will collapse and die at the same time unless somebody finds a way to break the doom. Oh, somebody please find a way to break the doom! Try even harder than this slave-mathematician tries. You'll all die as dead as he will tomorrow if you don't find the answer.

"Sit over the banquet tables as long as you wish, good people. Sit all night, for all that I care. But rattle your brains while you sit here. Very many of you people do have brains, and almost all of us Klepsis people have intuition, which is almost as good.

"Klepsis has been a covenanted piracy for two hundred years, two hundred years which we now decide not to count in our chronology. We lived a bloody and colorful legend, and *it is not now to be counted against us*. The result of our living so timelessly and vague is that those two hundred years do not count. *They did not happen*. I hereby declare them to have been non-years. We were clowns. And then we were clowns who weren't funny any longer. But I do hope that the First Day of Klepsis can bide all day.

"Thorn, please turn my hippopotamus out into the water pasture. Only a member of the royal family knows how to handle a royal hippopotamus. She'll refuse to go with a commoner. Do you want to receive the title Mistress of the Hippopotami, Thorn?"

"No, but I'll put old Aunt Rhodie here out in the water pasture," Princess Thorn said.

THIRTEENTH CANTO

Doomsday in the Morning

When white morning touched the top of O'Grogan's Mountain, there were already many people on that low mountaintop. Some of them were carrying their possessions in suitcases and backpacks. Well, some of their homes were already under the water of the raging ocean, and many of the people felt nervous about things. Klepsis had received several slight nudges, and whenever a planet is nudged, its human population feels a pang of alarm.

"The mountaintop is only about a hundred meters high here, but it may be that the tidal wave, the world wave, will not rise higher than this," said Bartolomo Portuguese who was from Tarshish. "The continents are close together on this part of Klepsis, and the tidal waves might not rise as high here as they do on other worlds when they go into their death throes. I've got off three dying worlds just in time, and I'll get off this one too, though I don't know how I'll do it. I didn't know how I was going to do it in the other three cases either. Oh, isn't there some way to call off your dog, Empress, to call off that stupid Malabu Worldwinger before he wrecks this whole world?"

"I will call off nobody," the Empress Angela stated firmly. "It may be that he will save us from doomsday even if he kills half of us doing it. And he is so exuberant and full of hope that I just hadn't the heart to explain the relationship of Tarshish and Klepsis to him."

"The earthquakes will get us if the tidal waves don't," Titus the Historian said. "The quakes are already splitting O'Grogan's Mountain while we stand on it here. It won't be tolerable for long. It isn't at all safe to stand here now. And the wind is blowing some whole people away. There go two more of them now, blowing through the air, hand in hand. What *is* the relationship of Tarshish and Klepsis that Malabu doesn't understand and I don't understand either?"

"I don't believe that the earthquakes this morning are quite as bad as they were in the Days of the Great Comet when I was a little girl," the Empress Angela commented. "But then, it's well known that 'Earthquakes in Childhood' are remembered as worse than they were."

"That's another tune that Juda O'Grogan-Brannagan sometimes plays with the little hammer on the bell in his bell tower," my Princess Thorn said. "I'd forgotten about that one. 'Earthquakes in Childhood,' that's one of the prettiest and most nostalgic of all that he plays."

There was much morning lightning, strange grumbling lightning that hit and bounced off the ground and hit again.

"It is planet-displacement lightning," the Asteroid Pythagoras said. "We get a lot of it on our asteroids. Our own asteroid is almost always being displaced by some force or other. As this planet rolls (and I believe that it has already rolled about fifteen degrees off its old axis) its magnetism is badly disturbed. This is disturbed-magnetism lightning, but not all of it. Part of it is sheer doomsday lightning."

Well, the earthquakes and the cyclonic winds and the strange lightning and the ocean that shouted and climbed out of its bed had already been evincing themselves for several hours. And there was the illusion that the lightning was scrawling prophetic words and messages as it crawled and rambled about the skies.

"Some of those things that the lightning is doing are pretty good," said Terpsichore Callagy, who was herself an amateur poet. "They are clever. And they rhyme."

"They are atrocious," Becky Breaksticks contradicted. "The *bon mots* are outright plagiarisms, and the rhymes are impure."

The slovenly sky seemed impressively near and was full of smoke and sulphur and small rocks. Everywhere on land there were prodigies, as there are every time that a world ends. A cork-island ox began to speak and to prophesy.

"See what the ox can do with the Doomsday Equation," Oliver Roundhead jibed good-naturedly. "Everybody else is working on it, and nobody has been able to do anything new with it this morning."

> *"Doom, doom, new-broom doom.*
> *Doomsday, doomsday, big bang boom."*

Thus the cork-island ox prophesied.

"Why, the ox is an idiot!" Oliver exclaimed. "He's probably right, though."

"By the way," Bancroft Romal confided to several of us, "our other plan is all set. The planet to be destroyed, if it comes down to that, is Gaea-Earth. It can be done instantly, but it will be done only as a last resort. I believe that we'll have at least a three-second warning when the worlds wind down to their end. A human death is always a kick, counter-kick, and then quietus. The whole takes about three seconds. We're plugged into Quasimodo's data as it is handled and interpreted on Astrobe. There is always the long-shot chance that the situation may be saved otherwise. Oh, I love to shave a thing close! I'm the trigger-man, you know. I've got the trigger wired into my brain, and you might say that I've got Gaea-Earth in my pocket. I can destroy that old world right now on half-a-second's notice."

A pack of bush-baby barbarians and sand-spit skulkers (these were tribes of humans that had gone feral) were making their way up the north flank of O'Grogan's Mountain. They had guns, but they weren't good guns. Fifty

years of rust shone orange on them in the morning light.
They had three wobble-wheeled wagons pulled by oxen.
They were carrying a gruesome head on the end of a long
lance. As they came a little nearer, it was seen that it was
the head of Prince Henry the Pirate, the recently fallen ruler of Klepsis.

"Stop the earthquakes, stop the cyclones, stop the lightning fires, stop the gobbling oceans," these feral people
jabbered, and several of their leaders stepped forward
from the others.

"We do not attack you. We do not invade you," they
said with sly sincerity. "The crooked-tongued Prince said,
'Come and invade them with me, and you will have meat
and gold, and heads to kick like footballs.' And we said
'Yes, we will,' but we lied, or at least we don't remember
now whether we meant it or not when we said it. But when
the earthquakes started and the lightning began to set all
the fires in our bushes, we figured we had better get on the
right side of things. We cut off his head then, and we bring
it to you now. Stop the earthquakes, high lady. Stop the
winds, stop the lightning, stop the gobbling ocean. It is
worse on us because we live in the lowlands. And give us
gold if you have some. *He* promised us gold."

"Oh, all right," the Empress Angela agreed. "Becky, let
them load their three wagons with as much gold as they
want. If their eyes are bigger than their wagons, though,
and their wagons break down from the weight of the gold,
they must leave wagons and gold and oxen all there. The
head? Oh, just put it down anywhere. I don't save them,
really I don't.

"Doesn't yesterday seem like a long while ago, though?
Oh, so much has changed since yesterday. You people go
back to your bushes and your sand-spits now. I'll stop the
earthquakes and the winds and the lightning and the
rampaging oceans. Yes, I give you my word that I'll stop
them."

"How long will it take to stop them?" one of the sand-
spit skulkers asked.

"About half a day. No more than that."

"Can't you do it quicker than that, high lady?"

"Shore-man, it took the sky thirty years to brew that lightning. It took the wind-master forty years to raise winds that big. It took the land sixty years to raise up those rock-splitting earthquakes. And it took the ocean ninety years to build up for such a rampage. And should I be able to stop all of them in less than half a day?"

"We guess not. But can we use the other mountain, the Issachar Mountain to the west to stand on? We haven't any mountain in our bush or sand-spits."

"Yes, go stand on Issachar Mountain," the Empress said, "and I'll stop the earthquakes and cyclones and lightning and rampaging oceans for you as soon as I get time to do it."

All the bush-baby barbarians and sand-spit skulkers went off towards Issachar Mountain in the west then, except for the wagoners who had gone with Becky.

There was an exploding noise. The David Watchtower separated itself from Ravel-Brannagan Castle and fell as a giant falls. Well, it had been weakened by the fires of the night before last, but there was still something providential about its fall.

After a little while, the wagoners of the barbarians went walking towards Issachar Mountain without their wagons or oxen. Their eyes had indeed been bigger than their wagons, and Becky had been a merciless dealer.

The waters of the saltless ocean ("Brannagan's Ghost still complains, whenever anything goes wrong on Klepsis, that it is because the people coming to Klepsis do not always bring sacrifices of salt to pour into its oceans," Princess Thorn said quite seriously), the waters of the saltless ocean had now completely surrounded Ravel-Brannagan Castle and inundated it clear up to the fourth story. It was still rising very rapidly and stormily. And the animals began to gather. Frightened by the rising water, some of them having been drowned by it, flocks and mobs of animals almost crowded the people off the mountaintop.

The Tarshish storyteller was there with us on the top of the mountain.

"Story-man, what is a good ending for the present story?" Titus asked him.

"I get most of my stories from my dreams, and from old legends. I have dreamed, many times and oft, everything here exactly as it has been happening. I dream it up to the point where the slave-mathematician is struck by lightning, and then my dream will stall and go no further. I only hope that the world won't stall and go no further forever. The old legends on it are pretty much the same. The endings of them are very weak and contrived. I just don't know how this episode is going to end."

Then there was a series of very loud meteorological explosions, from about a kilometer high in the air. And there was now a different feeling in the mountain-ground under us. We could also see and hear and feel a change in the tidal wave, the world-wave.

"Malabu is not simply rolling the planet now, trying to get hold of it," Alex Braveheart stated. "He has begun to move us slowly and relentlessly out of our orbit. Will we break up now, do you suppose? What odds will somebody give me that we don't break up?"

"Malabu is moving *Klepsis* out of its orbit?" I asked in amazement. "But he is supposed to be moving *Tarshish*. What is the matter with him?"

"Oh, for that matter, it is Tarshish that he's moving," Alex said. "They are oddly related. Tarshish is the what-is-it of Klepsis. Tarshish is the Lost Twin of Klepsis. Tarshish is the psychological under-mind of Klepsis. There are so many people who don't know that Tarshish and Klepsis are the opposite parts of the same planet, the opposite aspects of it. It was Brannagan himself who began the deception, and it was O'Grogan and his pirate children who kept it up. They had all their rivals in piracy running around through all the skies looking for Far Tarshish, which would be at the same time a treasure planet and a hellhole, an ideal combination for the pirates. And persons, shipmasters and haulers of people, those who did know the where of Tarshish, would take their travelers on a sedated and long-way-around course, orbiting each sun—Proxima, Alpha, and Beta—in turn while going from the Tarshish half to the Klepsis half of the same little ball. But there was truth in the deception. Tarshish *is* at the same time a hellhole and a treasure place, to at least the extent that Klepsis is."

Oh, it was a sick dizziness now. Our orb was being moved, and it resisted being moved. Big rocks were floating in the air, detached from their basis and unable to decide which of all the contrary forces to follow. The tidal wave, the world-wave, confused by the change of impetus, shot up many hundreds of meters into the air in narrow needles of water.

"Why did people let Malabu go then, and go under the pilotage of four hundred space-jumping short-tailed intuitives, to arrive at a place where he would do violence to this very world?" I asked.

"We let him go because it was silly-season with us," Alex said. "We let him go because we didn't think he could move a world of this size. Or rather, we wanted to see whether he *could* move such a world or not. And he can, a little bit at least."

"Well, there's a fast-looking little spacecraft stabled on the west flank of O'Grogan's Mountain just over there," Oliver Roundhead said, "and it looks exactly like mine. I must have spotted it there to thwart my silly inclinations. I think I'll just take a quick spin to the other side of the planet and call Malabu off his task. The changed rotation, and now the slightly changing orbit, have set up so much electrical and magnetic interference that there is no way we can get through to him on expresso or radio or vox-fox."

Oliver Roundhead took the fast-looking craft and zoomed off so rapidly that he simply melted away.

"Oh, this is heady, this is heady!" the Asteroid Pythagoras cawed. "We have such meteorological explosions and manifestations as these on the asteroids, and we love them. Sometimes one of our asteroids will bounce along in the empyrian like a rubber ball. And we have just such idiosyncratic lightning on our own asteroids. I'm homesick for all of it, and this is all like a big gust from home. I will just go up for a while and zigzag with the lightning and explode with the explosions."

"Wait, wait, catch her! Don't let her go!" Aloysius Shiplap from Gaea-Earth cried out, and three quick and powerful persons did pinion (literally) the Asteroid Pythagoras. "You are running out on it!" Aloysius cried at the big bird-creature. "You are about to be unmasked, so you are running out. The Doomsday Equation is a fraud, and now I begin to remember where that fraud began—in an obscure paper by an obscure bird on one of the bird asteroids. The Doomsday Equation is a fraud, and the Doomsday Equation was worked out by—"

"By myself, of course," the Asteroid Pythagoras bird growled. "I, the greatest mathematician in the universe, worked out the Doomsday Equation, a masterpiece of advocacy mathematics. It fixes the end of the humans, but not of the bird-men. And not, as one person has pointed out recently, of the dragons either. It will really be a great cleansing. I worked it out, and in order that everything might be done according to correct procedure, I presented it to a small but utterly competent symposium on my own Asteroid Doomsday. It was approved."

"And did nobody challenge it then and there, while it could still be challenged, before it got up trendy momentum?" Aloysius asked, mildly aghast.

"Three persons challenged it immediately," the Pythagoras cawed, "and the next moment there were three eyeballs dangling down three cheeks. The mathematical implications of the dangling eyeballs sank in quickly. The equation was approved without further arguments. I always liked that eyeball response. It goes like this—"

Like crackling lightning, the terrible beak of the Pythagoras struck three times, and her three captors had each a dangling eyeball and a sudden tempest of pain. The Pythagoras was loose from them easily then, and ascended twenty meters into the air on her powerful wings.

"To tell you the truth, I don't know whether my theory will stand up or not," the Pythagoras shrieked, "but it's going to be tested in a very few seconds, and I intend to watch that test from a few kilometers up in the air. Quasimodo is in the article of death right now, and the *En-Arche* Bell will be rung without hands in a very few seconds. I hear it. Why do you others not hear it? Can you not hear critical sounds a little before they happen? What do you do without such a cushion? A slave-mathematician is running up the buckling mountain now, buffeted by the winds and frightened by the lightning. He has a revision of the Equation in his hand, and I will be able to read it from seven kilometers up in the air. I have good eyes, even for a bird of prey. And I love to look at new and chancy versions of an equation."

The Asteroid Pythagoras immediately rose so high in the air that she was gone out of sight. She would zigzag with the lightning and explode with the explosions. And she would be able to read the emendation on the paper in the hand of the slave-mathematician with her infrared and highly magnifying eyes.

"I have correction, I have emendation," the slave-mathematician was calling in a loud voice as he ran up the mountain ahead of the fury of the churning water. "I have the equation in its correct form. The 'Doomsday' is herewith taken out of the 'Doomsday Equation,' and the doom need not happen."

The slave had almost reached the top of the mountain where all the scientists and many other persons were gathered.

Then, in that moment, in that first moment, the *En-Arche* Bell boomed, clanged, rang out a merry sort of toll from its bell tower.

"I could always stop time," Brannagan's Ghost said, "and I *have* stopped it now, for a very short while. It took a lot out of me, and I'll never be able to do it again. I've stopped it for a short moment only. If anybody is going to do anything about this, he'd better do it right now."

"The bell did boom half a tune before it was frozen," Titus the Historian cried out. "That means that Quasimodo is dead. That means that this is the end of the world."

And there was a lightning flash a dozen times as bright as any that had flashed before.

"No, Quasimodo isn't quite dead," Brannagan's Ghost insisted. "He doesn't die when the bell tune begins. He dies on cue, three notes from now. Maybe I can hold time for a while yet."

"No, no, it doesn't mean the end of the world, anyhow," my Princess Thorn contradicted all of them. "It means the beginning of the world. It was Old Brannagan here who built the En-Arche Bell Tower and hung the big bell in it. And he designed it to ring whenever the world should begin! Have you forgotten how you designed it, many-times grandfather? He named it *En-Arche*, 'In the Beginning,' from the first two words of the Septuagint Bible, the only Bible he ever read, one which he acquired on one of his very early piracies. Brannagan built the tower and hung the bell (it was from another of his early piracies) in a sort of intuitive transport, so his ghost once told me. Is that not so, Brannagan's Ghost? What do you say?"

"I say that somebody had better do something before I let time slip out of my control and the bell rings three more notes. It isn't easy to hold time."

"With that lightning, it looks more like an end of a world than a beginning of a world to me," Bancroft Romal spoke in a rather fearful voice. "Oh, I do have a nervous finger on the trigger. I thought I'd be cooler."

It was noteworthy that many of the people had now taken on 'the green face of fear,' people whom you'd never have suspected of such a failing.

"Tharrala Thorn, my perverse niece, tell me what the unspeakable sin was," the Empress Angela demanded. "I

must have my curiosity satisfied before the world ends and
I die."

"No, but I tell you what I'll do, Angela," Thorn said.
"I'll tell it to you the first time I meet you after we're both
safely dead."

"Nobody need die!" the slave-mathematician cried as he
reached the top of the mountain and arrived in the midst of
us. "The 'Doomsday' is herewith taken out of the Doomsday Equation. And the doom need not happen. Your writ
is false, Principality. Go back to your dungeon!"

As to the lesser of the catastrophes, it had already begun
to subside. Oliver Roundhead had arrived at the Tarshish
side of the planet and had convinced Malabu Worldwinger
that he must not move the Tarshish-Klepsis World out of its
orbit further. So the tidal-world-wave had begun to ebb,
and the wind and the waves quieted. The water level fell almost to the bottom of O'Grogan's Mountain.

But the Doomsday Principality had its lightning—
unsheathed and erratic lightning. The slave-mathematician
raised the revised equation high in the air in triumph. And
a blinding bolt of angry lightning struck down and set the
emendated equation on fire and at the same time burned
the hand of the slave-mathematician to an ember.

And the *En-Arche* Bell sounded one more beautiful but
horrifying note.

"Oop, I almost slipped. I nearly let the time get away
from me," Brannagan's Ghost apologized. "Two notes to
go. They must not sound!"

Aloysius Shiplap of Gaea stamped the fire out of the
equation paper and gathered up the fragments of it. "I
don't know whether there's enough of it left to
reconstruct—" he began, but the Doomsday Principality
had not yet surrendered. Furious lightning struck at
Aloysius and barely missed.

"Can you *tell* us the amended equation, slave?" Empress
Angela asked.

The slave made a motion that the lightning had made a
mute of him.

"Can you *write out* the amended equation, slave?" she asked.

The slave showed his right hand that was a hand no more.

"I believe that I have just enough pieces here to reconstruct the equation," Aloysius mumbled. "I'll have it in a minute. Oh, it's beautiful how it all goes together and each part illuminates every other part. Then the Doomsday Event can run and hide."

But a Doomsday Lightning hit Aloysius head-on. Oh, head-on! 'Twas life or death for him for a minute there. And then it was life. "I have it just about completed," the dazed Aloysius mumbled.

"Aloysius!" Terpsichore Callagy bubbled up, "that last lightning set your hair on fire. Oh, joy! Oh, glee! This is art like no art ever! Aloysius, you're not listening to me. I said that your hair is on fire. Aloysius, you become a piece of undying (even if you personally die from it) eschatologic art. Oh, the aeons are fulfilled when we can have a flash of art like that."

The *En-Arche* Bell tolled one more note before Brannagan's Ghost was able to bring slippery time to another precarious halt. And if it sounded its third after-note, that would mean that Quasimodo was dead.

"I've just about got it," Aloysius said. "Doomsday, run and hide! I've just about got it!"

"Has there ever *been* such a piece of outré art as Aloysius and his burning hair!" Terpsichore admired in ecstasy.

"It is all right, Terpsichore," Aloysius said. "I work best when my hair is on fire. I've got it, I've got it!" he gloated. "We're saved! Stand back, people; stand back, Terpsichore!"

"I'll *not* stand back. I'll be in the middle of it. Oh, what art! Look up into the middle of the convoluted lightning cloud, Aloysius. You can see the egg that the lightning comes in. Watch, watch, watch as the egg shatters! Oh, oh, it's coming right at us, scarlet murder as a form of high art!

Would it be artier if it misses us or if it hits us? There's no way we can lose. It's consummate art whether we personally live or die."

And the Doomsday Lightning, frustrated and angry, its prey about to slip away from it, gathered itself for what would have to be its final strike at Aloysius Shiplap.

"It's now or never," the Lightning mumbled, and struck in a jagged and erratic bolt—

AWARD-WINNING
Science Fiction!

The following titles are winners of the prestigious Nebula or Hugo Award for excellence in Science Fiction. A must for lovers of good science fiction everywhere!